THE INVISIBLE

THE INVISIBLE

AMELIA KAHANEY

An Imprint of HarperCollinsPublishers

HarperTeen is an imprint of HarperCollins Publishers.

The Invisible
Copyright © 2014 by Alloy Entertainment and Amelia Kahaney
All rights reserved. Printed in the United States of America. No part
of this book may be used or reproduced in any manner whatsoever
without written permission except in the case of brief quotations
embodied in critical articles and reviews. For information address
HarperCollins Children's Books, a division of HarperCollins Publishers,
195 Broadway, New York, NY 10007.
www.epicreads.com

alloyentertainment
Produced by Alloy Entertainment
1700 Broadway, New York, NY 10019
www.alloyentertainment.com

Library of Congress Control Number: 2014942410

ISBN 978-0-06-223192-5

Design by Liz Dresner

14 15 16 17 18   LP/RRDH   10 9 8 7 6 5 4 3 2 1

First Edition

For Jeannie and Cory, who taught me to be bold

There are no secrets that time does not reveal.

—Jean Racine

CHAPTER 1

Spring has finally come in Bedlam, and the air in the arena smells like newly blooming roses, popcorn, and manure. I'm in the bleachers at the Spring Fling Horse Show, watching the final group of jumpers lead their horses by the reins. At the front of the line is Martha Marks, the mayor's daughter, who I've known since we were little kids. Her black velvet riding helmet perched tall upon her head, Martha smiles slightly, her eyes all calm and focus, her riding jodhpurs with their leather knees pristine, her black riding boots polished to a shine under flecks of fresh mud.

I'm sitting between my mother and father in the third row, just behind Martha's parents, Mayor Manny Marks and Belinda Bullett. The mayor's giant head swivels around, and he flashes me that toothy grin he passed down to his daughter. Next to him, whippet-thin with her nervous bird's face half-hidden under her giant cloche, Belinda motions to my mother to lean in for a picture—a roving *Daily Dilemma* photographer stands below them on the bleachers, his flashbulbs popping for tomorrow's paper, which will feature lots of society ladies in their spring hats. My mother's is wide and white, like a straw-and-silk ring of Saturn, and Belinda's is dome-shaped, decorated with faux flowers, the straw colored antacid pink. When my mother leans down to pose with Belinda I can see the track marks on her temples just below her huge sunglasses from where she's been injected with fillers and plumpers.

"To stay young, I guess," she'd sighed last week when I asked her why she needed to do so much work on her face. "There's a lot of pressure on me to look this way. And it's good for the business." The business is Fleet Industries, the development company she owns with my father. Then she shrugged, as if to say, *It needs to be done, so why complain.*

When Martha turns her huge black horse to face the audience, I wave. "Go, Martha!" I shout. She grins, squinting out at the bleachers at the sound of her name. Her eyes find me in the third row, and she waves back.

She must think it's strange to see me here. I've never come to one of her competitions before. Horses have never been my thing.

But I'm not really here to see the horse show. I'm here to keep an eye on my father. Ever since I found evidence that he could be part of the Syndicate, Bedlam's notorious crime ring, I've been shadowing him every chance I get. Spying. Snooping in his office. But it's been two weeks, and so far I've found nothing. Just a man with a lot of money who likes to tell business associates what to do to build his buildings higher, bigger, faster, more profitably.

I spot him picking his way back down the bleachers after visiting the arena's snack bar. He holds a cheese plate and a plastic cup of fruit salad, three bottles of Exurbia Springs Water pressed against his gray suit. One of the bottles falls from his grasp as he's about to reach our row. Before I even think about it, I leap up and lunge toward him with my hand outstretched to catch the falling bottle. Fast. Probably too fast.

"Some reflexes!" my father says, startled.

"Just helping out." I shrug and give him a look like *what are you talking about* so he stops thinking about it. I'm usually careful not to move as quickly as I'm capable of, but sometimes I lapse for a second before I catch myself. I can move so fast now, do things a person shouldn't be able to do. It's one of the things Jax changed in me when she did the surgery, replacing my dead heart with a chimeric one she'd designed to beat faster, work harder than a human heart should.

It works. He sits down between me and my mother on the bleacher bench. "Just like old times, huh? Us three, all together on the weekend?"

I nod, careful to smile instead of scowl even as the thing in my chest twitches like a broken wind-up toy, full of misgivings and suspicion.

Nothing is like old times anymore. Not at all. But I don't want my father to question all the "family time" I've been partaking in recently. If he thinks I'm watching too closely, he'll be even more carefully guarded than he already is.

As he settles on the bleacher next to my mother, it's her I study, not him. She stares straight ahead at the jump course, her face hidden beneath her sunglasses, her hat pulled lower now, hiding the injection marks. Is she medicated today?

I decide she probably is, her brain soothed by an every-four-hours dose of Vivirax under her giant white hat and huge sunglasses. It's too early for wine, but she's so placid and calm right now that she borders on comatose. She fans her fingers out in front of her, examining her bloodred manicure. Shakes her head when my father waves the fruit cup in front of her face. "No thank you, dear."

"Suit yourself," he says back so quietly the mayor can't hear. He sends the cheese plate up to the bleacher in front of them. *What does she know?* I wonder. About my father. Is she as out of it as she seems?

My father was always the parent I used to think I could sort of rely on, but he isn't someone I can trust anymore. I need to figure out what my father knew about Gavin Sharp, once my boyfriend, then my enemy, now dead and buried.

It's been three weeks since Gavin's funeral, and though I've done as much surreptitious digging as I can, I still haven't found any connection between my father and Gavin, other than the fact that Gavin was his employee—something Gavin didn't tell me, but then why would he? Nothing he said turned out to be the truth, in the end. He fed me lie upon lie before his carefully orchestrated "kidnapping," and I stupidly believed it all.

Sometimes I wonder what made me such an easy target. Why I was so duped by a handsome face, by the way he held me, by all his promises and plans. Was there something written on my face that read *fool, rube, naïve*?

Whatever might have once been there, it's gone now.

Now I question everything, and everyone. Nothing anyone says feels like it could possibly be the truth. And my feelings about people—I question those constantly too.

I watch my father offer Belinda some fruit and pass out the remaining water bottles. "I was born to serve," he jokes. Belinda laughs politely, and I think I see my mother roll her eyes behind her glasses.

The top of the Syndicate chart in the book I found in Gavin's bag has two words at the top of it: *The Money*. It has to be a nickname, shorthand for someone shadowy and crucial. Someone I have reason to believe is my father. But could he really be funding the Syndicate?

I've searched his office. Looked through the files on his computer. It's all just contracts, plans, payroll for Fleet Industries. All of it seems ordinary, boring, the stuff you need to do to put up buildings. No more.

Not for the first time, I wonder if maybe it's all in my head. If maybe the chart I found in the back of Gavin's strange paperback book about police corruption and the mob—the one thing of his I kept after I let him drop to his death in Lake Morass—has nothing to do with my father. I keep it under my mattress and study it every few days as if I can glean the truth from his scratched-out names in ballpoint pen. Maybe it really is a coincidence that Gavin worked for him, and his "real" job with the Syndicate was during off hours.

A trumpet blast pierces my thoughts, and I focus back on the riding course. The riders each climb onto a little step to mount their horses as the announcer begins reading off their names. This is the final and most advanced level of the jumping competition. Martha sits up straighter on her horse when her name is called, and the group of twelve riders—three boys, the rest girls—dig their heels into their horses' flanks, gather up their reins, and move them toward a corral where they will wait for their turn on the course.

I close my eyes a minute and tilt my face up to drink in the heat of the sunshine on my forehead. Winter was so long, and the spring feels a little like awakening into the still-dark hours before dawn, sweat drying after a series of nightmares.

I remind myself things are not all bad. The Syndicate seems to have lost its power for the moment, now that Gavin, its captain, is dead. As a result, crime is down. All the papers say so.

And the only price I've paid, other than my freakish heart, is the way I shudder at the memory of Gavin landing on the jagged boulders in the lake, his mouth and eyes open in shock. It could so easily have been me, not him, whose skull pooled slick black blood on the white rocks. But he's gone, and I'm still here.

I shake the image free and turn my thoughts to Ford. Ford, who is the reason I have my chimeric heart, and the reason I'm alive today. He is alive, if not yet healthy enough to get out of bed. I picture him lying in his uncle's living room, the greenish hollows beneath his eyes. I go over there two or three times a week, whenever I can sneak away. Every time I hope for some improvement, but he's still so weak.

"Number four, Martha Marks," the announcer booms, and a swell of polite applause rises up from the bleachers behind us. The mayor and Belinda turn around briefly, acknowledging the crowd with politicians' waves, then turn back to watch Martha ride around the ring. She moves fluidly with her black mare as they canter up to each jump, easily clearing the poles, starting with the three-foot-high ones and moving on in the course to taller and taller obstacles. Her back is perfectly erect, her eyes focused, hands on the reins making small corrections, communicating with her horse.

I check the program and smirk at the name of her horse—Daddy's Girl. Martha's always been so proud of her father's political career, first as deputy mayor and then as mayor.

Martha barrels around the far corner of the course and loops in our direction again. The hooves of her horse cut into the earth, sending clods of it flying as she prepares to make this next jump—the highest in the course at seven feet.

My father and mother are both using this moment while the mayor is occupied to check e-mail on their phones, oblivious to the spectacle.

But as Martha gallops toward the high hedge, a sharp, sustained, ear-splitting whistle fills the air. I grimace and clap my hands over my ears, looking for the source, waiting for others to notice it.

But my father is still tapping away on his phone. My mother is doing the same.

The mayor and Belinda keep on cheering. Behind me, groups of people in funny hats eat and chat and watch the action in the ring, a few of them filming Martha as she closes in on the end of her course. Nobody else seems to notice the shrieking whine growing louder and louder. It's unbearable. I press my fingers against my eardrums, trying to block it out.

Is it all in my head? A new side effect Jax didn't warn me about? Nobody else seems to hear it.

Nobody but Martha's horse.

As Daddy's Girl approaches the final jump, her teeth flash in the sun and she rears up, following Martha's order to clear the hedge, but instead the horse twists in the air, whinnying loudly, and bucks Martha off. The bleachers erupt in gasps as Martha sails through the air and lands on her back in front of the jump with an audible snap of bone. Her face crumples, her blue eyes blank with shock.

The crowd erupts with shouts. "Roll! Roll!"

Because if she doesn't roll away, Daddy's Girl will land on top of her, hooves smashing her skull.

At the last second, Martha seems to process what's happening and rolls six inches to the right. It's enough. The trample of the horse's hooves misses Martha's back and hands by what looks like centimeters at the most.

I'm on my feet, my chest pounding, adrenaline pumping through me as I try to block the sound with my hands on my ears. Where is it coming from? I whirl around and around, wincing at the shrill whine, until I spot the speakers mounted on several poles around the arena.

The sound has got to be coming from them.

Frantically, I look around for some sort of control room, and my eyes land on a glass-enclosed booth where the announcers sit during games. I squint at the windows until human shapes come into view. There are three or four people inside, standing up and watching the crowd. They stand very straight, perfectly still. Watchful. The outlines of their bodies look young. Perhaps just a few years older than me. Not like the usual announcer types, who are older men in suits and ties.

And I could swear it looks from here like they are smiling.

As two men in dark suits rush from the sidelines toward Martha—the black curly wires snaking from their earpieces tell me they're the mayor's bodyguards—I look to my parents, wondering if I can slip away without them noticing. Martha flinches from the pain. She's broken something, maybe her ankle. The mayor leaps over the guardrail to join the bodyguards, leaving Belinda with us, pale and terrified. I've still got my hands on my ears, the sound growing almost unbearable, louder and louder every second.

Meanwhile, among the penned-in horses waiting their turn in the ring, there is a commotion. They whinny and snort, some of them rearing up, others kicking out. Many of them tremble violently, their nostrils flared.

The riders begin to dismount, jumping over the fence toward the show organizers, who yell on bullhorns for the riders to assemble near the judges' desk.

Everyone on the arena floor shoots worried looks at the horses, and they yell orders at a group of handlers they've summoned from the stables.

Just then, a chestnut mare with a tiny blue ribbon tied around the topmost section of her mane rears up on her hind legs, eyes wide and wild. On her way down, her hooves smash through the wooden fence. And then she's out, galloping on the course, hooves thundering. Eyes bugging out as if possessed.

The other horses follow her lead, charging out of the pen and galloping toward the bleachers, a row of frenzied hooves, manic nostrils flared. They move with grace and speed, their hooves biting the dirt as they race toward the far bleachers.

Toward *us*.

The entire crowd is on its feet now. I see a crying little boy launched into the air by his father, who carries him like a football under his arm and starts leaping over the bleachers, avoiding the walkways, which are clogged with people.

The horses are just a few feet from the bleacher rail now. Hooves thundering. Muscled hides shaking with the effort of the gallop. My father's expression is dazed, like he can't quite believe this is happening. But one look at the horses tells me they aren't going to let a little thing like a metal railing come between them and the bleachers. They're moving quickly, doing everything they can to escape the sound.

"We need to go!" my mother screams, lurching out of her medicated haze and onto her feet. Now is my chance.

I force myself to run like I would have before, at a normal

speed, until I've blended into the crowd enough to move faster and head toward the sound booth without her seeing me. On my way, I spot Serge, my father's driver and bodyguard, rushing toward my parents.

"Serge!"

When his eyes find me, I motion with my chin to the sound booth, communicating where I'm going.

He nods, and then continues toward my parents. Serge has experienced my enhanced speed and strength firsthand. He knows I can take care of myself.

The horses have cleared the bleachers now, but I'm closing in on the booth. I take a breath and start moving much faster, my heart whirring inside me, my ears echoing with the slippery scrape of hooves against metal, a drumbeat under the shrieking whine still humming deafeningly in the air.

I spot an older woman to my right who's fallen in the clogged edge of the bleachers. She could get trampled, people all around her moving fast. In three flying steps, I'm at the woman's side. She's wrinkled and ancient, struggling to right herself, but the crowd around her isn't stopping to help. Her huge robin's-egg-blue hat is crushed beside her and covered in footprints. I get a hold around her torso and pull her up. She's so old and dazed; I don't think she'll make it walking. So I hoist her up as inconspicuously as possible and carry her against my side the last eight rows to the top of the bleachers, where the sound booth is.

"What are you doing? I mean, thank you!" she cries when we reach the top of the stairs. "I—I—are you the girl from the papers?"

She means the New Hope. They were calling me that in the *Daily Dilemma* when I started rounding up members of the Syndicate. Back when I still thought they had taken my boyfriend. But I don't do that anymore.

"I don't know what you're talking about," I say, trying not to wince from the clamor in my ears. And then I'm gone, moving through the crowd until I reach a metal door with a plastic placard on it that says SOUND BOOTH.

It's locked. Still wincing from the whine coming out of the speakers, I gather up all my strength and take a running leap against the door. As my shoulder smashes against it, the door flies open. I crash into the room, too much adrenaline coursing through my body to notice how much it hurts.

Three guys whirl around from where they stand, in front of a complicated soundboard with microphones and dozens of switches. The skin around their mouths is smeared black with what looks like traces of shoe polish, their eyes glassy but focused, their expressions mildly surprised, nothing more.

"Can we help you?" the one nearest to me says. He's maybe twenty, a shock of black hair covering half of his pale, thin face. I open my mouth to say something, but then I see him reaching for something inside his jacket.

I run toward him, conscious of time slowing down until I can almost see the molecules of dust vibrating in the air in front of me. In an instant I am inches from him, close enough now to smell the chemical tang emanating from his pores. "Drop it," I hiss, wrenching his arm behind his back until he squeals. He tries to twist away, but there's no contest. I'm much, much stronger than he is, and in an eyeblink I feel him relax as he gives in.

His grip loosens on the gun, and I grab it with my other hand, shoving him away from me, hard enough so that he crashes against the wall near the door of the sound booth.

"You." I motion at the smallest of the three of them, a

blond kid around my age. He wears a black T-shirt with a drawing of a single heavy-lidded eye. Panic kicks in my stomach as the pounding of horses' hooves, the screaming of the crowd, and the whine from the speakers crowd my skull. "Shut it off."

"Or what?" the blond boy says. "You'll shoot?" His expression is so smug, it's like he's daring me to. His lips are smeared with blue-black oil. His eyes are dazed and indifferent despite the gun I'm pointing at him. "Go ahead," he dares me. Smirking. I cock the gun, deciding. Out of the corner of my eye I spot a huge chestnut stallion moving toward the booth, eyes wild, flanks straining up the stairs. People screaming, trying to get away.

Time is running out.

"That's what I thought," he sneers when I hesitate. "Why not embrace the chaos and enjoy the view?"

I make an involuntary sound of disgust in the back of my throat, and then turn toward the controls.

I take aim at the center of the soundboard where there are dozens of switches and sliders, bracing for the recoil. The last time I fired a gun was months ago, the night Gavin was killed. I squeeze the trigger, and the bullet explodes into the soundboard, sending white sparks flying and a plume of smoke rising up from the hole in the metal.

Instantly, the whine stops. I can think again.

For a half-second, I stare out the window at the horses starting to relax. People continue to run toward the exit, their faces etched with fear, but the horses have already slowed their runs from a gallop to a halfhearted trot. When I turn back around, the three boys have slipped out. I race to the door, but the crowd is so thick, it's impossible to imagine which way they might have gone.

"Anthem!" I look up toward the arena entrance doors, and there is Serge, waving, half-crazy from worrying about me. I nod and scurry toward him, my chest thumping with adrenaline and unanswered questions: Who were they? Where did they go? What did they want?

In the parking lot, the arena attendants have managed to round up half a dozen of the horses and stand with them under a cement overhang. I run my fingers along the mane of a black quarter horse as we pass by. I whisper *shhhhh* in its ear. It is trembling slightly, but nothing like before. All of them are calmer now that the noise has stopped. Next to the quarter horse, a white mare has a hoof-shaped red mark on her neck.

People hold each other in the parking lot as they move toward their cars. Children are crying.

I move with Serge toward a cordoned-off section of the lot where my parents are waiting with the mayor's family and his team for an ambulance. The men in dark suits—the mayor's bodyguards—keep pressing the wires on their ears and talking in hushed voices. The mayor is yelling into his phone. Belinda bends down to tend to Martha, ghostly pale and lying on a stretcher on the ground. She moans softly, obviously in a lot of pain.

The ambulance screeches into the lot before I can say anything, my words lost in the squeal of the siren. It pulls up next to us. The doors pop open, and two medics jump out to unlatch a gurney. In a moment, they lift her stretcher up on top of it and start strapping her in.

"Anthem," Martha says as they hoist her up. "Tell everyone at school I'm fine, okay?"

I nod.

"You were amazing," I say. "You would have gotten the blue ribbon."

This seems to make her happy. Her eyes twinkle, and she's about to say something else, but they are pushing her gurney into the ambulance. The last things I see are the mud-caked soles of her riding boots before one of the medics shuts the door.

My father's hand clamps down on me. He grips my upper arm tightly, his other arm around my mother, who's been silent as a stone since we left the arena. I wonder if she's popped another dose, maybe something stronger than Vivirax. Maybe a Calmalin, which always leaves her nearly catatonic. After a moment, I squirm away from my father.

As we walk through the parking lot, the sun beating down on our heads, I notice two little kids pointing at the sky. I look up. A message, written in puffy purple smoke, floats above us. So innocent looking, that purple. The skywriting of extravagant lovers. But when I read it, a deep shiver moves through my veins.

WE ARE THE INVISIBLE, AND WE ARE EVERYWHERE.

"The Invisible," I say out loud. *Who are they?*

"Garbage," my father mutters, looking up without breaking stride. "Someone thinks he's a hero for causing trouble. It's happened before," he adds.

I shoot a look at Serge. His jaw is clenched. His eyebrows rise when he meets my stare, before we both look quickly away.

I swing around for one more look at the parking lot as I get into the car. Everyone's looking up at the sky now. Everywhere, lips beneath sagging straw hats read the slogan in the sky.

Conversation swells loud all around us. As I get into the car, I look over my shoulder, paranoid. *We are everywhere.* Suddenly, I feel certain that today was just a warm-up for something more ambitious. Something deadlier.

CHAPTER 2

Ford's uncle Abe lets me into the apartment early the next morning. He's off from his shipping job at the PharmConn factory on Sundays, and it looks like he's getting an early start on his day—a green apron smeared with pancake batter covers his massive belly and barrel chest. His bushy gray mustache fans out when he smiles at me. "Come on in, Anthem. He's sleeping, but he'll wake up for you."

"Any better lately?" I ask, searching Abe's face for clues. I haven't been able to make it out here since Thursday.

He shrugs. "Maybe a little." But the strain of worry is evident in his bloodshot eyes. He is trying to stay positive for Ford, and for Sam and Sydney, Abe's daughters, still asleep in the apartment's only bedroom.

Abe sleeps on the couch at one end of the living room, and Ford has a small, curtained-off spot near the kitchen where his bed is pushed up against the alcove wall along with a tiny desk and a rickety wooden chair. I desperately want to believe Abe that Ford is indeed a little better.

I walk toward the curtain and knock on the wall next to it before I pull it back. "Ford?"

"Mmm." I hear him stir in his bed. "I know that voice."

My chest buzzes with anticipation—even in his weakened condition, seeing Ford gives me a charge every time. I let myself linger there for another second before I pull the curtain, hoping to find a healthier Ford this time. But when I lift the curtain and move into the darkened alcove where his bed is, the wheeze in his chest sounds worse than before. I force a smile.

"Morning," I whisper, standing just a foot from the bed. I grope in the dark until I find the wooden back of the desk chair. I turn the chair around so it faces the bed before I sit down. "How are you feeling?"

"Better, now that you're here." I can hear him smiling in the dark. A silence opens up that Ford breaks after a few beats. "I stood up for a whole shower yesterday."

"That's progress." When he first came home from Jax's lab after his coma, he couldn't stand up at all.

"Guess so," he says, but he sounds nonplussed. He must be miserable not being able to do what he normally does, which is run and train and generally power through his days. Though he doesn't say it, I know that in his mind, without exercise, he may as well be dead.

I find the lamp on his desk and switch it on, careful to keep my face neutral even though my heart sinks as I take in how pale he is, his gaunt cheeks. He must have lost at least twenty pounds by now. Maybe more.

"You look good," I lie. I search his face for evidence that

he's getting better. But if anything, he looks weaker and sicker than ever.

I think back to when I woke up from my surgery on Jax's gurney. I was off and running—more like flying, actually—the same day. Why couldn't Jax do the same for Ford, who didn't even need a transplant? Who wasn't even clinically dead?

"You'll be better in no time." I hope I look like I'm sure of it. I don't want to betray my new suspicion that he might never fully recover from Gavin's bullet, and that he'll have me to blame for a miserable life spent hobbling to and from his bed. If he hadn't followed me to Gavin's house that night, everything would be different now. I might not be here at all.

"How long has it been, anyway?" Ford asks. He can't remember the first week, when he was in a coma, and time has been sketchy for him ever since.

"Three and a half weeks."

"These things take time, I guess," Ford starts, lifting his head from the pillow and then collapsing back down in exhaustion.

I try to think of something to say to him, something to cheer him up or at least distract him. I'm about to tell him about the horses, the skywriting, ask him if he's heard of the Invisible, when I hear little feet scampering on the planks of the wood floor.

"Sam and Sydney are up," I whisper. Ford makes an effort to sit up taller in bed, and I help him by stuffing another pillow behind his back.

"Guess who's here, girls?" Abe says to them, and then they're running toward us, two mop-headed balls of energy in matching pink cotton nightgowns. Sam is five, serious under her big pile of curly black hair. Sydney is seven, a bigger version of Sam, and more of a joker.

Sam dives onto Ford's bed atop the covers, and Sydney gives me a hug, her curls tickling my neck.

"Hi, you two. What's shaking?" I ask. Their energy is infectious enough to lift my mood a bit.

"Sam, show Anthem your new moves!" Ford demands, a cough rattling in his throat.

"Good idea!" Sam leaps off the bed and pulls the curtain back all the way, exposing the alcove to the rest of the room. Abe rummages in the fridge, putting ingredients for a second batch of pancakes on the counter. "Let me get my music."

She scampers into her bedroom, and Sydney follows. "You mean *my* music," she corrects her little sister as she runs after her.

While they're gone, Ford grabs my hand. "Thanks for coming by," he says. His eyes look ablaze with fever or emotion, I'm not sure which. "It must be getting kind of boring for you."

"Are you kidding? This is the best part of my week." I'm blushing again, and I'm not quite sure why. But when I sneak another peek at him, I think Ford might be blushing, too. This is harder for him than for me, I remind myself.

He's made it pretty clear that our relationship is more than just a friendship to him. But his protracted recovery is clouding his mind. It must be. How can you love the person who almost got you killed?

"When's the last time you saw Jax?" I don't say *because I think something's wrong*, but I'm sure it's written all over my face.

"Last Friday," Ford says. "She told me to wait and see how I'm doing in a week or two."

"That's it?" I say lightly, wondering if maybe Ford looks worse than he feels. Could this really be normal, part of his recovery after losing all that blood?

Ford shrugs, and suddenly I feel angry with Jax. Can't she

do something more than just wait and see? The scientist who invented my chimeric heart should be able to do better than this. Extra vitamins? Plasma? Antibiotics? There must be something she hasn't tried yet. Something that will fix him. I make a mental note to pay her a visit.

"Abe thinks I'm doing better. Right, Unc?" Ford raises his voice a little to reach his uncle across the small expanse of the room.

"Yup," Abe says over the hissing of batter in the frying pan. "A little."

"I could take you to see Jax right now," I suggest. It'd be nice to see Ford out of bed. To breathe fresh air with him. "Today."

"Abe will do it." Ford shakes his head, staring down at his sallow hands on the bedspread. They're losing their calluses, no longer the hands of a boxer. "When I'm ready. I'd rather he sees me limping than you."

"Okay, weirdo," I say, busying myself with a stack of pictures on Ford's desk, frustrated by his stubbornness.

I find a shot of him in the ring, his stance victorious after a knockout. Back when he boxed for money. Before he was driven underground by the Syndicate, when he stopped throwing fights for them.

"Look at you here," I say, more to myself than to him as I stare at the photo. He's pouring sweat, his opponent laid out on the mat to one side of him. Ford's sculpted arms are raised in victory, one glove still on, the other clutched in his hand. His mouth guard swelling his smile.

"Yeah." He smiles now, but it looks pained. "Hope I can get back to training soon."

Ford wants me to think he's strong, but I already know he is. I've seen him at death's door. I carried him to Jax after he was shot, his blood soaking through my clothes. Most people would have died from the blood loss then and there. At least that's what she told me. He needed more than a gallon of transfusions when I got him to her lab.

"Want to come to the table?" I ask. I want to see him walk. If I see it, I'll know he's really getting better.

Before he answers, the girls come back from their room, dragging a cracked plastic record player covered in stickers. "Wow, that thing is ancient."

"It was my mom's when she was a kid. Probably was her mom's before that," Ford says. The girls carefully place the needle on the record, and the tinny twinkle of a tune—"Dance Me to the End of the Road," I think it's called—comes out of the record player.

Sam has tied on the tutu I brought her—one of mine from level one, a foamy blue wisp of tulle—and assumes first position, pausing to look me in the eyes and grin before she puts her game face back on and spins to the music. Sydney joins in after a minute, and soon they're both spin-jumping off the couch in fits of giggles.

"Bravo!" we shout. Ford smiles, the glint in his eyes brighter now. Abe, too, pauses to watch as he puts pancakes on plates. The small dark room in the basement of the run-down building is filled with music, laughter, and the smell of batter sizzling in the pan.

Ford inches toward the edge of the bed, wincing as he pulls himself to his feet. It's an effortful maneuver. So much so that he almost falls.

I rush to help him up, to steady him, but he shrugs me off and indicates he can do it himself. "At least I'm out of bed, right?"

"It's great," I agree as I watch him hobble toward the kitchen table. His movements are tentative, painful, as if each and every step requires everything he's got. The last person I saw walk this way was my grandmother after surgery. That was two weeks before she died.

Ford's *not* getting better. Even if he doesn't want to admit it, the truth is plain as day. The realization kicks me in the gut as I watch him hobble around like an eighty-year-old. And believing time will fix this is just wishful thinking.

My insides ache when I think back to the shooting, to the moment he burst into Gavin's office. All because he was protecting me. It's my fault he's in this condition. And now I have to do everything I can to fix it.

It's 4:45 A.M., and the boy has been inching along on his belly inside a metal tube for the better part of an hour. It's making him sweat. The tube is part of the ventilation system in the top of the recently shuttered Hillside Palisades Mall. The sweating is making his mask itch, so he stops crawling and pulls it off to blow air upward onto his wet forehead.

If his calculations are correct, the next opening in the vent is the former Big N' Tall Shoe Palace, the unofficial den of the Hammer, one of the Syndicate's top lieutenants. Rumor has it the Hammer likes to sleep in the mall.

The boy pulls his mask back over his face and keeps crawling, hoping there aren't too many guards watching over the Hammer. Hoping they don't hear him coming. His arms protest the continued push forward, but his body still hums with anticipation. If he takes down the Hammer, he's one step closer to dismantling the Syndicate's central power structure.

Finally, he reaches the slatted vent above the Big N' Tall. It's dark down there, but he thinks he sees a flicker of light between the vent's metal slats. Slowly, he reaches for a dime in his pocket.

Taking care to be absolutely silent, he uses it to unscrew the vent's four corners. After he removes the last screw, he holds his breath and slides the vent's plate away, making no sound, save a tiny scrape of metal.

He pulls the wool mask down over his nose and mouth and sticks his head into the store, relieved to spot the extra-large shoe racks on the wall. He's found the Big N' Tall.

There's a metal trash can in the center of the room, a low fire burning inside it that smells chemical and toxic. A tent is set up in one corner of the store. Behind it, stacks of footlockers. Must be around thirty of them. He wonders what's inside. Likely pharms, if he had to guess. That's what the Hammer deals in, after all. Droopies, giggles, smokestacks, BodMods, and whatever else they're pushing. And when his corner boys don't come through, he deals in making examples of them.

Other than the tent, there's nothing here except a bunch of empty office chairs strewn around the room.

The boy flexes his arms, makes sure he's got his strength after all that crawling. Then he lowers himself into the room, hanging from the ceiling a moment before dropping down, wincing at the muted thump his feet produce when they hit the carpet.

"Go see what that is," he hears a man say from outside the store.

He races to the wall of footlockers, but though he's fast, he's not fast enough. A girl enters the store, young, skinny, strung out on something. And she carries a rifle. She spots him before he can dive behind the footlockers. She looks shocked to see it's him. His mask is known. He is known. He's been in the papers for a solid three months now. VIGILANTE CAMPAIGN FOR JUSTICE. HOPE FOR THE CITY. THE HOPE CONTINUES CRUSADING. The headlines never seem to get old.

Her eyes widen, and she falters, lowering her rifle a half-inch. A Syndicate tattoo rides her collarbone like a necklace, a yellow bruise from an old black eye on the ridge of her cheek. "It's you," she breathes.

He nods, doesn't say anything. Tries not to look down the barrel of her gun. His is in his boot. He considers grabbing it, but so far he opts to wait. Something about her tells him she's better than this.

I hate him, she mouths, eyes flicking on the tent, then back to him. He wonders if the Hammer is the person who gave her that black eye.

Then she faces the door and calls to whoever sent her in here, "Nothing here. Must've been a mouse or something."

Before she leaves, she points to the tent. Folds her hands together, rests her face on them to indicate he's sleeping.

Careful, she mouths before she goes. When the door closes behind her, he takes out his gun. Holds it in front of him as he unzips the tent.

Then everything speeds up the way it does when his adrenaline rises. The eyes of the Hammer—a short man with giant, steroidal arms; a buzz cut; and a red, greasy face—flutter open. He reaches for something, but the boy beats him there, yanking a sawed-off shotgun from the Hammer's sleeping bag.

He pulls the Hammer out, presses a gloved hand over his mouth with one hand, the gun in the other pressed into his sweaty temple. "Don't make a sound," he mutters. The mask is enough to tell the Hammer he'll do it. He's killed several of them, but he prefers not to.

The girl out there might keep the other guards occupied. But she might not. He doesn't want to kill anyone. He wants to take the Hammer alive. Deliver him to the cops. See justice served.

The Hammer breaks free and runs toward the door. He's slow and clumsy, though, and the boy is quicksilver. He slams the Hammer over the head with his gun twice. It's all it takes to lay him out cold.

Now he has two choices. Get the big man out through the vent, or charge through the mall.

Eyes darting toward the front of the store, where several tall, bulky shadows move behind the paper covering the windows, he opts for the vent. He hears the girl talking on and on, diverting their attention. He was right about her. She's one of the good ones.

It takes three minutes, and all the strength he has, to boost the unconscious Hammer up on top of a stack of chairs. Then he climbs on top of him, slides into the ceiling through the opened vent, and pulls the impossibly heavy man through.

In fifteen minutes, they'll have cleared all the vents, and the boy can get him to the police with a long list of incriminating evidence he's compiled. And a little something extra—two packages of pink-and-blue striped giggle pills he's found in the Hammer's pockets.

One less Syndicate capo on the street. Which means he's one rung closer to the top of the organization. To ending them for good.

Hours later, he wakes to her getting dressed. He pretends he's asleep, watches her precise movements through slitted eyes, her small hands buttoning the white blouse of her school uniform, her body blotting out the dim winter light coming through the window, leaning over him, his vision bleary and shot through with stars, light coming in around the edges. That's how tired he is.

The smell of coffee and he sits up. She's filled a blue aluminum camping mug with it for him. "Morning," she says, and grins. The light spills through her tangled white-blond hair, and he cannot recall her ever looking more beautiful.

"Thanks." He sits up, takes a sip. Black and sweet, three sugars.

She leans down and fingers a fresh cut above his eyebrow, careful to hold the coffee away from him, not to spill it on the bed. "You okay?"

"Just a scratch," he says. "Shallow."

Her big blue eyes are playful, capable of detecting people's bullshit a mile away. Especially his. "Put some disinfectant on it."

He nods. "You're up early."

"I have to go," she sighs. "Math test."

"Where do they think you were last night?" Her parents, he means. He's terrified they'll find out. Hire a private investigator, then a bodyguard just for her, and a hit man for him. Or more likely, they'll lock her up at home. Hire private tutors. Keep her forever in that gilded cage of an apartment.

"At Aaron's." She shrugs. "They're so wrapped up in work, they barely care where I am."

She sighs and her breath blows dust motes through the chilly air of the squat. The rattling space heater in the corner does all it can to warm the place, but it's still cold.

"Brought you something." She unbuttons the top two buttons of her cloak, pulls a zippered leather case from her inside pocket, and hands it to him. It's heavy. The stack of bills inside is two inches thick.

"I can't keep—" His voice is hoarse now, embarrassing him. In his chest, his heart stutters. A swell of gratitude smacks up against a wall of pride.

"Don't. It's nothing to me. To us," she interrupts him. "You know that." She shrugs as if to emphasize how little the money matters, her expression faraway as she walks to the window, checking, he assumes, to make sure she wasn't trailed.

His belly rumbles, thinking about eggs in a pan. Butter sizzling. The thought moves him to nod, to tuck the pouch of cash underneath his mattress. He has to take her money. He can't get by without it. "I'll pay you back."

She doesn't bother responding. Never does, when he says this.

"When this is over," he says, "we'll go somewhere far away."

"Maybe we won't have to." She leaves the window and re-buttons her cloak. "The city's changing. You're changing it."

He nods, humoring her. Knowing there will be a price on his head for eternity here. "Maybe."

If he stays here much longer, it won't end well. No matter how much moving around he does, from apartment to squat, residing farther and farther from the center of the city, their network is vast. The reward for him is substantial. How many South Side kids would rat him out to get enough to buy their families food for a year? "I hope you're right."

Her eyelashes are blond at the tips. He never noticed it before. There are so many things to know about a person. Especially when it's *the* person. The one you can't get enough of. Most people, he doesn't want to know a thing about. But with her, he catalogs everything. Each factoid given its own drawer in his mind, labeled specially for her.

How he wound up this hooked on her, of all people, is still a mystery to him. Since he was a little boy he knew what he was meant to do. After his father was killed in front of him, he suspected it would fall to him to do what the police would not.

A girl, especially someone like her, was never part of the plan. But he can't help it. It feels too good to be near her.

They are from different worlds in every way. Him, the one they call the Hope. A ridiculous name, since he has less hope than almost anyone. He's certain it will catch up to him, that he is destined to die in the act. To die fighting them.

And her, Bedlam royalty. Her father in many ways responsible for the way the money rolls upward in this city, all concentrated at the top, in real estate, banks, and politics. And the rest of them with nothing. Gina Fleet, raised in a glass tower built of dirty deals.

Gina Fleet, whose father would be shocked to learn what a radical she really is. More radical even than he is. He's got his reasons for what he does, only some of them to do with making the city better. But Gina believes in it. She calls it a *movement*.

And then her coat is zipped, hat pulled low on her head. She kisses him on top of his head. "I left the paper on the table," she says. "You're everywhere in it."

Before he can answer, she's closing the door. Heading back to her other life. Without her, he might have stopped already. But she makes him feel like it can maybe be done. All the violence, ended. The crime, the fear, all obliterated by his own fists.

And then what? he wonders. *What happens after?*

CHAPTER 3

Monday morning arrives with a torrent of pounding rain, the dark skies matching my mood. The halls of Cathedral Day School smell like the gym locker room, the air close and sweaty and the floors slippery with tracked-in rainwater, everyone's galoshes wet and squeaking on the slick stone floor. There are only nine more weeks until the end of the semester, which means graduation for us seniors. Nine more weeks of wearing the regulation pleated plaid skirt, the white blouse with cap sleeves, the scratchy burgundy or gray cardigan, the coordinating-with-the-cardigan kneesocks.

Nine more weeks until I never see most of these people again.

If I don't get into the Bedlam Ballet Corps, I'll be heading to the U with Zahra. If she doesn't flee the city and head south to try to be an actress, that is.

After I take my books out of my wet knapsack and put them in my locker, I thread my way through a group of beefy rugby players nearly bursting out of their uniform blazers as they jostle and slam one another. I pass by Z's locker, but she's not there.

I wait around a minute or two, avoiding eye contact with Olive Ann Bang, the principal's daughter, as she struts by with one of her henchgirls, Clementine Fitz. In my peripheral vision I see Fitz lean over, whisper something to Bang, and give me the side-eye, but I turn away and face the lockers. These girls are toxic. Ever since I staged an "intervention" with my ex-boyfriend Will's parents and had him sent to rehab, they've been giving me disapproving looks. They likely have no idea that he planted a camera in my room, discovered who I became after the surgery, and used the footage to blackmail me. But even if they knew the truth about what Will did, they'd probably still take his side.

Nine more weeks, I tell myself, *and I never have to see them again*. I wait a couple more minutes but Zahra doesn't show, so I head to homeroom.

On my way, I pass a group of Martha Marks's friends gathered in a tight cluster, huddled around a video playing on one girl's cell phone.

I edge closer. "Anyone hear from Martha today?" I ask Alexandra Veern, one of her best friends, but she shakes her head and shushes me, gesturing at the phone held in the middle of the cluster of people by a petite blond girl wearing pearl earrings. I recognize her from the horse show the other day. Her whole posse has their eyes glued to her phone.

"Have you seen this yet?" hisses Alexandra.

I shake my head, and she pulls me by the elbow until I'm in the circle, able to see the screen.

I stand on tiptoe and lean over Alexandra's shoulder,

assuming it's a replay of Martha's dramatic horse-bucking incident. But instead it's a torrent of still photos, each with a few damning words stamped diagonally across them in bright red. A slick electronic beat and a few chords in minor keys supply an eerie soundtrack, and every picture is punctuated by a deep, electronically modified voice reading the stamped words. I hold my breath as the jumble of words and pictures starts to pile up, dread calcifying in my bones.

A six-year-old boy picking through burnt rubble from a fire. HAPPY CHILDHOOD.

A homeless mother with an infant in rags clutched to her breast. HAPPY FAMILIES.

A guard with a BulletBlower 3000 pointed at an old man with a cane. FUN FOR ALL AGES.

Then the scenes change to North Side pictures. Everything tinted a sickly green. The words turn grayish yellow.

A group of laughing adults dressed in tuxedos and gowns. Voiceover: AND WE ARE ALL SO HAPPY.

Two five-year-old girls wearing pearls, flanking an ornate cake with flowers dripping from its tiers. Voiceover: SO HAPPY IT HURTS.

The mayor laughing with a group of cronies, his mouth open wide, a gleam of gold glitter smeared across his teeth. SO PROUD OF OUR FAIR CITY.

And then the still images stop, and the music thumps faster. We see a large desk draped with a flag. The camera pans up to a white T-shirt with an open eye on it, the bottom of it done in black, fading to gray, and then disintegrating at the tip of the top lashes. A flood of sweat begins to pour from my torso as I flash on the three drugged-out creeps in the sound booth at the arena. The unblinking, all-seeing eye. This is phase two of whatever they've got planned.

The camera pans up above the shirt. A neck. A masked head. Molded white plastic. The mask a crude black-on-white drawing of a grinning face. A crayoned red mouth. Black dots for eyes on the blank white plastic surface. In a different context, the mask might look innocent. But here, after what I've just seen, it sets my teeth on edge.

Could this be a Syndicate thing, some sort of new campaign to fill the void I helped create when Gavin fell off that cliff?

The smiling mouth never moves, but the robotic monotony of the artificially deep voice that begins to drone beneath it sends a chill down my spine.

"Citizens of Bedlam City: Things are about to change. We are a group of people dedicated to making the invisible visible. To making the comfortable less comfortable, and the unhappy a little happier. Ask yourself—am I *too* happy? Too smug? Too comfortable? Do I have so much that I don't know what to do with it all? Could someone use a little of what I have?

"We are here to help. We are here to right the wrongs. To balance the scales. We are the Invisible, and we are everywhere."

The screen on the girl's phone goes static, then white.

"Spooky-cool," one of the girls sighs.

"Right? I bet he's hot under that mask," another says.

"My brother ordered a T-shirt," someone offers. And the cluster of girls breaks into excited chatter. Their talk circles around me, not touching me. Not penetrating the growing sense of alarm punching through my head. I'm conscious of the skin on my arms crawling, my hands shaking slightly, a slick of sweat blooming in the small of my back.

This is definitely not a Syndicate thing. It's too professional. Too performance-based. And the goal is too vague. The Syndicate operates with one goal in mind—money. They steal from the wealthy and the poor alike. They're not interested in making changes like this. This person—persons—is after something bigger.

I step away from the crowd of girls and move down the hall, disgusted by how excited they seem about the video. *We are a group of people dedicated to making the invisible visible. To making the comfortable less comfortable.* Do they not understand that the people who will be targeted are *themselves*?

I move through the crowd, my head buzzing with panic and confusion as I push through the crowd. When the homeroom bell rings, I head mechanically toward Mr. Brick's classroom. As I walk, I start to feel like I'm hearing the word everywhere. Roderick, Cathedral's resident pharms dealer, is talking about it with his pill-head friends, and I turn to look at him. "Invisible's the only one doing anything other than just sitting by, watching the city go to hell," he's saying to a medicated-looking red-haired boy, his voice full of sober conviction. Just above the lapel of his blazer he's sewn a small patch, the single gray eye in a circle of white, its gaze infuriatingly calm.

When I turn the corner I spot Zahra, her black hair shot through with hot-pink pieces, closing her fringed umbrella near a side door, droplets of rain spraying out in front of her. She slips on the wet floor, cursing under her breath as she grabs on to a wall of lockers to keep herself from wiping out.

I rush toward her, relieved to be able to talk to someone I can count on to be cynical about all this. "Have you seen this video going around?"

She raises her eyebrows, her lips turning up at the corners. "Saw it last night. Why are you always the last to know stuff?" she jokes, clapping me on both shoulders and squeezing, her violet eyes ringed in silver liner that looks left over from a night out with Dando, a bartender she met a few weeks ago. "Kinda cool, right? Maybe something will finally happen around here."

My stomach is starting to hurt. "Stuff already happens around here," I say. "Lots of stuff, actually."

"Only on the news," Zahra says. "Never, like, here, or to us."

That's a good thing, I want to remind her, but I don't want to sound like a bore or a prude. If there's anything I learned since spending my nights in the South Side, it's that things happen all the time, and most of them are terrible. Zahra is lucky not to know about them.

"I'm okay with that," I say at last. "Look what happened to Martha. She could have died if she hadn't moved out from under that horse."

"That *is* pretty messed up." Z nods, digging around in her purse and pulling out a compact. "But I'm sure that wasn't supposed to happen. I think it was a prank that got a little out of control. Have a sense of humor, Ant. At least they're not boring. And come on, it's not like anybody died."

Yet. I think. Nobody died yet.

"Maybe you're right," I say, not wanting to argue the point. "After everything that happened, I guess I might be on edge."

Z knows I had a relationship with a South Side boy who turned out to be a con artist. She knows we broke up. She even knows that he's dead now. She just doesn't know the crucial fact that I'm responsible for his death.

"Sorry," Z says, laying her cool hand on my arm in a gesture of apology. "I should be more sensitive. You're so strong about . . . everything . . . that sometimes I forget."

"It's okay." As we head toward homeroom through the emptying halls, I realize all I want is to live the life Z thinks we live. I want to live in a boring city, a place where nothing all that interesting ever happens. So far, no such luck.

CHAPTER 4

I wait until the hallway is quiet and slip out a side door during what is supposed to be my independent study period. I walk out the main security gate and wave at Meechum, one of the Cathedral Day School guards, who sits on a swivel chair in the security booth at the school's entrance, a mini-TV playing muted footage from the Invisible video. Meech wears a BulletBlower 3000 slung across his belly, but the way he leans back in his chair with his feet up tells me he's not on particularly high alert.

"Doctor's appointment." I force a smile I hope looks relaxed and wave a piece of paper in the air that I've ripped from my notebook, pretending it's a pass from the school secretary. Then I keep walking, not giving him a second to stop me.

"See you soon, Anthem," Meech calls after me. "Feel better."

Well, that was easy. I suppress a smile as I move from school cobblestone onto the city sidewalk. I walk with long strides, arms swinging, at a pace a regular person might think of as a fast walk.

But I'm not regular. It feels agonizingly slow.

The minute I round the corner of Church Avenue and head onto Thorne, I pull the black hood of my jacket up over my head and take off, knowing I have a big distance to cover and not a lot of time to do it if I want to be back in time for physics next period.

And in a heartbeat I've sped up to the pace that feels most comfortable for me. A pace that's half-run, half-flight.

All I hear when I run like this is the whirring of my internal hard drive, my regular breaths, and, maybe two or three times in the space of a city block, the thud of my thin sneaker soles making contact with the sidewalk.

I favor streets in the North that are mostly residential, empty at this time of day. I'm always weighing my speed against getting caught. But every time I sense a pedestrian or even a car, I slow my run to something that feels like the sprint of a normal girl. By the time I reach Hemlock, near the river, I decide to experiment, first with two men sitting on a bench, both nodding on droopies, soon to be chased by cops back to the South Side, most likely. I whiz past them on the other side of the street and sense no reaction, no swivel of their necks, their eyes not registering me at all.

I keep moving, pushing myself even faster, amazed. *Maybe when I move like this, people can't see me at all.*

When I race over the Bridge of Peace, halfway to Jax's lab in the space of five minutes, a record for me now that I'm not slowing down, there are two police officers in a cop car parked on one side of the bridge. And in front of me, an orange-and-white barricade.

I take a deep breath and speed up, leaping easily over the barricade, willing myself to move faster, faster than ever. Conscious all the time of the boys in blue sitting in their car. I stare straight at them.

There is no swiveling of their necks. No staring back. Not even a glance in my direction. They don't notice a thing.

"Oh! It's you." When Jax lets me in, she looks like she's seen a ghost. She sticks her head out the door and looks up and down the alley, then slams the door hard. Her thick glasses are crooked on her face, and her Bedlam University Hospital sweatshirt is on inside out. But it's her eyes that strike me most. She looks . . . confused. Jax is a lot of things—flighty, brilliant, and nervous, to name a few of them—but she has never seemed the least bit confused before.

"Did I come at a bad time?" I hesitate in the lab's dim front room, one eye on Jax, who turns in a slow circle, the other on Mildred, Jax's caged monkey, who is screeching and scratching her chest and eating a carrot all at once.

Jax stops turning and looks at me, the weird blank confusion in her eyes eventually focusing into something like recognition. "No, sorry. I—it's just that I've received a bit of an odd letter."

"What is it?" I say, my stomach clenching in anticipation. Maybe someone's found out how I got to be what I am. Found out who made me that way, in this lab, three months ago.

Jax just keeps opening and closing her mouth. She has a plastic pipette lodged in the silver curls piled on her head. I wonder for a moment if she's been threatened and is afraid to tell me. "Jax?"

"It's nothing," she sighs. "Forget I mentioned it. Just a prank, I think."

"Are you sure?"

Jax can be secretive and moody. I would be, too, I remind myself, if I'd been through what she has. I grab her hand, once again noticing the tattoo on her wrist. The tiny red heart. The name of her daughter. The one who died during the experimental surgery Jax performed to try to save her from a rare condition. *Noa.* When the police began investigating, her husband insisted Jax should be arrested. So she hid. And she's been hiding ever since, grieving her daughter and deprived of anything close to a normal life.

"I'm very sure." She turns to me, rolls her shoulders back, and smiles determinedly. "You have my full attention now."

"Okay," I say, letting her off the hook for now but reminding myself to ask about it again later. I tell her about Ford, how he's not getting better. How he can barely hobble out of bed. "It's been a while," I say gently. "Shouldn't he be healed by now?"

"He told me he was doing better," Jax says. "I should have known it wasn't true. If it were, he would come by and show me."

I shake my head. "He's so weak. If anything, I think he's worse." I ask Jax if there's anything she could try, anything at all to make him well.

"I've been working on fortified blood. It's at a very early stage, though . . ." She trails off.

"I don't know how long he can continue like this," I say honestly.

"His white blood count was very low, when we tested last," Jax concedes. "I'll bring him in. Maybe try him on a suboptimal dose, since I'm not done testing."

"Thanks," I say. I give her a tight hug. "And Jax, if you ever want to talk, I'm here."

She smiles, too brightly. Hiding whatever it is, pushing it

away for now. "Thanks, Anthem. I love it when you come to visit. I think I'll do some research on my own, then we'll talk."

I nod. For Jax, research is safety, normalcy, comfort. I tell her I'll come back and check in soon. Then I leave and race back across town, my mind clinging to the hope—faint and half-formed—that Ford might finally get better.

CHAPTER 5

I move around the kitchen island at home that night, ravenous after ballet practice and feeling a little woozy from low blood sugar. I surreptitiously check my fingertips for signs of torpor, when my fingers turn blue from the slowing of my heart, something that happens to me sometimes if I don't eat enough or if I spend too much time being still, but they look okay. Maybe a tad gray, but not the periwinkle they can get sometimes.

"I saw that," Lily, our cook, says after I grab a sautéed Brussels sprout straight out of the pan she's cooking them in.

"Sorry." I grin. "Just one more." I pop another one into my mouth, the hot oil slicking my lips. Just then I hear the elevator doors sliding open in the hall. They're home.

Lily nudges me gently out of her way so she can reach the plates in the cupboard. "They'll be here soon."

Lily won't hear them for another thirty seconds at least, not until they're on the other side of the thick front door to the apartment. I just nod, chewing and preparing myself for another meal with my father rambling on about work while I look at him and wonder.

The curse of my sonic hearing is that I hear stuff even when I don't want to. Like when my parents discuss my emotional well-being in their bedroom and they think I can't hear them.

How is she doing these days? my father will ask my mother. *After everything with that boy. Is she suppressing her feelings?*

My mother's touching if off-base reply: *She's just much stronger than we give her credit for. I think she's moved on.* She's sort of right on both counts, even though they have no clue what really happened with Gavin. In many ways, I *have* moved on. Even though there's a moment at least once a day where I flash on him falling, moving on is all I have. My only hope of staying sane.

But mostly when I bother to listen to their conversations, they talk shop. Today it's no different. Inside the apartment at last, they're discussing (as usual) some detail of the stadium project Fleet Industries is doing. They both sound irritated. Also pretty usual.

"I sent another letter. Why don't you get Phillip to follow up about the stadium jobs proposal, take it to city council?"

"You've said this three times today, Leenie." My dad sounds defensive. "I told you I'm handling it, and I'm handling it."

"Fine. I just . . . Lyndie wants to move on another press release because of the protests, she said—"

"Next week it'll be done. You have my word." My father's tone is sharp, designed to close the subject.

"Great," my mother says tightly. When they come into the kitchen she gives me a kiss on the part in my bunned hair and heads straight for the wine cooler under the counter, to her chardonnay.

"Smells good in here," my father says, brightening for me and Lily the same way he always does, wiggling his thick eyebrows and doing a little jokey shuffle-dance.

I used to like this little act. Now it just seems rehearsed.

"No hello for your pop today?" he says pointedly, a lock of his dark hair escaping its gelled formation and springing down across his forehead.

"Hi," I say, ducking as he tries to grab my bun and twist it—another of our old games.

"Crab cakes." Lily opens the oven and dons a silicone glove to pull out the metal tray warming inside it.

My stomach emits a loud burbling growl as the platter hits the counter. My mother pulls the cork out of a wine bottle with a pop—

But at the exact moment the cork is released, we are all plunged into darkness.

Out the window, one by one, the blocks sprawling in all directions from where we are in Fleet Tower go dark. All the way to the Midland River, where the darkness bleeds into the inky black of the water.

And beyond the river, the normally muted South Side suddenly looks brighter, as if the power outage on this side of the river is because the South is getting more wattage somehow.

We haven't blown a fuse. The whole neighborhood has.

"Uh-oh," my mother says. Even in the dark, she is pouring the wine. I hear it glugging from the bottle into her glass.

It's a new moon, and the only light we have to see by is the faint glow coming from two miles away, the intermittent street lighting of the South Side.

"I'll just go and get the candles in the pantry," Lily says, and I move toward the sound of her voice to follow her.

When we return, our arms piled with boxes of candles and a big box of kitchen matches, the TV built into the wall of the kitchen—one we hardly ever use—is now on, displaying only black-and-white static, buzzing loudly.

"Why does that work?" I ask. "And not the lights, I mean?"

"It turned on by itself," my father mutters. He rummages in the kitchen junk drawer under the counter. "Where's the damned remote?" His voice is edged with panic.

"But why . . ." I start as Lily lines up votive candles on a piece of tinfoil on the counter and strikes a match. "Lily, have you ever seen . . ."

"Course not," she whispers, her green eyes wide in the glow of the static from the TV. "Because it's impossible."

But then the static stops, replaced with that same drawing of the eye. Placid, unblinking, unfeeling, watching. *Invisible.* My skin begins to crawl as an assault of pictures moves across the screen, these more disturbing than the ones I saw this morning. Pictures from the South Side Riots—a rash of violent clashes that broke out in the city when I was a baby. By the time I was one, they'd been squelched by the police crackdown that's continued until now. Doubling the amount of police in the force and giving the police more power ended what I've always been told were the scariest months the city has ever seen. The images are horrible, mesmerizing: A young woman lying on asphalt, the top of her head caved in, blackness seeping around her hair. A policeman with a baton raised, about to come down on a ten-year-old boy, the cop's face twisted in anger, the boy's scrawny arms covering his head. Feargas clouding around a group of what looks like thousands of people marching outside of city hall, their eyes wild and wide, mouths open as if screaming.

The images get faster and faster.

Dozens of black-and-white stills in quick succession, each of them depicting dead or collapsed people on city streets. Many of them young, younger than me.

A few shots of what look like twelve-year-olds getting Syndicate tattoos, their faces hard, their eyes fearful.

As I watch, I sink into a chair at the kitchen table next to my mother, who has poured her wine into a jelly jar and now holds it to her lips with two hands, drinking it the way a small child drinks juice.

"But how is it happening?" I hear my father ask wonderingly. "It's on all the TVs. How have they switched the TVs on?"

Nobody answers him. I pull my arms around myself, a cold shiver rocking through me.

Now the photos show the kind of people I know. We've passed the riots. On to the parties. The balls. The orphans singing for the mayor and his ilk. Tuxedos, champagne, orthodontically perfect smiles. Then shots of South Side children polishing shoes, their foreheads black with grease marks.

I look out the window for a second, and my throat seizes—in every apartment in all the towers on the block, there are TVs broadcasting the same assault of pictures. People crowd around some of them, their profiles in shadow. Other TVs broadcast to empty rooms.

But *how*?

I shake my head hard and turn back to the screen, wanting to understand.

The images combine with similar phrases like the ones I saw this morning on the girl's phone:

SOME PEOPLE ARE SO COMFORTABLE IT HURTS.

THE GAME IS RIGGED.

THE SCALES ARE OUT OF BALANCE.

SOME OF US ARE GOING INSANE AT THE SIGHT OF IT.

And on and on. The music thumping. The images flying.

And then, again, the masked man behind the desk. The desk draped with the flag of Bedlam. Four white stars in a square formation. One for each bridge. The red and blue halves of the flag split diagonally. His mask, the crude child's drawing of a face, the features uncannily askew, everything just a little wrong in the placement. The chin area of the mask curling up slightly, jutting into a rounded triangle that reveals a small swatch of his chin, giving the effect of a face being peeled from a skull.

"To those of you sitting in the dark right now, and you know who you are . . ."

I feel gooseflesh rise on my arms when there's muffled laughter from behind the mask.

"You have an assignment. It's a simple one. And it won't hurt you a bit. Go to your banks, withdraw half your money, and give it to someone who has less than you. Let's come together to even the scales, shall we? You have forty-eight hours. If you complete the assignment, you might get to keep all the things that make your life so easy. And if you decide not to do your homework, there will be . . ." A long pause here. I meet my mother's eyes and see vivid horror etched in them. ". . . consequences. Bedlam will start to live up to its name."

The man in the mask folds his hands together on his desk, sets them down on the Bedlam flag. Then the illustrated eye flashes for a second on the screen, followed by static.

And just as they all turned on out of nowhere, the TVs shut off all by themselves.

Then all around the neighborhood, the lights come back

on. Our own lights flare on a second later, and we stare at one another around the table, blinking.

"Forget it," my father says. "A prank. Let's eat."

The whole thing is over just as quickly as it began. Except that none of us are able to forget what we've just seen.

"We will not be cowed by terrorists," the mayor huffs into his microphone at a press conference less than an hour later. We haven't left the kitchen, having turned the TV on to watch while we ate dinner so we could see the reaction to this bizarre transmission. Two laptops sit open on the table, displaying more news. "We will find the person or persons responsible for these ridiculous, baseless threats, and they will be held accountable."

My father bursts out laughing and gets up. He pauses behind my mother and puts his hands on her shoulders. "Some trick. Gotta give them that," he snorts.

"I'm glad you find this so funny, Harris," my mother breathes, shaking his hands off her shoulders and standing up. "I don't see why you're laughing when there's a maniac making threats. I may have to cancel the masquerade ball, if this keeps up." My mother's been chairing a committee for a charity ball this weekend. I look at her sharply. Can this really be her biggest concern right now?

"Everything will be fine, Leenie. Internet consensus is that they hacked into the TV satellites," my dad says. He seems almost to be relishing the theater of it all. "Manny's calling them terrorists for the ratings. They're just a bunch of punk kids."

Something in me can't hold back when he says that. I think of the party at Gavin's house, for new Syndicate recruits. Kids younger than I am being handed guns. All the blood money Gavin used to outfit his house in the latest technology. The kids I met there, some of them fourteen or even younger, who worshipped the Syndicate, as if the crime organization was their ticket to righting the wrongs the world had committed against them.

"You'd know all about punk kids, right, Dad?"

I pull myself up tall, looking up into his green eyes, his charmer's smile faltering into a glazed, expressionless grimace.

"What's that supposed to mean?"

"I think you know," I say. My hands are starting to shake.

"I don't know what you're implying, but if you have something to say to me, I'm all ears."

I press my mouth closed, suddenly aware that my mother and Lily are looking at me strangely. This isn't a conversation I want to have in front of them.

"Fine. I'll be in my office. Too much female hostility up here for me at the moment." He crosses the kitchen and heads for the stairs down to the lower floor.

My mother shoots me a bewildered look and heads to her room, where I'm sure she'll take a pill and fall asleep.

"You okay?" Lily says softly.

I nod. But I'm not. Not really. I can't keep doing this, I decide as I drop the dinner dishes one by one into the sinkful of suds Lily's prepared. Sneaking around and trying to catch my father in the act has gotten me nowhere. It's time to confront him.

When the last dish disappears into the scummy water, I head down the stairs and knock on his office door.

"What." Not a question, and barked in an unfriendly tone, but I push the door open anyway.

He's sitting in the dark, tapping on his keyboard, some sort of spreadsheet on his computer screen. His face glows in the only light in the room, coming from the three computer monitors set up in a row on his desk. He keeps his eyes on the screen when he talks. "Hello, *dear*. Are we continuing the game of Ambush Daddy?"

"Do you give money to the Syndicate?"

My father stops typing and swivels his chair around to face me.

"Where is this coming from?" Amusement and condescension flit across his face and then vanish, replaced with his thousand-watt real-estate developer smile.

"I heard it somewhere. That you give money to the Syndicate." I am thankful for the darkness of his office—my face is on fire.

"From whom, exactly?" he asks, laying his hands open-palmed on his knees.

"I . . . I can't remember. It was a while ago."

"Anthem, why don't you have a seat?" He gestures to the leather club chair pushed up against one of the walls.

I collapse into it, my legs suddenly like toothpicks holding up a boulder.

He takes a deep breath. Lets it out. Crosses his legs, uncrosses them. "We have been in a position to keep you very innocent of some of the dirtier parts of living in this city. And I'm happy we were able to shield you from them. But you are getting older, so I'm going to tell you something now that may shock you."

You are a crime boss. Mom is in on it. Everything I've always been told is a lie.

"Everyone with any kind of business operation in greater Bedlam gives money to the Syndicate. We don't like it, and we don't like them. But we do it. All of us."

My mouth falls open. I'm shocked by the bluntness of his honesty.

"All of who?"

"Everyone. Anyone who needs to get things done here. Because if we don't pay them off, they make our lives impossible. What do you think a mafia is? It's organized crime, and it depends on coercion to keep itself operational. And we—the businessmen and -women of Bedlam—have been coerced into paying them to leave us alone."

"How long has this been going on?" I say robotically. It's starting to sink in. He's not "the Money," not the ringleader of the Syndicate. If he was, he would deny any involvement. He's bad, but not in the way I thought.

"My whole adult life. Ever since my first job after the boys' home, when I worked construction. There have always been payoffs."

My whole adult life. My father never talks about his childhood. All he ever says is "I'm glad it's over." I know he spent his teens in a boys' home outside the city, that he left home at twelve because there were too many mouths to feed, that he's a self-made man. But that's about it.

"But why don't you call the police?" I say, my throat a desert, my tongue sticking to the roof of my mouth. "Why pay them off when you can have them arrested?" Though of course, I know why. The police are on the Syndicate payroll. Not all of them, but definitely a few. Detective Marlowe, for one, whose name is also in Gavin's book. And probably hundreds of others. The only cop I trust even a little bit is the officer who interrogated me with Marlowe after Gavin died. Officer Rodriguez struck me as incorruptible. I still have her business card in my wallet.

"We do, if things get really ugly. But small payoffs, they're the cost of doing business. The Syndicate knows they can only push me so far before I snap and call in the law, and for the most part they respect my boundaries. If I called the police every time someone wanted a payoff, I wouldn't be able to run Fleet Industries." His lips twitch into a sad half-smile, and he shrugs, as if to say he's sorry that the world isn't the fair, just place I've always thought it was.

I nod. It's an ugly reality, but not the one I expected. "And the funeral you went to? Your employee who fell off the bluff at the lake?"

"What about him?" He sounds testy.

"I happen to know he's . . . he was . . ." I struggle to get the words out. "He was high up in the Syndicate."

My father shoots me a suspicious look and lets a silence fill the room before he answers. "And how would you know something like that?"

"I just . . . do." I watch my father absorb the fact that I'm stonewalling him. Like he's reassessing me. I guess he's surprised that I have secrets, too. He looks at me strangely, as if he's got a new respect—or maybe wariness—of me.

"I heard about that, too, just after his body was found," he says at last. "But I knew nothing about the guy when he was working for me. And then at the funeral I realized that Serge and I were surrounded by Syndicate thugs. I was shocked."

I nod, silent. Hoping he'll say more.

"We employed him as a caretaker for our Morass Bluffs project, which had been stalled for over a year." He leans in closer. "But kitten, why are you so curious about him?"

"Because . . ." I stop midsentence, wondering what I can possibly say that will make sense. *Because he was my boyfriend, the one who conned me into thinking he was kidnapped? The one you didn't want to give the ransom money for?* "I don't know. I just heard it somewhere."

He sighs. "I wish I didn't have to give the Syndicate anything. I hate them. They're murderers and thugs. Someday soon, I hope I won't have to. If the mayor can just crack down harder. Get the police to do a big sweep of them. Ferret them out." He looks up at me. "Maybe you'll help do something about it when you're older. Maybe you'll join the city government."

Or just go out at night and tie up bad guys, I think, my chest squeezing my heart like a vise. "Maybe—anything's possible."

I rise from the chair. My father stands up, too, and he gives me a short, tight hug. For the first time in a while, I feel like I used to. I'm Harris's daughter again—comforted in my father's arms. No longer naïve, but also no longer scared of him.

When we separate, he says something so quietly I have to ask him to repeat himself.

"I said this Invisible thing is just amateurs. Fame-seekers, pranksters. It'll blow over soon."

I nod. "I hope you're right."

CHAPTER 6

When the blue numbers on my bedroom clock flash two A.M., I slip out of my bed and get dressed in jeans, suede sneakers, and a hooded black jacket. I've watched Invisible's dispatch on the Internet dozens of times and spent the past three hours turning over every word of it in my head.

Will people really start giving their money away? Is it just a thought experiment, a prank?

I've tried, but I can't possibly sleep, thinking about it all. It's time to get a new perspective. And there's only one person I want to see.

Running through the South Side, my feet barely touch the ground at all. The air on my face is like a wind tunnel. Parked cars and buildings are no more than smeared blurs in my vision. My heart pumps ten times faster than normal when I'm at rest—right now, moving this fast, it must be at one thousand beats per minute. I feel it humming under my ribs, a hot motor powering me.

All over the South, a giant Syndicate party is in full swing. The revelry outside the South's many bars is louder and more boisterous than I've ever seen it. Homemade fireworks pop low in the sky along the riverbank, throwing watermelon-size sparkles into the black sky.

Groups dressed in the black, gray, and brown favored in the South spill out of bars on every corner, stumbling along in the slick streets. On Oleander and Ivy, a bleary man harmonizes with a younger woman on an old Bedlam protest song:

We will fight, against the might
Of the rich, who wish we all would disappear.
We will fight, every night
In quarters far and near
And call upon the angels bright
To hold us tight
Against the bombs, the water cannons, and the gas
Because it's with knives
And with our lives
That we pay 'em back for all that's come to pass

It's because of the video, I realize as I speed down an alley and pass by a group of people a year or two older than I am, hair dyed in blues and purples and pinks. They are drunk, two of the boys in the group with SYN tattoos on their necks, shouting something about a payday or a paycheck. The words are all garbled.

But they can't actually think someone's going to walk up to them and give them a suitcase full of cash . . . can they?

No, I realize. Of course not. They know that will never

happen. The payday they're talking about is the one Invisible is threatening to give the North Side if—*when*—nobody does the "assignment." Not payday or a paycheck. Pay*back*.

When I get to Ford's apartment, the light in the living room is on. I tap softly on the window, and instantly the curtain is pulled back and I'm met with Ford's face, his teeth glowing in the lamplight, smiling broadly. A thrilled shiver ripples through me—it's great to see him up and around.

He buzzes me inside and I move down the hall toward the apartment, where he's standing in the doorframe. His color isn't so green anymore. Even in the hall fluorescents, I can see a pink in his cheeks that hasn't been there for weeks. His posture is the one I remember from before the shooting, straight and tall, no longer stooped and slumped as it has been for too long.

"You look better." I fight the rush of heat creeping from my chest to my face as I move to embrace him. "A lot better."

Ford pulls me to him and squeezes, hard but not too hard. An electric jolt of want ripples through my body and I can't resist leaning my head on his shoulder a minute, just breathing in the fact of him standing up, healthy at last. Then I pull away, though it's clear he doesn't want me to.

Don't want him, I command myself. *Just don't. You need a friend, not complications. Not the pain of losing him when it doesn't work out.*

"I am. Much better, in fact." Ford pulls me into the apartment and shuts the door behind us. "Jax decided to give me some kind of special blood she came up with. I went in yesterday morning. It's working. Really well, actually. I started feeling better almost right after she gave me the transfusion."

I nod, feigning utter ignorance. Inside I'm cheering for Jax, and congratulating myself for insisting she try something more.

We both stand in the living room, my hands in his, blinking at each other, grinning. "Special blood, huh? Must have been extra-special," I joke.

"Glad you're here," he says. His voice cracks on *here*. "You put me in a good mood. You've always had that effect on me," he adds shyly, looking down at our hands, our fingers still wound around one another. I pull my hands away, suddenly self-conscious about how close we're standing. The part of my heart that's still damaged after being conned so ruthlessly by Gavin jangles out a warning: *Proceed with caution.* But the rest of me doesn't want to hear it. My fingers are thrumming, warm from Ford's touch.

"I also put you into a coma, though."

"No you didn't. *He* did that." Ford's face darkens at the mention of Gavin. "If he hadn't died the way he did, I'd be out hunting him down right now."

I shake my head. "I wouldn't have let you."

"I would have done it anyway," Ford says, his eyes shining in the low lamplight. "He was Bedlam river scum."

"Anyway, he's gone," I remind him. "It's just us now."

Just us, alone in a room. I think of what Ford said when he was briefly conscious, just before he fell into the coma: *My whole life, I've been waiting. . . .*

My feelings about Ford were buried under so many layers of panic and worry before, but with those stripped away, all that's left is a fuzzy warmth in my midsection and a need to be close to him. I start to lean in, feel my eyelids sinking down as I give in to the spell of our attraction . . . but then the doorknob clicks behind Ford and little Sam comes out in her nightgown.

"I had a bad dream," she says, rubbing sleep from her eyes,

"that there were bad guys in here. I wanted to check."

"Hey, munchkin," Ford says, scooping her up in his arms and motioning for me to join him on the couch, Sam between us. Her hair smells like shampoo, still wet in two messy braids. "No bad guys here. Just us good guys." He winks at me.

Settling into Ford's lap, Sam grins up at me. "He loooves you, Anthem."

"Easy there, tiger." He rolls his eyes and grins at me, his neck flushing a deep red. "The kid's been reading a lot of fairy tales."

It's okay, I think but don't say. Because I probably love him, too.

CHAPTER 7

At four in the morning, the revelry on the South Side has died down. I whiz through the silent blocks of dilapidated row houses with trash swirling in the streets and driveways, not a soul around to see me, floating on a pillow of happiness about Ford being healthy again, the relief so druglike that I'm not even paying attention to my surroundings. My legs are pumping as usual, but it takes so little effort now that my mind is free to wander, my thoughts disconnected from my body.

As I run, a bizarre image pops into my head: Ford meeting my parents. Everyone getting along. Would they see that we make sense, even if we are from different worlds?

I'm running down Hemlock toward Hyacinth Lane when a scream punctuates the silence. I slow down to a jog, and then freeze altogether, listening in the cold night. I hear the shattering of glass. Then another sound, a quiet *zzzz-zzzz* that starts and stops.

It's coming from up ahead, the cul-de-sac devoted to the

massive property everyone calls Marks Manor, because it's the mayor's mansion and Mayor Marks has been in office for so long.

When I reach it, the enormous house looks undisturbed from what little I can see beyond the sloping lawn and trees and fence. I flip my hood up, conscious of the possibility of cameras. But then there's another scream, and the hairs on the back of my neck stand at attention. It came from inside the house.

For some reason, I look at my watch—4:21 A.M.

My fingers begin to pulse. My heart stutters painfully. The scream echoes in my ears—was it Martha?

I run toward the iron security fence surrounding the house and leap. I manage to grab on to the top of it, just to the right of the gate. Once my feet get purchase on the bars it's easy to shimmy over the top. I drop down and land soundlessly on the grass, my heart whirring with panic as I pull my hood tighter around my head and sprint toward the house. If I keep moving fast, the cameras hopefully won't be able to pick up my image.

The lawn has been spray-painted with a message. The paint is wet and purple on the soft blue-green grass.

This ridiculous and baseless threat
brought to you by the Invisible.

My blood freezes in my veins as I recognize the words from the mayor's speech. They've come for revenge.

I dart soundlessly to the side of the house until I reach the door. It swings open on its hinges.

My mouth goes dry as I run through the marble front room, sweeping staircases rising from either side. I take the one on the right, toward the residential rooms. I used to play here occasionally with Martha when my mother brought me with her to charity luncheons. The image of Martha as an eight-year-old, her room covered with horse-jumping ribbons, her braids askew as she bounced on her pink bedspread, swims into my mind.

I'm up the stairs in a second. I pause on the landing, then dart down the carpeted, dark hallway to my right. I don't see the feral-looking boy of maybe nineteen until he barrels around the corner and nearly cuts me with a blade he holds in his hand.

I leap away from the blade and then I'm on top of him before he even sees me.

"Where is she?" I whisper, twisting his wrist until the blade, a small box cutter, thumps to the carpet. I scoop it up and hold it to his throat.

He smiles a vacant smile, his eyes scarily blank as he motions behind him. "In her room. With the others," he says matter-of-factly.

"Take me there," I growl, pressing the blade against his pimply neck.

"You're too late," he says.

He's said it so calmly and clearly it makes me pause for a moment. Something is not right, but I can't understand it yet. "Who do you work for?"

"You'll see," the boy says, squirming against me as I move him down the hall. "You're very good at this. You should join us. He'd love to have you."

"Never." My hands shake with rage and apprehension and I pull the blade back a bit, afraid I'll accidentally cut his jugular.

That's when I hear the tiny muffled ping of a bullet with a silencer. Followed by a sickening thud. Followed by the sound of glass sliding open. A window.

I hurl the boy as hard as I can against the damask-covered wall, the hallway blurring as panic rocks through me.

He smashes face-first against the wall with a howl and the snap of bone. I don't stay to see if he's out cold.

I fly down the hallway, passing room after vacant room, all the doors flung open. The mayor's suite is on the left. A huge bedroom flanked with a bathroom and a dressing room on either side. I peek in for a second, my breath held, half-expecting to find the mayor and Belinda lying in their bed, murdered.

But the bed is empty. There's no time to figure out where Manny and Belinda are. I leave the empty room and dart down the hall, listening, hearing nothing but the insane whirring of my chest, when I come to the only closed door. It's carved mahogany. I frantically try to yank it open, desperate to get inside the room, suddenly certain it's Martha's. But the door is locked.

I start hurling my body at it, my hands shaking like crazy. I hear shouting that sounds like it's coming from below, from the lawn.

I take a running start and slam my shoulder against the door. On the second try, I succeed, and the whole thing falls forward into the room, with the frame still around the door, having splintered away from the wall.

It's Martha's room. I remember it now, the way the walls are perfectly round because it's located in the turret. It looks just the same as it did when we were ten. The curved walls, the ceiling that comes to a perfect, swooping point in the center. There are more horse-show ribbons now, and more snapshots of Martha.

I move inside, stepping over the door I destroyed, my breath stoppered in my throat.

The lavender bedspread is pulled back. I see a tangle of white sheets. Nothing more.

My chest loosens. She is still alive. They've got her. I need to go after them.

But when I move toward the window I nearly step on her. Martha. On the floor. Crumpled where she stood. Her body folded, jackknifed unnaturally in two. Wearing a white camisole with small pink roses, matching cotton pants. Blood spattered all over both.

"Martha!" I cry. *Nononono.* I drop to my knees, a high-pitched sound coming out of my mouth that I can't seem to control.

Surely this is fixable. A doctor. Technology. Look what they did for Ford. All of these thoughts whisper through me as I pull my sleeves down over my hands, somehow having the presence of mind to remember I don't want to leave fingerprints here.

I lift her shoulders, still warm, then put my hand over my mouth to hold in the scream. There is no fixing this. It is done and final. A hole in her forehead. So clean and small, but for all the blood.

I sit down on the floor, let her upper body fill my lap on the pink shag rug.

I cock my head toward the open window to Martha's room, the white curtains billowing in the wind, listening. Whoever did this is already long gone. The faint tones of approaching sirens reach me, maybe ten blocks away now. A clatter of foot-steps two floors below. A slamming door. The blank-faced boy from the hallway, I'm certain of it.

I look down at Martha. The curl of the cowlick in her bangs is still parted funny, the detail so utterly Martha that I can't help but reach out and touch her hair. Her face frozen, ghost-white, streaked with a black half-mask of blood. The features are hers, but the shocked expression, the frozen eyes don't look anything like who she was. Her upper body stretched across my thighs is already stiffening.

I move out from under her, letting her body slide to the pink shag carpet. I cough, and it's like a deranged bark. I think of Martha's parents. Are they still alive? Where are they?

I lay her down on the ground, horrified to leave her here like this. But the cops are on their way. I can't be here when they arrive.

I pull the sleeve of my coat down over my hand and wipe Martha's doorknob before I race downstairs, the sound of sirens moving closer ringing in my ears. I slip outside and look around the manicured grounds. There's no movement aside from the Bedlam municipal flag flapping on a pole, the four stupid stars, in the stupid square formation, the blue half and the red half even on the diagonal plane. What were they supposed to represent? Prosperity and unity or something idiotic like that? Could two words possibly be more hollow than those?

I race toward the back fence, running even faster when I notice it's lined with surveillance cameras, their red lights blinking. I flip my hood over my hair, and run with my hands shielding my face, so fast I hope I'm a blur, until I reach a willow tree near the fencing, using it to climb over.

Careful to face away from the cameras, I take off again, my heart thrashing against my ribs—the pain so real I'm afraid they'll crack.

CHAPTER 8

I pull the covers tight around my ears to mute the hissing sound that's invaded my Dreamadine-assisted sleep. But the hissing becomes a monotone snarl and I unseal my eyes, which feel like they are full of glass shards. I emerge from under my blanket, check the glowing numbers on the bedside table clock—6:09 in the morning, and I fell asleep after five A.M.—to find the source of the electronic howling: My computer monitor is blaring black-and-white static, like an old TV.

A shiver passes through me so hard I convulse. Then I am perfectly still. Watching the static, bracing for more threats from the Invisible.

I don't need to see it, I realize, the drugged lid of sleep unfastening from my brain. *I can turn it off.* I stagger out of bed, my head spinning, and try to turn off my monitor. But the button does nothing. The static just grows brighter, louder.

I look through an open crimp in my tangle of blinds and see that all over the neighborhood, far below my room on the eighty-seventh floor of the tallest building in Bedlam, it is the same as in here. Everywhere there is a half-open curtain or tangled-up blind, every unobstructed view inside an apartment or a house or an office building reveals a tiny screen twitching with static.

A moment more and the static stops. Then up pops the same masked man. Sitting at the same desk. "Good morning, Bedlam. Wakey wakey, eggs and bakie. We are the Invisible, and we are everywhere. The girl in the big white house was unfortunate collateral damage. These things happen, and they make us sad. A moment of silence, then, for the city's daughter." Long pause, bowed head. I glare at his curly brown hair.

"But enough about her," he continues, his voice bright again. "This is a special transmission for the girl in black, Bedlam's New Hope."

Oh no. I peek out the blinds again and see him on every TV. Everyone in Bedlam is being woken up with this. I think of my parents in their room. They must be hearing it, too. A message broadcast to the whole city, but meant just for me.

"Whoever you are. I'm looking for you. I hope we find one another before things get a whole lot darker." And then that same insane giggle warbles out from behind the mask. My arms prickle with gooseflesh as the computer goes static again and shuts off.

In the blackness of my monitor, I see my own face. My mouth pressed thin with determination. Fury burning in my too-bright eyes.

I crawled back into bed eventually, my heart racing. I closed my eyes, knowing full well I would not sleep. But when my mother shakes me awake from a dead sleep at eight, I'm surprised to realize that somehow, I slept. While Martha's body was loaded into a van and driven to the morgue, I slept.

"We need to talk," my mother says, her eyes calm and Viviraxed, but her voice strong, her posture erect. "There's been another video. Did you see it?"

Oh god. My stomach recoils and all traces of my heavy sleep dissolve. *They know it's me.* "I . . . uh, I saw some of it. I was half-asleep."

My mother nods. "Harris, come in here," she calls out to my father, then stares at me anxiously as she perches lightly on the corner of my bed. She is in full makeup. Her injection sites have healed and the skin of her face is frozen and taut, her body Pilates-perfect, her blazer pressed. She is cloaked in the full Helene Fleet armor. I sit up in bed when my father comes in, balancing two espressos on a little tray.

"From Lily," he says courtly as he bends to present us with the steaming china cups.

"Thanks." I take it, grateful for the caffeine.

"Anthem. We don't want you to be alarmed or scared. But you need to know that some strange things happened last night," my mother says, her words breathy and careful as if she's bracing herself for my reaction.

I nod, trying my best to look like I don't know what's coming.

"Martha has been killed," my mother goes on, wincing at the awful words. "They shot her, execution style."

"What? That's . . ." I shake my head, feigning disbelief. "No."

"It's awful, I know. Unthinkable. What Manny and Belinda must be going through, well, it's . . ." Her voice cracks. She's been through a dead child. Before I was born, my sister, Regina, drowned in Lake Morass. They never figured out why. My mother squeezes my hand.

I change the subject. "Where were they?"

"Who?" My mother looks at me blankly.

"Manny and Belinda." I clear my throat, sitting up straighter. "Were they there when it happened?"

"They were at a conference in West Exurbia, staying in a hotel," my father cuts in. "And they'll regret that conference for as long as they live." My father's voice cracks when he says this. His eyes are red and puffy, I notice. I've never seen him this emotional, not even at our yearly trips to the cemetery to visit Regina's grave.

"And the girl who was turning in all those criminals a few months ago? The one they were calling the New Hope? They believe she was involved somehow. All the surveillance at the mayor's house was erased by the killers somehow. They can't figure it out. But they have footage of some men running away, what looks like a girl coming later, moving very fast so it's hard to see her. She was trying to stop it, by the sound of it, and going by what they said to her last night in their . . . what do they call it?"

"Transmission," I mutter, my voice husky and raw. "I think they call them transmissions."

"It's awful, what's happened to Martha," my father says. "But what they've done to the museum shows us how much muscle they actually have."

"The art museum?" Have they done something else?

My father nods. "They've . . ." His mouth squeezed into an angry knot, he can't seem to get the words out.

"What?"

"Maybe we'd better just show you," my mother says. She gets up and moves to my windows, pulling up my blinds. I follow her. When I reach the window and see, I gasp. Several blocks over, we have a perfect aerial view of the museum, and half of it is just . . . gone. Charred to a black crisp. Nothing but the burnt concrete foundations remain, metal rods extending from it like ganglia, like the frozen tentacles of sea anemones. Through a gray haze of smoke and pollution, half the dome sticks out, along with half the plaster wings. The other half—nothing but foundations—crawls with tiny people. Police, I assume.

My father moves to join me at the window. "There are two museum guards still missing—suspects, I'm sure—but that's it. Nobody saw a thing until the museum imploded. Think of all the art they destroyed. Irreplaceable."

I nod, my chest thrumming so fast and hard that I regret having downed the espresso. "But why?"

But even as I say these words, my thoughts latch on to the logic of the act. *Half your money.* Taking away half of the North's excess.

"Why do scum like this do anything?" my dad says under his breath. "Need for attention. Insanity. Who knows?"

"As chair of the gala," my mother says, "I'm going to do what I can to redirect the funds to the museum this year. God knows they'll need all the help they can get. We can't have a gaping hole there. Whatever's left of the structure will be destroyed."

I stare out at the festering hole in the city's skyline, the black smoke and char like a wound.

"Anyway, kitten," my dad cuts in, "the city is on high alert. Serge is driving you today. And he'll be there to pick you up.

Dance class will be cancelled, I'm sure. You're to come straight home after school, okay? Just until they figure this out and catch these creeps."

"Okay," I say, as if I actually believe the city and its useless, bought police can do anything at all to catch Invisible. I think of Gavin's handwritten list, the names of all those cops he paid off. People like that can't be trusted to care about anything.

You want something done around here, you have to do it yourself.

CHAPTER 9

At school, everyone looks ashen. Eyelids are swollen from crying. Martha's locker has become a shrine—teddy bears, horse memorabilia, pictures, notes, candles, and dozens of bouquets spill out onto the floor, the pile six lockers wide.

"Attention, students, please report to the chapel for a special morning assembly," Principal Bang's monotone bleats through the loudspeakers. It's going to be about Martha, of course. I skirt around the edge of the flower pile, wishing I'd thought to bring something.

Everywhere, girls are crying in the hallways. I feel sick when I see Team Ice, the group of juniors who were Martha's closest friends, hugging one another, shoulders shaking. I run to the bathroom and make it into a stall just before heaving up whatever's in my stomach.

Afterward, I flush it down and grimace at the bitter taste. While I'm crouching in the stall on the cold tile floor, I eavesdrop on a conversation between two girls standing at the sinks.

"Still, I bet he's hot."

"Wasn't *him* who offed her. One of his people. The thing at the museum was ridiculous. I mean, that took guts."

"Serious guts. He's like Robin Hood or whatever. Evening the scales."

"I heard he's only twenty-one."

My empty stomach lurches when I hear one of them emit what sounds like a dreamy sigh. I push open the stall door and size them up. They're barely pubescent fourteen-year-old girls, freshmen, one of them brandishing a pink lipstick, the other brushing on a shimmery eye shadow.

"I heard he's forty and has a deformed face," I say. "Also that he likes to shoot young girls in the head." I bring my index finger up to the shorter, blonder one's forehead and press an imaginary trigger. "Bang bang. Serious guts."

"Stop it." She steps away from me, glaring. "Leave us alone."

"If you don't like the idea of a gun to your head," I say as I wash my hands, "you might want to reevaluate crushing on a killer. It's a great way to ruin your life. It's also stupid and sad." *Trust me. I know.* Gavin was exciting and dangerous, and look how much fun that turned out to be.

"Whatever," they mutter, and hurry out. The taller girl drops her lipstick and doesn't notice, and I stare at the black tube as it skitters across the tile. The bathroom door swings shut on its stoppered spring, leaving me alone with my reflection: hollowed-under eyes, colorless cheeks. But my eyes glow that vibrant green again. The color they get when violence courses through my mind and limbs.

I'm moving with the mob of other Cathedral students toward the chapel, everyone's conversation a little more muted than normal, when I catch sight of Olive Ann flipping her blond hair to one side and reaching out to embrace someone. A tall boy with blond curls. *Oh no.* Of all the days in the calendar, *today* is the day Will returns from Weepee Valley?

I speed up, cutting through groups of students, careful to keep along the rightmost edge of the crush of people filing through the courtyard, and catch him in profile.

It's definitely him. I circled it weeks ago on my calendar at home, but I must have forgotten. Will was released from rehab over the weekend. He looks calm and clean-cut and, if I'm not mistaken, a little bit tentative in his movements. As if he's nervous to be back.

Scared he'll spot me, I peel away from the group and squeeze between two benches toward an overhanging section of roof to the right of the chapel. I wait there, my eyes glued to the back of Will's head, until he and Olive have gone inside.

All I can think is that he'll find a way to get his revenge on me, for what I did to send him there.

I pull out my phone. *Where R U?* I type, sending the message to Zahra.

Panties on, Fleet. Nearly there.

It's ten more minutes before Z shows up, but I'm happy to be waiting out here instead of in the echo-filled chapel full of crying kids. I can hear through the crack under the door: Principal Bang makes a speech about Martha being taken from us too soon, then goes on for a long time about grief counseling. Next, Martha's best friend, Jojo, gets up to say a few words and basically cries through the whole speech.

It's awful. I feel like I might throw up again, except there's nothing left in me but white-hot fury.

When Z finally comes clomping over the cobblestones of the courtyard, she looks upset.

"This is bullshit, huh?" she says, waving her hand toward the chapel, then circling it to encompass the courtyard, the whole school, the city, the world. I'm surprised to see her violet eyes are red and her eyelids swollen. Zahra never gets emotional. "Poor freaking Martha. Of all the people on Team Ice, she was the best of them."

"She was," I agree. My voice is hoarse with tears, but I swallow them down.

"Remember when she was like seven and our dads were all doing that charity golf game and she crawled inside a golf bag and got stuck?"

I laugh and it sounds like a wail. "I remember a lot of things about Martha." Especially the way she died, I think, trying to push the image of her frozen eyes out of my thoughts. I can't make the memory go away, not really, but I have to try not to dwell on it or I'll fall apart.

"And to think I thought Invisible was going to make things interesting." Zahra rolls her eyes.

"You couldn't know that this would happen." Nobody could. Not even me, who doesn't trust anyone and who sees danger everywhere.

"Zahra." I change the subject. "I saw Will."

She raises her eyebrows. "How'd he look? Still psycho?"

I motion to the chapel. "Weirdly calm. Deer in headlights."

"An act, I'm sure," Z sighs. "He's milking the rehab thing. Still the same douche on the inside."

We finally head into the chapel and scoot into the last row, where there are a few seats left. Debbie Lunelle is sobbing at the altar, eulogizing Martha.

"She was so good, never talked bad about anyone, it was like she was an angel, and now . . . and now—" Debbie breaks down, the sound of quiet crying breaths pushing into the mic.

I look around. All the teachers' eyes are shining with emotion. Mrs. Perkins, the junior world civ teacher, is openly weeping into a pink hankie.

Just then, something white passes in front of my face and lands on my knee, between the folds of my plaid Cathedral uniform skirt. A flower. I pick it up and examine it. It's a cut daisy, the stem about an inch long. I look up at the ceiling. There's a black tarp hanging there, in the very center of the chapel, fastened at three corners. A few more daisies spill from one of the corners.

It isn't like Cathedral to do something like this. Especially not inside the chapel, which is reserved for solemn morning masses and dignified graduations and award ceremonies.

Was this Principal Bang's idea? I turn to Z and point upward, rolling my eyes. But then another corner of the tarp comes undone, and we're all doused in daisies. And along with the daisies, tiny slips of paper.

Debbie is still making her speech, but I'm not listening until she stops and screams out, "WHAT IS THIS?"

She waves a slip of paper in her hand. Everyone is picking daisies out of their hair, rumbles of conversation growing louder.

"Is this a prank?" Debbie yells. "It's not funny, you guys!"

I pick up one of the slips from the ground and my blood freezes in my veins when I read the words, hand-scrawled in blue ballpoint:

Like the humble daisy, the Invisible grow every time it rains.
Expect us, children. We are everywhere.

"I need to get out of here." I jump to my feet, shoving my way past Zahra's knees on the end of the aisle. I want to get outside and see if they're still nearby. But the aisles immediately cram with people. Everyone wants to get out.

Principal Bang's voice is projected from the mic. "Please form an orderly line to exit the chapel. School is cancelled for the rest of the day while we investigate this matter."

I suddenly remember there's another exit behind the pulpit. I skirt the edge of the pews and head straight toward it, but lots of other kids are doing the same.

"Hey, Red," a deep voice too close to my ear says from right behind me. I speed up, pressing forward in the crowd, but I can't get through. Will moves up in the throng until he's next to me. "I . . . I know you don't want to talk to me," he says haltingly.

I sneak a sidelong peek at him. His light blue eyes are clear, no longer bloodshot and crazed. He's smiling nervously. "Let's not do this," I say. I just want to get out of here.

"I just wanted to say sorry. About everything. I wasn't myself. I'm better now, and I guess you're part of the reason why. I hope we can, I dunno, be friends, someday."

"I'm glad you're better," I say tightly. And I am. Really. But that doesn't mean that I trust him or want to have anything to do with him. Planting a hidden camera in my bedroom, black-mailing, stalking, countless threats—it's not something we can come back from. We'll never be friends.

I see an opening in the mass of people and I take it.

But when I finally get outside, the riot police have already colonized the courtyard. They've got a ladder against the chapel wall. Six of them are up on the roof. Their gray coveralls, their gas masks. Their enormous, gleaming Uzis.

When I turn around, there is a bullhorn in my face, a riot policeman screaming into it: "PLEASE EXIT THE CAMPUS IN AN ORDERLY FASHION. PHOTOGRAPHY IS PROHIBITED."

Invisible will be long gone by now.

CHAPTER 10

Zahra and I are walking toward the Scrambled Yolk, our usual diner, when a familiar voice calls my name.

I look across the street. "Ford!" Heat rushes to my face. I didn't realize how badly I wanted to see him until now.

"Hey. I was in the neighborhood and heard the sirens. Everything okay?" His eyes are clouded with worry, but his cheeks are flushed with health and vitality.

I'm speechless for a second. I haven't seen him out of his apartment since before the shooting. "You were *not* in the neighborhood," I say finally, touched that he cares so much. "Did you come to check on me?"

"Is that weird?" He smiles feebly. "I saw that the girl who was murdered went to your school. It's getting kind of freaky out here."

"It's sweet," I say. And I mean it.

"So you're okay?" Ford is practically bouncing on his tip-toes when he pivots slightly toward Zahra, who's been standing here the whole time, silent, with a bemused smile of her own. "Hi." He puts his hand out. "I'm Ford. You must be the famous Zahra."

"Why yes, that would be me." Zahra reaches out and shakes his hand. "You're the guy who got shot, are you not? Anthem's been worried about you. She didn't tell me you were . . . um . . ." Zahra turns to me. *A stone fox?* she mouths, her eyes widening in mock-panic. Turning back to Ford, she says: "An athlete."

Ford shrugs, still bouncing from the ball of one foot to the other. "I used to be."

"Well, *Ford*," Zahra says his name like it's an exotic delicacy or punch line to a great joke, "we were just going to get some breakfast and discuss some insanity that just went down at our school. You should come with us."

Z starts pulling me down the sidewalk, leaning in at one point to hiss, "You kept him a secret!" in my ear.

I snort-laugh at Zahra and grab Ford by the arm, and for a moment I'm able to forget about Martha dead in her room, to ignore the sick feeling that Invisible is closing in on all of us. All I feel is a surge of simple happiness over being with Zahra and Ford together, of Ford being well, of my two favorite people colliding at last.

At the Scrambled Yolk, we cram into a red vinyl booth. Zahra insists I sit next to Ford, and though I roll my eyes at her obvious delight in embarrassing me, I'm happy to do it. To feel the fact of him, alive and healthy and flushed. We all order the Unemployment Special—two sunny-side-up eggs, toast, hash browns, and coffee for $4.95.

"So what happened at your school, exactly?" Ford asks Zahra. I concentrate on adding creamer to the coffee the waitress has plunked down for us, then gulp it down, draining the cup in one long swallow. I'm nervous, watching them talk. Zahra will tell it better.

"You heard about Martha Marks, right?" Zahra asks.

"Yeah." He looks from me to Z. "Were you two friends of hers?"

"We knew her," Zahra says. I feel my hands clenching and unclenching under the table, picturing Martha's vacant cold eyes. I feel guilty now, for allowing myself to have a moment of happiness today. "Anyway, they had this memorial service for her and there was this prank—"

"It wasn't a prank," I interrupt. "It was a threat."

"Well, whatever it was, it said 'Invisible is everywhere, blah blah blah' on these little pieces of paper and then there were our friends the riot police, bum-rushing the school, and we were free to go. And now we're here," Z sighs. Invisible is still an abstraction to her, I realize. Even with Martha dead. Like politics in another country. Like precalculus. For a second, I envy her that.

"Pieces of paper, huh?" Ford knits his thick brows together. "They never would have cancelled school over paper at my high school."

"Where'd you go?" Z asks through a mouthful of toast.

"West Bed."

One of the giant public schools in the South. People at our school call it West Dead because of all the knife fights. I should know where Ford went to high school. It suddenly strikes me as weird, how little I know about his past.

"They killed Martha," I say quietly to Ford. "And now they're making their presence known at school. I just wish we knew why—"

"Three Unemployment Specials," the waitress says, interrupting our conversation. For a while, the three of us are quiet, all of us tucking into the food like we haven't eaten in a year. Ford folds his toast around a fried egg and eats the whole thing folded up like a pizza slice. I'm pleased to see him chowing down like this—he's eaten like a bird since the shooting.

He's keeping up with me as I mow down my hash browns, then use my buttered toast as a tool to shovel the eggs in my mouth. I'm starving, and I feel comfortable enough around Ford that it doesn't matter how I eat.

"Gotta tinkle," Zahra says out of nowhere. "I'll be back. Ant, I have no cash. Can I pay you back?"

I nod, and then Ford and I are alone. Our food is demolished.

"Penny for your thoughts." He elbows me in the ribs.

"Ow!"

"Sorry," he says. "I just can't believe I'm out at a restaurant, with you. With the famous Zahra."

"I know," I say. "Me either. It's—it's great." I grab his hand in my two hands, running my fingers along his knuckles, squeezing and not wanting to let go.

"I was there, Ford, but I was too late."

"Where?"

It all comes out in a rush. Marks Manor. The scream I heard. The gunshot in the forehead. Ford's fingers grip my hand now as I almost choke on the words. "I've got to find them."

"Okay." Ford nods. "I want to help."

And then there's nothing more I need to say, and we're just staring at each other. Our faces serious and composed as everything in the restaurant crystallizes and individuates and slows. The clatter of plates, the light streaming in through the fingerprinted windows. The squeak of the booth as Ford moves toward me.

Which is when I notice the waitress standing over us, looking at her watch.

"Can you guys settle your bill? We kind of need the table."

"Sure thing." Ford straightens up, embarrassed to be caught about to kiss me—*was* he about to kiss me?—by the waitress.

I shove him hard in the shoulder this time.

"Ow!" he yells. We're both biting back grins as we divvy up the check.

Outside the diner, the warm spring day has begun to melt into a pastel-colored afternoon. The middle soft and sweet, the edges of things sharper, a little bit sour. His hand finds mine and it feels like a promise.

"Be safe today," he says, his ropy arms wrapped around my shoulders for a brief chaste hug. My stomach flips when his scratchy cheek meets mine. And then he leans in and kisses me. Softly. He tastes of coffee. Everything he's felt all these months comes out in this kiss. The softness of it. The care. And I respond in kind. My hands run over his soft short hair. The kiss is like a punch in the gut; the way I want him suddenly feels wrenching and deep. We keep on kissing, right there on the sidewalk, under an elm, outside the restaurant I've been coming to with Serge and my parents since I was eleven years old.

And I want it to go on forever. His hands around my shoulders. In my hair. My body thrumming with adrenaline and pain from Martha's death and an ache for Ford all at once, until I pull away slightly, dizzy from it all. I have an urge to laugh, and I do. It feels good.

"What's so funny?" he whispers.

"I'm just . . . I guess I'm just really . . . this is good. You. Being here. Us." Saying it makes my knees go watery.

He nods. Looks at me with soft eyes. "I know just what you mean."

"Get a room, you two," Zahra interrupts us, stepping outside the diner. We both laugh awkwardly and move away from each other then, but I can still feel the heat of him on my skin long after we part.

"So. Ford. Very cute," Z says once we're in the backseat of the Seraph. After we both fielded calls from our parents, my father sent Serge to pick us up at the diner. Ford declined a ride, instead heading off to the boxing gym for his first day back. "Anthem's got a boyfriend," she singsongs, teasing me.

"Shhh," I hiss, pointing to Serge in the front seat. "And he's not my boyfriend," I protest, but my blush says otherwise.

"Call it what you want," Z says. "I know what I saw. He's so . . . *nice*, too. I approve a hundred percent. You have my blessing."

"Are you sure I shouldn't just get back together with Will?" I joke.

"Hmmm, psycho daddy's boy who is the embodiment of all that is evil about prep school, or sexy boxer boy who looks at you like you just cured cancer? You know, it's a tough decision, but I think I'd go with Ford," she says in mock-seriousness. "Does he have any boxer friends?"

"What about Dando?" I pretend to act shocked, but Z knows I'm not. She grows bored of whatever boy she's with fast—usually in a week or two, tops.

"Dando is getting on my nerves," she sighs. "He has weird teeth. And this annoying way of laughing, sometimes. And I don't like the undershirts he wears. V-neck, yuck."

"Sounds awful," I say dryly. "I don't know how you've stood it this long." I feel so close to Zahra right now, I wish I could tell her everything about what's happened to me, here in the car. I imagine the whole story spilling out here and now, the way she'd react if she knew about me falling into the river. If she knew about my hummingbird heart. About my . . . abilities.

It'll be fun to show her someday.

But then Z gets a call from her mother, and I'm snapped back into the moment. Both Z's and my parents are on edge after what happened at school. It's hitting closer and closer to home.

"Okay, okay. Got it. I'm in the car. We're almost there. It's okay, I'm fine!" She hangs up and rolls her eyes. "She's so worked up about the school closing, my god." Z sighs. "Want to come over and hang at my place for the afternoon under the watchful eye of Melinda Turk?"

"Sounds fun, but my parents want me home, too. My dad sounded like a vein was going to pop."

Z sighs sympathetically. "They're all bonkers right about now."

"I think they might be right to be worried." I wish I could piece together Invisible's actions and figure out his next move. "What do you think they meant with the flowers and the notes?"

"On the one hand, it was a little like they were saying sorry, you know, for what happened to Martha." Z chews her cuticle and looks out the window, where several Cathedral kids are still waiting for rides and loitering outside a newsstand. The headlines scream at me through the Seraph's tinted glass:

MAYOR'S DAUGHTER FOUND SLAIN IN HER BEDROOM.

BAND OF VIOLENT CRUSADERS PRIME SUSPECTS.

ART MUSEUM EXPLODED BY "INVISIBLE" MADMEN.

"INVISIBLE" CALLS OUT THE NEW HOPE—AUTHORITIES STUMPED.

"Then why say they are everywhere and getting stronger?" I counter, shivering as I turn away from the newspapers.

"Right. On the other hand, it was just rubbing our faces in what they did and trying to scare us. Where's the New Hope when you need her?" Zahra sighs wistfully.

I hope she doesn't notice the blood rushing to my face as we pull up in front of her house. I think back to a month ago when I was still going out nights, looking for Syndicate thugs to round up. When I was still avenging a death Gavin had faked.

The Syndicate has been quiet lately. There's been very little in the papers about them. Just a few minor robberies in the South, some looting when Invisible made their announcement, and a turf war with some dealers near Hades, the abandoned mall that's now a black market for all manner of contraband. They must be regrouping now that their top lieutenant is dead. Or perhaps their brand of crime is just relegated to the back pages of the papers, what with Invisible taking up all the headlines.

"Bye," Z whispers. "And hey, enjoy this. You're allowed to. Even with all this horrific stuff going on. Be happy with your boxer."

A swell of gratitude prickles at the back of my eyes. "Thanks," I say, and then Zahra's wobbling up her front walkway in her too-high platform shoes, her plaid skirt swishing in the spring sunshine.

"Anthem," Serge says, rolling down the partition. "What happened last night?"

"I don't know what they were planning," I admit. "But when I arrived at the mayor's mansion, they shot Martha point-blank."

"So they're organized."

I nod. "Very. And if they're capable of doing it once, they can do it again and again. You heard what happened at school. They are intent on becoming a threat. I'm just not sure what their game is."

Serge nods, his hand absently rubbing his chin. "But they're different from the Syndicate. Not in it for the money, it seems."

"No," I agree. "It's more than that for them."

When Serge turns the car onto Thorne, there's a traffic jam starting and the car slows to a crawl. I gaze absently out the window as a group runs past on the sidewalk. It's a big bunch of joggers, their knees high in the air with every step. There are maybe twenty of them in the pack, racing by on the sidewalk. I'm only halfway paying attention, but I register that they're all in black, even their socks and shoes. There are many piercings among them. A lot of dyed black hair, glowing bluish in the sun.

As they run, they shout encouragement to one another: "Way to be!" "Feel the burn!" "Push it!"

When they move away, my thoughts move to my kiss with Ford. Wanting more time with him, already. Missing him and also reminding myself I didn't—*don't*—want things to move too fast.

I start to dig my phone out of my pocket to send him a text when the car is rocked by a sonic boom—louder and more powerful than thunder.

Then a second bang rocks the car. I look out the front window. Up ahead on the crest of the hill is the North Bedlam power plant. A fireball rises from the top of it, opening up like a mushroom cloud in the bright afternoon.

"Are you okay?" I ask Serge.

He nods. Heat ripples shimmy across the shiny hoods of cars. Then he turns the wheel hard and pulls the car sharply to the curb, out of the traffic jam and into a bus stop.

"I'm going out there." Serge grabs his gun from the hidden compartment of the glove box and puts it inside his jacket. I follow him when he steps out of the car. Thorne Street is long and straight and leads up into the Bedlam hills. Several blocks up, the power plant is engulfed in flames. They leap from the white dome of the plant, along with huge white sparks. An ominous black plume of smoke pours straight upward into the perfect blue sky. It's almost beautiful.

Everywhere, cars are pulling over, people are getting out to stare. The air is filled with the smell of burnt plastic, smoke, and leaned-on car horns.

Suddenly I flash on the joggers in black. *Feel the burn*, one said. Their shoes were not running shoes. They were out-of-date leather dress shoes. Why would anyone wear those to go jogging?

"Did you see that group of people running?" I ask Serge as I wheel around, my muscles tensed for liftoff from the hot sidewalk.

"I did," he says. "Very odd."

I crane my neck for a glimpse of them, but they're long gone. Thorne forks up ahead—I have no way of knowing which way they went.

"We need to get you home." Serge raises his voice above the

din of people pouring out of apartment buildings and offices and businesses. "Without electricity, the city will grind to a halt. Just like during the riots."

The riots. When I was a baby and before I was born, the city was full of them. The Hope got everyone stirred up, is how my father puts it. People demanded things from the city—higher wages, more services. The police cracked down hard on the riots. There were curfews, power shortages.

I nod. The cars on Thorne Street look like they will be in a dead stop all day, stuck in an endless traffic jam. But we are close enough to walk.

Everywhere, people are leaving their homes and businesses, coming out of all the buildings to look at the power plant in flames. Shopkeepers wander around with flashlights inside, or sit in their doorways holding baseball bats, bracing for looters.

I turn again to try to spot the pack of runners in the distance, but it's useless. They could have gone anywhere. Meanwhile on the street, the mood has shifted from shock to fear. And anger too. Like a match has been struck, and it's only a matter of time before the whole city burns.

CHAPTER 11

It's dusk when the visual drama of the power outage starts to show, the North Side completely dark, the normally dim South Side a carnival of lights in comparison. I press my forehead up to the glass in the kitchen as the TV blares, and stare down to the street a million miles below, where riot police run drills and there are no pedestrians out walking in the sweltering, ash-swirly air.

I've been home all afternoon with my mother and two of her socialite friends, Phyllis Sheltz and Fernanda Cuesto, who came over a few hours ago to do damage control for the masquerade ball. It was supposed to be held this Saturday, but now that the city is on lockdown, they've had to postpone it.

In the darkening streets, teams of riot police patrol in formation, spreading through the North Side like ants. School is cancelled tomorrow. Life as we know it has stopped. Our building is one of the few around with an emergency generator, so we have power for now, but it won't last long. Serge has been out stockpiling fuel. Lily has been buying up canned goods and nonperishables at inflated prices. It's like we're in a bunker, preparing for the end of the world. There's no word yet on when the electricity will come back. The plant explosion was "massive and total, with seven individual bomb sites," says the news anchor on the kitchen TV, where I'm camped out, watching.

"The police have not yet released the names of any suspects for the murder of Martha Marks, but many are speculating as to the identity of Invisible," the news anchor reads from his teleprompter.

"The North Side's four hospitals are still running on generators. Bedlamites have been lined up for hours at mobile charging stations that have been set up at major intersections," the anchor goes on. I press my nose against the window glass and peer out at the South, all lit up, glorious and prosperous-looking in contrast to the gray-black stillness surrounding me here.

This is what we must look like to them. Normally. Since we have more working streetlights, more businesses, brighter wattage in every way.

The TV shows more footage of Invisible's past few videos, and I watch them closely for clues. The curtained backdrop behind his desk. The flag draped over it. The way the camera zooms upward, starting at his hands. Do I know those hands?

Think, I urge myself.

One of the Syndicate thugs, changing course? I shake my head slightly. No. I've been able to tell all along that this is different.

"It's just such a shame," I hear Fernanda say to my mother as they walk down the hall toward the front door. "We worked so hard."

"We're not cancelling, we're just postponing," my mother reminds her. "There are worse things. At least we still have running water and backup generators. At least our children are safe."

"True, true," Fernanda mutters. "Imagine being the mother of that poor girl."

"Horrific," my mother says. "Just horrific. The mayor and Belinda are beside themselves."

My arms prickle with goose bumps as I stare down at my hands. I know all too well what scene awaited them when they came home.

The next day, with the power still out on the North Side and school still cancelled, Madame calls a rehearsal. I walk to Seven Swans at nine A.M. Even with a dozen buildings running on generators, the streets are eerily devoid of life. All I hear outside is the boot steps of the riot police as they march in endless drills around the neighborhood. Whenever I pass by a group of them, they stare me down, their plastic shields on their helmets raised so I can see their dumb eyes watching me, their fingers tickling their batons at their waists.

Toward evening, the silence takes on an air of menace. The curfew in Bedlam is eight P.M., with the only exceptions for emergencies and city workers. Occasionally a person wrapped in a coat will scuttle by Fleet Tower at night, eyes downcast, before disappearing into the shadows.

I'm glad to be heading to rehearsal. We're supposed to perform *The Four Seasons* in less than six weeks—it's something to focus on. My body craves movement, and I'm certainly not getting much of it sitting at home with my mother.

As I move down Hemlock Avenue, I spot a huge graffiti eye,

maybe five feet high by ten feet wide, placid, unblinking, and totally realistic, so much so that it seems to follow me as I walk. It's painted in black and white on the brick wall behind the Bank of Bedlam. THE INVISIBLE ARE WATCHING, it says underneath it in purple letters. I reach out a shaking hand to touch the iris. The paint is still wet.

I yank my hand away and hurry toward the ballet studio, gritting my teeth in frustration. Whoever did this was *just here*. And yet I'm still so far from finding them. I spent hours this morning looking at their video transmissions, but so far nothing has clicked from the few scant details on the walls behind the desk. It could be anywhere.

Each of the twelve dancers in level six is off her game. Constance is all over the place, her limbs flailing. Liv's fouettés look like she's doing them in slo-mo. Jessie is so wildly off the count that Madame makes her do the routine twice by herself while we all watch.

For the first couple of hours, I manage to hold it together and rein in my hummingbird-fast heart and my new abilities. I focus on keeping my mind here in the mirrored room of Seven Swans and not off in the clouds with Ford or in Martha's bedroom or out on the silent streets where the Invisible are no doubt painting additional all-seeing eyes all over town.

But as rehearsal stretches into the third hour, I start to lose focus.

And pretty soon I catch myself hovering a second too long in the air. I quickly readjust, hoping Madame hasn't noticed the extra beat it takes me to come down. It doesn't look fully human—even I can see that, in the studio mirror.

I flick my eyes to Madame, and I'm relieved to find her focused on critiquing Constance's form at the moment.

Concentrate, I order myself. *Move like an ordinary human being.*

From then on, I put 80 percent of my focus in class on keeping myself in line with the others. We keep doing the same *chassé-jambe* sequence again and again. It requires symmetry and control, and I've got it down. At least the first ten times, I'm on the count. Matching the speed of the others.

But on the eleventh or twelfth go-round of the same section of the dance, my mind drifts again, pulling me back to the sidewalk outside the Scrambled Yolk. Back to Ford. My feet kick out too far. I jump too high. Hover in the air a beat or two too long.

"Anthem!" Madame shouts in exasperation, breaking me out of my thoughts just as I land my *grande jeté.* "We do not need pyrotechnics!"

The other girls glare at me when Madame says stuff like this. I shrug it off, but make a point of doubling my efforts to focus on keeping in line with gravity.

I pick one of the weaker dancers, a small, dark-haired junior with heavy eyebrows named Tish Tanger, and tell myself not to go any higher than her. I peg myself to her movements.

All the while as I watch myself dance with my fellow level sixers in the studio mirrors, the back of my mind is working, always working, on the question of Invisible's identity.

Over the past two days, I've spent hours watching the last two transmissions on repeat, slowing them down to isolate them frame by frame and look for clues. In one of the shots of the most recent video where the masked man says he's looking for the New Hope, there is a large, scratched-out *D* on the wall. Too straight and ordinary-looking to be graffiti.

I noticed it this morning, and paused. Zoomed in on the *D*. Then I listed words that end with it on the back of an envelope on my desk.

Dead

End

Bad

Doomed

I stood up when I realized what it was.
Condemned.
Which could be anywhere in the South. There are hundreds of condemned properties. Even here in the North, close to the river it's not hard to find block upon block of warehouse space that's been condemned and awaits the wrecking ball. And then I focused on a tiny, squiggly tag done in metallic-paint pen next to it that looked familiar but was too small to read. I couldn't place it. I still can't, not quite, but it feels like my mind is circling around it, getting closer.

As I'm fanning out across the studio floor, it hits me at last.

The scrunched letters. The paint pen. The shape of the scrawl.

I know the tag. *WrastlDown.*

WrastlDown is a Lowlands tagger with a huge mural a block away from Jimmy's Corner, where Ford and I used to box. In the corner of the mural—all faces and googly eyes popping out of windowed buildings—the artist put his signature in paint pen. The letters scrunched and squeezed tight. WrastlDown. The Leonardo da Vinci of the Lowlands. It's the same tag. I'm sure of it.

Invisible must have filmed the transmission in the Lowlands, somewhere flooded out and empty.

"Anthem!" Madame's face blazes with incredulity and irritation and I'm snapped back to the mirrored studio, the candles set up all around the edges, the room sweltering from lack of air-conditioning. "My office, now. I need to speak with you."

"Oooh," Constance singsongs under her breath. "Miss Prima Perfect's going down."

I ignore her and stare at the floor as I follow Madame to her office, still turning the room with the desk in it over in my mind. How many blocks away is Lowlands? Twenty? More?

"No lies. I want the truth. What is it you are taking?" Madame says, her accent crisp, her words precise so there can be no misinterpreting. "This is unacceptable."

"What?" I search her face, shocked that she would actually accuse me of using drugs. "Nothing. I swear."

"Nobody can move like this," Madame hisses, her eyes frantically searching mine. "So high in the air."

"I . . . I'm sorry. I just . . . it's just something I figured out how to do."

She towers over me in her three-inch character shoes. Her whole body radiates suspicion. Her black shawl abandoned over a chair, her bony caramel shoulders tensed, arms crossed over her black cami.

The silence between us is heavy and hot in the airless room.

"Very well," Madame says tightly after a long assessing pause. "I am watching you very closely. If I hear anything about illegal substances among you girls, the consequences will be immediate. And irreversible."

I nod, making my face blank and empty. The default weapon

of every teenage girl. "Got it. Sorry. It won't happen again." My body slouched, my eyes dulled, waiting for her to shoo me back to practice.

In my head, I'm halfway over the river, already flying toward Lowlands.

CHAPTER 12

I'm prowling the streets of Lowlands, my heart on fire, Serge's gun pressed between my boot and my sock. It's 2:33 in the morning.

I've told Ford nothing about tonight's expedition, even though this is the neighborhood where he goes to box. Now that he's well, he would insist on coming with me, and that's not a risk I'm about to take, since last time he helped me he wound up shot.

Everywhere here is marked by a musty dampness that hangs in the air, and by a black line on every structure, just at my shoulders, that shows where the water rose during the last big flood.

I make a loop around the neighborhood, bordered by the river on one side, the freeway on another, and Oleander Way to the east. Then I circle back, moving down each street and alley so fast that there's only the occasional toe-touch of rubber to asphalt. So fast, I assume I can't be seen. The Lowlands are almost totally deserted because of the floods a few years ago that kept it underwater for weeks. Most all the buildings here are condemned, or should be.

The South Side gets all the flooding these days, but before I was born, things were different. Back then, it was the North—my neighborhood in particular, which isn't far from the river—that was always flooding. Back then, the North was underwater at least once every winter.

When my father was first getting into real estate, he and a group of other developers came up with a redevelopment plan to add height to the land north of the river (which they were smart enough to buy up "for a song," after a particularly flooded spring, as my dad puts it whenever he tells the story) by trucking in garbage from a few landfills, adding layers of soil over the top, then paving over the new higher ground.

Building on top of the hills he created in the North is what turned my father into the king of Bedlam real estate. Or at least that's how my parents tell it. I've heard the stories a million times. They like to leave out the part about how building the hills in the North made it so the South became the flood zone.

After my father's redevelopment of the North, everyone wanted to live there. When the river overflowed again a few years later, people who could afford it picked up and left, and the South Side became more and more neglected, and more dangerous.

When the most recent floods hit a few years ago, Lowlands was submerged for weeks. Now there are only a few blocks with electricity here, toward the center of the neighborhood where there's a little hill. That's where Jimmy's Corner is. Ford might be boxing there at this very moment.

I see something move out of the corner of my vision and come to a stop behind a Dumpster, landing hard on my heels. An animal comes into view, flitting in the tall grass growing in a vacant lot behind a chain-link fence. Its black eyes blink curiously at me, two shining beads disguised in its black mask, just a raccoon. Pretending to be someone else, or nobody at all.

You and me both, I think, reaching a hand in the pocket of my black Windbreaker to make sure the mask I've made is still safely stashed there. It's only a four-inch-wide strip of stretchy black mesh with holes just big enough to see through that I cut from an old costume, but the effect is startling, since it obscures my eyes and nose so completely. In my closet mirror, I felt a strange ripple of pride when I put it on. Combined with my black hood, it disguises me well.

I edge away from the Dumpster, away from the vacant lot, keeping my run slow now so I don't miss anything. Up ahead, I spot a droopie den, marked as is the custom in Bedlam with two shoes with laces tied together and flung over an electricity wire—though without electricity, the wire is only decorative.

I slow to a walk that I hope appears casual and concentrate on getting my breathing under control, quieting any lingering sounds of exertion. The nice thing about droopers is that they are docile and unguarded with their speech.

Two pallid, vacant-eyed teenagers are sprawled on the brick front steps. One of them, the girl, braids the hair of the other, a boy. Neither speaks or raises a hand in greeting when I walk up to them. They stare so listlessly out at the street that it's like they're staring inward, at whatever visions or chasms lurk in their minds. The girl's fingers work slowly and skillfully through the mane of the boy's dirty blond hair. She's giving him cornrows. A package of tiny rubber bands—MegaMart brand, $.42 FOR 42, the sticker says—spills out onto the steps.

I approach slowly, hesitant to get closer than ten feet away in case I'm wrong and they're not as drooped out as they look, and are hostile or territorial, or worse, ready to empty my pockets any way they can.

"Hi."

The boy doesn't look up, but his hand flaps in a low wave.

"'Lo, girlie. You looking to score?" The girl smiles big and fake. "I can get Pepe, just needa finish this project here."

"No, don't bother . . . um, Pepe," I say quickly, jumping lightly from one foot to the other. "I'm just looking around for this guy I used to know."

"Mmmkay." The girl shrugs, her fingers moving strand over strand in a five-sectioned pattern that I have to admit is impressive. "Not that many of us in Moldlands."

"Right. But I think this is where he said he'd be," I say, thinking again of the condemned sign, of the tag that I know I've seen before around here. In fact, I've seen two just tonight, since I've been out here. *WrastlDown* sprayed in silver on a peeling black wall. The shorter version, *WDown,* in black marker on what was once a phone booth, now just a urine-scented shelter made of cracked glass.

"Shay!" Someone calls down from a higher floor. "Go to the corner and get some chips!"

The girl squints upward.

"Fine." She stands up, pulling the boy up with her by his hair. "You're paying," she says to him.

He snorts and follows her.

"So . . . have you seen anyone new hanging around here the past few weeks?" I say, moving with them to the corner.

"Just those guys with the videquip. Shooting a movie or somethin'," the boy says. He can talk after all.

"You know, that sounds like who I'm looking for. I'm supposed to be in their movie," I say, wincing at how obvious the lie is. I try to mimic Shay's and the boy's slouches, mirror their vacant faces. Maybe they're too drooped out to notice the way my story keeps changing. "Where were they, do you know?"

The boy hawks a loogie, and I look away as he spits it into the gutter. "You take Ivy Street and turn—"

"You're going to need to buy us some chips first," Shay says, elbowing him in the ribs. "You are so high, you don't even think," she whispers at him.

"I am not," he protests, his braids already unraveling. "I *wish* I was," he snorts. "I hate thinking."

In the MiniServ the girl points at random things she wants me to buy her, her limbs loose and wild from the droops. "Four SnoPops—no, wait, six. And those JumboCrisps. And the Chocobuzz. Three cans." And I do without a word, my arms full of stuff. Six bags of chips, two BrainFreezes, and the rest of the stuff all paid for and bagged by a clerk who might also be on droopies judging by how slow he's moving, we step out into the night, and I clear my throat. "Okay," I say. "Now tell me where you saw the videquip."

"It was, like, a few days ago. But they were in the old hospital. On Gypsum Street, the entrance to the ER. Mold city. Here, I got extras. You'll need this." He digs in his jeans pocket and pulls out a frayed blue surgical mask, the edges where it's been folded lined with grime. Blinks at me, then stumbles off the curb.

"He is so out of it," sighs Shay. "That all you want, girlie? We gotta split."

"Thanks," I say to the boy. And maybe I imagine it but I think he does a drooper's version of the Hope sign. Hand over his heart. Fingers crossed.

I check his eyes. There's a flash of clarity there. Then he cough-laughs.

I shake my head slightly, finger to my lips, and back away. He just waves, his eyes vacant again. Too high, I hope, to care all that much about who he thinks I am.

Inside the hospital, everything is black. The ER waiting room linoleum is slicked with glistening mud, and black mold marbled with green and gray crawls up the walls. I'm glad for the surgical mask I've put on. Even if it's filthy, the air in the hospital is filthier still. And even though it's dark, I pull out the black mesh mask from my pocket and tie it over my eyes. I must look like a demented raccoon surgeon, but there's no one here to see. All that's here is the dripping sound of water leaking from pipes, running like slow tears down the walls.

I shove open the double doors leading to the back of the ER, pushing against a toppled gurney slimed with mold and mud until the doors give. Could anyone really be here, in this foul space? With every step forward, there's less light to see by, and more squeaking of rats or mice. I shudder as I step in deep mud, my sneakers sliding. After a few steps, I slip and nearly fall on my face, grabbing on to a bar against the wall.

Then I freeze. My spine turns to ice. Someone is whistling the jingle for Buzz Beer.

The words are so ingrained in me, I think them as the low whistle marks the syllables. It's coming from above me.

Along with shuffling footsteps. I move down the hall, barely able to see, opening every door I pass in hopes of finding the stairwell.

When you need a lift, it's Buzz time
When you ask for more, it's Buzz time
When the party's on, it's always time
for Buzz Buzz Beer.

When I find the stairs I climb them cautiously, stopping every few steps to listen. The whistling continues.

Slowly, I push the door open and assess the second floor. Up here is less muddy, less ruined. The walls are still veined with mold, but the floor is dry and dusty.

Something—a shadow, a rat, a person?—moves around the corner, down the hall. I keep singing the Buzz Beer song in my head to keep calm, and pull Serge's gun out of my boot. The black plastic is warm. My chest kicks with revulsion at the thought of shooting someone, but I will if I have to. If there is no choice.

I creep to the corner where the hallway turns and edge slowly around the wall, just enough to see with one eye. Ice shoots down my spine when I spot someone in the shadows twenty feet away. I don't dare breathe. I don't dare move.

It's a guy. Not as young as me, but close. He is thin but strong. His shoes are encrusted with mud. And his head is crowned with the same springy dark curls as the man in the Invisible's transmissions.

My hands flood with sweat as I try to decide. Do I run? Do I continue to stand here, frozen against the wall?

But then he steps into a room halfway down the hall. He hasn't seen me.

I dash-fly down the hall, willing my feet not to touch the ground, dizzy with my own speed.

My heart revs painfully when I reach the doorway to the room. It's a former hospital room, with a plastic hand sanitizer dispenser still attached at the entrance. But inside, there is no bed. No curtain. Just a desk. Draped with the Invisible flag with the wide hazel eye, unblinking.

The man—really a boy, around the same age as Ford, maybe twenty—is adjusting a camera on a tripod. His back is to me. Stage lights shine on the desk, impossibly bright in the moldering room. My breath hitches as I move toward him. I spot the telltale graffiti on the wall. The condemned notice decorated with the tag: *WrastlDown*.

The mask he uses when he does the transmissions lies on the desk, faceup. A hard white plastic shell he wears over his face, because he is a coward.

I stand there, ears ringing, watching as at last he turns in an achingly slow arc to face me, a calm and open expression on his face as he studies my mask.

"You came." He puts his hand out. Blinks. "Nice to meet you."

How could this unassuming boy be Invisible?

Then he flashes a grin. His teeth are stained. His eyes have a glassy, drugged quality to them. "You're as predictable as we thought."

I nod. Blood pulses through me, every extremity tingling with anticipation. "Then you know what I'm about to do to you," I say.

Before he can answer, I am upon him.

I leave the gun in my waistband for now, jumping up and coming at him with my muddy feet in the air, my sneaker making contact with his shoulder. He staggers against the desk, sending his white plastic mask flying to the floor, and I hear something in him crack, maybe a rib.

A broken, choking sound emerges from low in his throat.

But he straightens up and starts to fight back, batting his arms. He gets a fist punch to my neck before I swat him away like a slow-moving moth, pushing him over the desk so he lands on the floor on the other side. He's a surprisingly poor fighter. When he looks up at me, there's still that odd, pained smile pulling at his mouth.

I yank the flag with the eye off the desk and come at him, fast enough so he sees I'm not all human. To his eyes, when I move like this, I'm just a blur.

"Jesus." I detect a tremor in his voice. "What *are* you?"

"Just a girl you pissed off. Did you predict this, too?" Before he can answer, I pull my right hand back so it's just above my shoulder and release, just like Ford taught me, aiming for a knockout. My fist explodes against his temple, and he smashes against the wall, eyes still open, before sinking to the floor, lids fluttering closed.

I hum the Buzz Beer jingle as I use my keys to cut the flag into long strips. The satin is strong. It will do as rope. The sprinkler heads are attached to metal pipes on the ceiling. I tie Invisible's wrists and ankles, then tie two strips of the flag together and toss it over the metal sprinkler system. I fasten the long strips to the knots binding his wrists and ankles and test each of my knots. I learned these knots in Scouts when I was nine, things I never thought would come in handy.

Knots, kindness, how to build a fire. All of these are so much more important than I realized.

His head lolls on his neck, shoulders pulled back because his hands are tied behind him. I walk behind the desk to fetch the mask and put it on him. Invisible. Masked and in his own room.

Then I take the camera, unlatching it from its tripod and zipping it into my Windbreaker. I double-check the other two cameras are off, then leave the room and shut the door behind me, making a note that he's in room 327.

In the hall, I call the tip line. "Room 327 of Lowlands Hospital. The person who calls himself Invisible is in there."

I race to the stairwell and move higher and higher, careful to hold on to the camera inside my jacket with one hand, until there are four stories between me and the third floor. Finally, I reach the roof. I push the stairwell door open and dash across the tar-papered surface of the roof until I find an alcove on the water tower that is just the right size for a small person like me.

I take off the surgical mask and put it in my pocket.

The other mask, the black one, I keep on. It feels like protection, somehow. Then I wedge myself into the alcove and wait for the police helicopters to arrive.

It takes twelve minutes. I time it on my watch. Soon there are dozens of riot cops pouring out of two helicopters, glass riot masks lowered, their Uzis raised.

"This is it," I say to nobody, my words sucked into the air filled with the beating of chopper blades, deafening revolutions in the black night. "No more."

This is the last of it, and all I'm willing to do. Their leader is toppled, just like Gavin was. The police will have to do the rest on their own.

I watch the blades of the chopper swoosh round and round above the spotlights, six helmeted cops hoisting the still-unconscious boy with the curly dark hair on a stretcher, his hands bound tightly in white plastic ties. I feel a sensation of unwinding deep in my chest. Something like what people must mean when they talk about a sense of peace.

CHAPTER 13

By the time I scurry down a fire escape on the side of the hospital, it's after four A.M. I take off running through Lowlands, one arm curled around the bulky camera still hidden under my jacket, feeling giddy and triumphant. Something nags underneath—him telling me I'm *predictable*, maybe—but I tell myself to ignore it.

My legs take me the six blocks to Jimmy's Corner as if I'm on autopilot.

Standing on the threshold, I listen, looking up at the lighted upstairs windows until I detect the *thwunk thwunk thwunk* of fists hitting a big unyielding bag.

I know those hits. This sequence of sounds is perfectly familiar, the way a lullaby is, or the school bell, or the sound of your family's car starting. *Low low, high low. Low low, high low.*

They are his.

My skin tingles in anticipation, a syrupy warmth spreading through my chest and down into my legs, to my knees.

I dig my keys out from my jeans pocket and find the one Ford gave me months ago when I first started training, the one that unlatches all of Jimmy's bolts. In a minute I'm flying up the stairs, slowing as I push open the door.

He's at the big bag, the red one I once knocked across the room, the first night my own impossible strength shocked us both. Pounding away, his face red and fierce and dripping with sweat as he one-twos from foot to foot, he hasn't noticed me yet.

I move toward the ring in the center of the room and grab one of the ropes surrounding it to steady myself for the rush of desire and relief I feel when I'm near him. How funny that you can start off so completely platonic with someone and all of a sudden you feel like a million tiny magnets are just under your skin, pulling you toward him.

His hands are wrapped with white surgical tape. He wears a gray tank top with holes around the seams, wet with sweat around his chest, and his usual black training pants with the white stripe. *Slam-slam-slam-slam. Right right left right.*

His face is a sweaty mask of ferocity and focus. A vein pops up on his shoulder, traveling up his neck.

It feels too intimate watching him, having him not know I'm here. I clear my throat: "Ford."

When he looks up at me his eyes are hooded and entranced, still in the fight zone. Then he softens, and blood rushes hotly to my cheeks.

"Green." His nickname for me.

A dimple pops through on one smooth cheek. He moves toward me, hands still clenched. Muscles almost as defined as ever. But how can that be, since he's only been back in fighting form a few days? Has he been living at Jimmy's for the past forty-eight hours, lifting weights?

He's in front of me now, tall and imposing. I sway a little on my feet. The air between us seems to hum with electricity. He hasn't even touched me. Yet.

"I'm glad you came." His voice is husky.

My hands shake as I unzip my jacket, carefully taking the camera out, placing it on the mat beside me.

"What's that?"

A long beat of silence. How do I tell him? "A souvenir."

"Of what?" His slow smile melts me. "What did you do?"

"Took care of things," I say, relief catching in my throat. Or maybe it's pride. "Of Invisible."

Ford's jaw drops open. "That simple, huh? Where is he now?"

"With the cops. Unconscious," I add. "Or he was a little while ago. He'll have a headache when he wakes up."

"Nice." Ford nods, pride in me shining in his eyes, but something darker there, too. "You didn't want backup?" he says lightly. "I would've been—"

"I needed to go alone," I interrupt him. "I'm still . . . you were so sick." And slowly, slowly, I'm moving toward him, until my hands find his arms and the heat of his torso is near enough to feel.

"I'm better now," he says, his breath warm in my hair. "Better than ever." And then he's pulling me toward him, closer, closer. Until there's nothing between us but the clothes we wear. "I'm glad you're okay. And that you kicked his ass," his voice low. And then his lips traveling on my neck, until we find each other.

Kissing Ford is like pressing my lips against a tropical storm. Wet, wild, thunderous, unpredictable.

Before I know what's happening I am against the ropes

of the ring, the soft vinyl floor pushing against the backs of my knees, and I don't quite know where he ends and where I begin.

Everything we've never said, we're saying now, with hands and lips.

I am feeling him press against me, my heart twisting and flipping and spinning. He pulls away and puts his hand to the scar on my chest, the place Jax cut into for the transplant. He caresses it with a calloused knuckle.

A tiny moan escapes me.

And then we are kissing again, my legs wrapped around his torso, moving against him, breathing him in like he's oxygen.

The ropes aren't holding us, and I slip under them, Ford following me, and then we are lying on the air-filled boxing ring, the smell of old matches—blood and sweat and dust—billowing up around us. I am on top of him, his head in my hands, his skin on fire. My eyes closed, he grows warmer and warmer and I'm somewhere else, a place I've been before but never, ever like this—

Until I hear him yelp. My eyes flutter open just as he pushes me away, *hard*. I fly off him, nearly to the edge of the ring, and land hard, on my tailbone.

"Ow." I frown, frozen, confused. Blinking dumbly.

"Sorry," Ford says. He's up on his feet, pacing. He's bright red. Even his shoulders and neck, not just his face. His expression is strange and intense, that vein pulsing in his neck again. He opens his mouth to say something, then shuts it abruptly.

"What is it?" I say.

He shrugs, suddenly looking ill and miserable, then turns away from me.

"Did I do something wrong?" I say, my voice small.

"Nothing. You did everything right," Ford says to the wall, still facing away from me, his head hanging low. "I'm sorry." He turns around. "I'm just . . . not totally myself right now." His voice is thick with remorse. Hands clenched in fists, the white tape on his hands contrasting with the red-purple shade his olive skin has taken on. He looks up at the drop ceiling, as if seeking answers there. His expression hopelessly confused. "I'm sorry. I—you can't possibly know how happy this makes me. How long I've wanted this. I just, I just . . . I need to get myself together, I guess."

"Okay." I nod, unsure what to do. What is he holding back? Normally I feel like I can read Ford better than anyone else, but he's totally opaque to me right now.

"Let's try this again another night," he says, keeping his distance from me. I move forward. He backs away. "Sorry."

"Ford." I try again. "Just tell me. What is it?"

He shakes his head. "Go home. Don't hold this against me, okay?" Then, more quietly: "I'm crazy about you. Have been from day one. Just, I need to slow it down. For now."

I scoop up the camera, swallowing down a dozen confused questions. I believe him when he says this. Maybe things were just moving too fast for him. I didn't know boys ever really felt that way about this kind of stuff, but what I know about boys could fit on the head of a pin. If he wants to take things slow, I can do that. I want to do that. I just wish it didn't feel so strange, and so much like something's wrong between us.

I wave good-bye, backing awkwardly toward the door.

"I can't believe you found him, Green. Way to be," he says as I go.

"Next time I'll show you the footage," I say. Before I leave, Ford smiles at me, and something in his face is horribly off, like he's in serious pain and trying to cover it up. I turn away so I don't have to see it.

CHAPTER 14

I wake late the next morning, weak from hunger. My fingertips are turning a faint blue that extends all the way to the nail beds. I stagger to my desk across the room and open my desk drawer to grab an oatmeal cookie from a box I've stashed. I chew it without tasting it and wait for my dizziness to subside as the sugar hits my bloodstream.

When I go to the bathroom I discover the electricity is finally back on. I flip the light switch on and off a few times, enjoying the bright immediacy of the power compared to before, with the generator in the building, when everything was dim and delayed.

How perfect, I think as I wash my face. I capture Invisible and the power comes back on, all at once.

When I pad out of my room and down the hall, I hear my parents in the kitchen, talking to Lily.

"Got to be the same girl from before."

"No question," says my dad. "What I'm wondering is, what's she on?"

"What are you talking about, Harris?" My mother snorts. "Is there a drug on the market I don't know about?"

"Gotta be. No human being can run like that without drugs."

I press my back against the wall in the hallway and freeze, hoping they haven't heard me come out of my room. They've obviously seen some footage of me. Do they suspect it's their daughter?

"She's amazing, whoever she is," Lily declares.

"Think it might actually be a small, feminine-looking man?" my father muses, his mouth full. "What kind of girl goes head-to-head against these people?"

I bristle, feeling indignant before I realize I should be relieved he's so clueless. I walk the rest of the way to the kitchen, stand in the doorway, and make a big show of yawning.

"The kind of girl who can do *that*," my mother says, pointing at the TV, which is muted, but flashing surveillance footage of a person moving with impossible speed down a dark street. So fast she's a streak, a blur. It's all surveillance footage, different black-and-white, grainy captures from several different angles, spliced together by *Channel Four News Roundup*.

Then the TV cuts to the anchorman, who wields a stylus pen and begins circling things on the screen. His lips move but the sound is still muted, and the footage is replayed, much slower this time. He draws arrows, circles the figure. She's still blurry. Then the footage plays slower still, and crops and zooms in on the figure until I can make out the shape of a nose, the black eye mask, the legs and hooded head of a girl-like figure, grainy and black-and-white.

My mask is on, and I know I'll need to wear it whenever I go out at night. My hood bounces, but enough of it covers my hair. The footage is all in black and white.

"Morning, kitten," Dad says, reaching out to ruffle my tangled hair before turning back to the TV.

"She's incredible," Lily sighs as she continues to watch the footage. "They're going to try hard to find her. Probably want to know how she's so fast."

I shudder in my seat. Jax was right. And Will was, too, when he threatened to expose me if I didn't do what he wanted. If anyone ever finds out that girl is me, my life as I know it is over. My blood, my bone marrow, my brain matter will be tested; I will be poked and prodded, possibly for years.

And Jax—if I ever told them what she did to me—Jax could become a very successful doctor. Or a liability, if they decided what she's figured out how to do was far too dangerous for any one person.

But so far, it seems like my secret is still safe.

In the elevator an hour later, my mother's sugared lemon perfume fills the space. She's wearing a gray silk shirtdress with heels. Her collarbones jut out, and she looks thinner than ever. She's insisted I go with her to her tailor to get a dress made for the masquerade ball, which is back on, now that Invisible has been captured. The ball will now raise money for the museum, and it's even being held there, since their ballroom wasn't damaged. I don't care what I wear, but I'm willing to do what she wants, if only to try to get back to normal.

She stares up at the lowering numbers, but when we get toward the bottom she reaches out to grab my hand. It's a surprising gesture. I can't remember the last time I've held her hand.

"Everything will be all right now," she says, her words ever so slightly slurred even at this hour. "School will be back on tomorrow."

"That's great," I say, squeezing her thin fingers back. Though I don't know what *all right* means for me. I can't stop thinking about the look on Ford's face last night, the terror in his eyes when he pulled away from me so abruptly and told me to leave. "You must be relieved."

"I'm relieved." She nods, wisps of her ash-blond hair moving around her face. When she faces me, her eyes have a haunted look that lasts only an instant before they're blank again. "That the person who killed Martha is going to be locked away forever. It was terrifying knowing he was out there. Waiting."

I nod, realizing how shaken she still is. She's still dousing her fears with extra-large doses of Vivirax, I would guess, judging by her flat monotone.

The elevator door opens into the lobby, full of brilliant sunlight shot through with rainbow hues from Fleet Tower's colored glass walls.

"Enjoy it out there, you two." Cass, the morning doorman, smiles and tips his hat as we pass.

"Thanks." I smile back.

And on Foxglove Court, the soft spring sunlight feels yellower and warmer than it has all year. Lots of people have left their buildings to go out walking. The eerie quiet in the streets these past three days is over at last. An older woman waves hello to my mother. "Isn't it wonderful?" she says.

"It is," my mother replies. She smiles wide, and even through the Viviraxed haze her relief is palpable, along with a few more wrinkles than I've ever seen around her eyes and mouth. The Invisible fears and all the curfews have prevented her from getting her usual injections, and she's starting to almost look her age, or as close to it as I've ever seen. "Will I see you at the masquerade party, Leora?"

"Oh, yes," the woman says. "We would not miss it. And such a good cause."

We keep walking down Foxglove Court. The whole neighborhood seems to be out today, everyone smiling and dazed in the bright sun. Two uniformed doormen slap each other a high five. A little girl chases a smaller boy around a tree in the center median. She must be six or seven and wears a glittery black mask. Is that because of me?

"How about something green?" my mother is saying. "For your dress. You look so good in emerald. And it's springlike, the color of new life and all of that."

I pull a newly popped leaf from a sycamore tree as I walk, admiring its softness. "Green sounds nice."

Of course, green makes me think of Ford. His silly name for me.

And then I get the craziest idea. It unfurls slowly, a tiny wisp of a thought that grows larger until I'm convinced it's right.

"Mom," I say shyly. "I might want to bring a date to the ball. Would that be all right?"

My mother stops dead in her tracks, and for a second I fear I've said something to dampen her mood, made her afraid for me again because of what happened with Gavin, the boy she never approved of, the boy who caused me to vanish for days on end.

"I don't see why not," she says hesitantly. Then she clears her throat as if getting ready to say something important. "I . . . it wasn't right to try to convince you to stay with William. I see that now. And I know you went through so much with that other boy. The one who . . ."

She can't say it. *The one who was kidnapped. The one we wouldn't pay the ransom for.*

She knows so little about what happened with Gavin. I told my parents he was released and we broke up. And, desperate to believe me so they could stop worrying, they bought it.

This is my mother's way of trying to connect. I nod. "Gavin," I say, my voice tiny.

"Of course. Gavin." It feels wrong to have his name rolling around in her mouth, even if it turned out to be a fake one. "Anyway, darling, yes. Bring whomever you like to the ball. Someone from school?"

Her tone is upbeat now, eager. I don't have the heart to tell her who it is. But I'm hoping he'll win her over in person.

"I think you'll like him," I say instead. I flash for a moment on the vein pulsing in Ford's neck, the redness of his face when he said *I'm not myself tonight*. I'll invite him to the ball anyway. And my two worlds will fuse, like a new heart to the tubes surrounding it. Like hummingbird DNA inside human cells. Everything will reconfigure just a little, until it's something new and better. Something extraordinary, maybe.

"I'm sure I will," she says. Her ankles wobble in her heels as we turn the corner onto Thorne Street. The tailor is half a block away now.

"He's a really good guy." I fling my palmed leaf away and watch it spin through the sunshine.

CHAPTER 15

Mr. Tanaka, the tailor, made me a gown from emerald-green silk shantung, raw and rough in places, smooth and delicate in others. When I walk into the masquerade ball a week later, held in the Museum of Fine Art's undamaged ballroom, the dress fits me like a second skin, the skirt ragged and long with knots up and down the bustled train, the bodice snug and slightly asymmetrical, the effect body-hugging and slightly cleavage-creating just above the soft-shoe shuffle of my heart.

I've worn ball gowns my whole life, but never enjoyed it much. Usually it's like I'm playing dress-up, pretending to be older and ending up just feeling like a fraud, or when I was much younger, pretending to be a fairy princess. But this time, in this dress, I feel like . . . me. Not like a fraud. Not too young. Tonight I'm a version of myself I can live with.

Maybe it's the mask I'm wearing. This time it's silver, the corners sharpening toward my temples into cat-eye points. My hair is in an artfully messy, voluminous pile on top of my head.

We arrive exactly on time to the ball. Immediately upon entering the room, my mother and father are waylaid by an older woman with an electric-blue asymmetrical bob and matching eye shadow, her lips injected to clownish proportions.

I wander away from them after giving her a polite smile, and I circle the perimeter of the massive room, weaving around the scattered guests slowly wandering into the ballroom, a napkin in my hand as I pluck various rolls and puffs from the silver trays offered by the cater-waiters.

The plan is to meet Ford here. I made sure to double-check that his name is on the list at the museum door.

The museum ballroom seems to have suffered no bad effects from the bombing. The ceiling is hung with thousands of purple blown-glass orbs; the walls display large pieces of art specially chosen to highlight some of Bedlam's finest artists. My mother and Fernanda lobbied to change the name of the party to the Heal the City Masquerade Ball, which helped to turn it into a huge benefit to help the museum gain its footing again.

I spot Olive Ann with her mother, Winnifred Bang, the principal of Cathedral Day School. Olive is in a short white cocktail dress, her shiny white mask decorated with albino pea-cock feathers. Principal Bang is in a dark pink suit with a mask on a stick in the shape of a moon. They are arguing quietly in the corner of the room, near the shrine dedicated to Martha Marks, standing in front of her picture but not looking at it, their mouths pinched and angry-looking in the same unfortunate way.

I avoid the shrine as I wander the room. It makes me too sad.

There are people I recognize from school starting to circulate in the ballroom, masked but a few of them identifiable. I wave hello to Callie Flaunt, wearing a thin glittery strip of red over her eyes, whose mother owns a chain of North Side boutiques, and to Jean Keener, a lacrosse jock who plays on the boys' team but who looks great in her silver ball gown, a full-face black mask on a stick held in one hand. It's kind of sad and nostalgic, somehow, seeing everyone dressed up like this. The school year is almost over. Soon most of these kids will just be people I used to know. I wonder how much I'll miss them.

"You are the hotness!" Zahra's voice rings out from behind me. I turn around, overjoyed to see her in a typical Zahra boundary-pushing ensemble.

"You are . . . wearing a leather romper." I state the obvious.

"Yeah, but it's a *sparkly* leather romper. You hug me too tight, I cut you," Z jokes, her ringed fingers forming the shape of scissors. She is a giant flashing diamond, a walking jewel, her black leather shorts-and-strapless-top combination all studded with crystals. Her mask is equally studded, covering most of her forehead down to the tip of her nose. And her black hair is set in pin curls. I reach out and touch one, and it's the texture of concrete, totally shellacked to her head.

"How long did this take?" The knot of nerves inside me loosens slightly. I'm still nervous about Ford joining me here but more at ease now that I'm with Zahra. "I love it."

"Hours," she sighs. "It involved actual pins. You look great, too—I like your hair all crazy like this." She pats at my wild updo, tucks a tendril behind my ear, and for a second it's like we are nine again, and she's doing my hair. "And this dress! The asymmetry is to die for. I've died. I'm dead right now, actually, and have been reanimated in spirit form."

"Thanks, but don't die." My hands flutter out in front of me to pat my knotted skirt.

Within the jewels of her mask, her eyes catch on something behind me. "He cleans up nice, your boxer."

I whirl around to see Ford lingering by the door, staring straight at me. In a tux he rented. Black tie. And black sneakers with white stripes.

So very Ford.

I feel the blood rising to my face as I walk with Z toward him, taking care not to move too fast, certain I'll trip over my train. I don't want to call attention to myself or to him, in case he's nervous.

But he looks great. Relaxed. Almost like he's comfortable in the tux, though I know it's the first one he's ever worn.

When we reach him, threading our way past ball gowns and tuxes topped with masked heads that could be anyone, close friends or total strangers, he pretends to stop breathing, coughing as he looks from me to Zahra. "Sorry. I can't really handle how good you guys look," he jokes, his eyes lingering on me.

"I could say the same to you," I breathe, enjoying his proximity. We've only seen each other twice since the time at Jimmy's. It's been chaste, but all the heat and strangeness of that night at Jimmy's is still between us.

"Will is going to be so jealous," Zahra whispers in my ear.

"Let's not worry about Will," I mumble, my eyes still locked with Ford's. I don't care what Will thinks anymore. My only concerns tonight are that Ford has a good time and doesn't feel too alienated by this North Side crowd, and that when he meets my parents, it's not a total disaster.

"Thanks for coming," I say, just to him. "And renting the tux and everything. It fits perfectly."

He blanches. "It smells a little weird. Sorry."

I move closer and the smell hits my nostrils, faint but

instantly recognizable. "So that's not *your* Sniff For Men Cologne?" I smile at him. I'd know that smell anywhere—several of the Cathedral boys wore it in middle school, before they realized it smelled like a wet dog rolled in nutmeg.

"Nope. Guy before me used a ton of it, though."

"It's not that strong," I reassure him. "And besides, I kind of like it on you."

Ford's smile droops, and he leans in, his mouth an inch from my ear. "Green. About the other night?"

"Don't sweat it," I interrupt him. "I'm not. I'm just happy you're here."

"I just . . . I want you to know I think everything's sorted out now. With me, I mean."

"Let's just take it day by day." I don't want to talk about the other night, not here. I just want to enjoy this one. "It means a lot to me that you came."

Ford's about to tell me something else when Z interrupts us.

"We need to make introductions." Zahra links her arm in Ford's and starts pulling him away from the doorway. "I'm going to take care of introducing you to our illustrious classmates. Anthem's too shy and serious—she'll just botch it or make it awkward."

That's probably true, so I follow along, happy to let Zahra take charge.

I watch as she marches Ford over to Serena Swelling and Annette Gotts, both just a little lower in the Cathedral pecking order than Olive Ann and Clementine Fitz. Both of them wear stilettos that are way too tall, and they almost fall over as they shake Ford's hand, their thick coats of lip gloss gleaming as they flirt with him.

"He's cute, Anthem." Annette smiles at me when Zahra starts moving Ford along, baring her oddly small teeth below her gold mask, her brown curls pulled back with a gold feather headband. "Good for you. And I love your dress." Then she squeezes my hand.

"Thanks," I say, startled by her warmth, which seems genuine. This is a girl who hasn't said more than *can I borrow your math homework for a sec* to me since the eighth grade. "You look great, too."

It's the end of the school year, I realize. Everyone's loosening up. Some of Cathedral's petty turf wars and ridiculous labels are falling away, behind us now.

As we make the rounds and grab mushroom balls, caviar on toast, and cheese puffs from the small silver platters carried by the cater-waiters, I realize we're moving closer to the shrine set up to honor Martha. Below a row of lit candles and blown-up pictures of Martha in her riding helmet, her school uniform, her prom dress are family photos. One of them draws me toward it—ten-year-old Martha on the beach with Manny and Belinda, all three of them squinting at the camera, grinning and sunburnt. Martha's gap-toothed grin and blue eyes. Her whole life in front of her. Gone, now. Because of one lunatic.

A ripple of anger moves through my chest, and I sway on my green satin high heels, turning away quickly, looking for Ford and Zahra. The mayor and Belinda are notably absent at this event. Nobody's seen them since the mayor issued a statement immediately following Martha's death.

I move along in the crowd, shaking thoughts of vengeance from my mind as best I can. Telling myself to relax for now, to enjoy the party. The huge room has filled up, and bejeweled, begowned women and men in black tie are swirling all around me, so many of them that for a minute I've lost sight of Zahra and Ford.

The cater-waiters thread between everyone, quickly empty-ing their trays and heading back for refills.

When I find them again, Ford hands me a glass of pink champagne. "You look like you've seen a ghost," he says.

"Just thinking about Martha." I smile, straighten up. Trying not to look like someone who wants to throttle and choke any-one. "I'm good, really."

I take a sip, then a gulp, and feel the bubbles dissolve on my tongue. I drain the glass and feel a tiny bit lighter in my heels, the champagne hitting my mostly empty stomach hard.

Zahra's laughter in my ears, Ford's arm around my shoulder, the pink champagne—all of it feels good enough to be in the moment.

"This kid has some serious poise," Zahra reports. "Even Olive Ann didn't rattle him."

"Everyone's really nice." Ford grins, and Z and I burst into laughter.

"What?"

Nice isn't how I'd ever describe Cathedral kids, but I'm glad he thinks so. "Nice to *you*," I finally say. "That's great. I'm so happy you came."

Just then I notice my mother gliding toward me in her black lace gown, her face calculated and deceptively calm as she eyes Ford.

"Are you ready to meet Helene?" I lean in and whisper in Ford's ear.

"You mean your mom?" he whispers back.

I nod. Then I grab his glass and down half his champagne as my mother says hello to a series of gray-haired men between us and her.

"I'm looking forward to it." He straightens his tie. The look he gives me is all reassurance and ease, but still, I worry. What if she's snobby and mean to him? What if he says the wrong thing?

"You've *got* this," Z says, standing on my other side, giving my hand a squeeze. The quartet in the corner starts playing Beethoven, and it must be a sign. "He's every mother's dream."

And then she's here. A glass of chardonnay in her right hand. "Hello." My mother eyes Ford, eyebrows raised. "I'm Anthem's mother, Helene. I'm so glad you could join us here tonight." I can read her mind—she's thinking *handsome*. Also, *stranger*. Also, *sneakers*.

"I . . . Mom, this is . . . my . . ." I open my mouth and stammer a minute. The champagne has done nothing for my powers of speech.

Ford saves the moment from total awkwardness: "I'm Ford. Nice to meet you, Mrs. Fleet. And thanks so much for the invitation. You've raised an amazing daughter." Then comes his smile. His twinkling, sincere brown eyes.

Z is right. He knows how to charm people.

"Please, call me Helene," she says brightly. "And thank you for saying so. We're very proud of her."

Ford starts asking her all about her fund-raising efforts for the museum, and she answers him, then asks him about himself, his hopes and dreams. Pointedly not asking him where he's from. Or how we met.

And then my father saunters over, all smiles. His teeth white and bright, hair gelled into a swish. I sneak a look at Ford, and he's respectfully sticking out his hand.

"This must be the mystery date," my father says, winking at me, giving Ford a slap on the back, shaking hands with him.

"Mr. Fleet. An honor to meet you." Ford clears his throat and stands up straighter so that he's almost as tall as my father.

"You too, m'boy." *M'boy?* I shoot a look at Zahra, shrugging, my eyes wide. This is going so much better than I'd imagined. Even my father seems to be holding back, making polite conversation, not invading Ford's privacy or mine. "How long do you think it'll take the museum to rebuild the missing wing? Think they can do it in nine months?"

"Hard to say, sir," Ford says with a laugh. He doesn't know the first thing about construction, and doesn't want to say the wrong thing.

"Because we're going to bid on it and say nine months. Even though between you and me I think it'll take eighteen, ha ha!" My father's had some whiskey. He's relaxed and chatty. The thousand-watt Harris Fleet grin is beaming out from his face like the lights of a spaceship seeking intergalactic fellowship.

"I'll bet you can pull it off," Ford says, matching my father's playful banter. Nobody's grilling him, so he can relax. Nobody's asking where he came from, or what his intentions are.

South, North. None of it seems to matter, suddenly. At least not now, not tonight. Maybe my parents learned their lesson with Gavin and are just hoping it isn't serious with Ford, or hoping not to get into an argument tonight. One or the other. Whatever the reason, I'm glad.

Z elbows me hard in the ribs as my father asks him what he thinks the best way to rebuild the museum is, and actually listens as Ford suggests multiple cranes, all lifting in a row. He uses his arms to show how they'd do the job. My father nods, rubbing his chin, suggesting additional tractors, wedges, and pulleys they'd need to use. "If we get the job, I'll call you, and you can remind me what you said tonight," he jokes.

Ford laughs, and it doesn't sound fake. I've always liked his laugh, the way it's from his gut.

"Parents' dream," Zahra whispers. "Told ya."

"I've read a lot about Fleet Industries, the new stadium project," Ford says.

He has? I look at him sideways, but he presses on. "You're breaking ground soon, right?"

My father nods. "After many headaches. If you're interested, come down to the office one day; I'll give you a tour and show you the plans for the stadium."

"Wow, really?" Ford shoots me a look, and I shrug. I'm just as surprised as he is. "Thanks, Mr. Fleet. I'd like that."

"Call me Harris." My father smiles at Ford, then turns to me and winks almost imperceptibly before he breezes away, waving across the room to two old men.

"Excuse me." My mother smiles at Ford. "Those investors look like they want a minute," she says, then follows my father into the crowd.

"I think that went okay," Ford says. "They're nice."

I nod. They can be nice, when they decide to be. And I'm relieved they put on their charming personas, just now, with Ford. Who knows, maybe my parents genuinely liked him. Maybe they'd want to spend more time with him, in the future. Maybe he can come over to the apartment and hang out and it doesn't have to be a big deal, or awkward, or anything.

It's a happy few minutes, my feet pas de bourréeing under my long gown as I move around the party with Ford and Zahra, a cater-waiter politely replacing my empty champagne glass with a full one, the champagne starting to make all of me fizz and effervesce. I let myself wonder if the pieces of my life are coming together, becoming something new and better.

I'm not immediately on my guard when a tower of champagne glasses shatters on the far side of the room. A woman screams, but I don't think twice.

Then I notice four of the cater-waiters—three young men, one woman—moving quickly toward the center of the room. Which wouldn't be so strange, except they're not holding trays anymore. And there's something odd about the black aprons they wear tied around their waists. They look lumpy, weighted down with something.

Across each of their faces is a creepy, pasted-on smile.

CHAPTER 16

"Please step back," one of the smiling cater-waiters says, his voice clear and loud as a bell. They form a horizontal line as they move forward.

"You heard him; step back, please," repeats another, this one unsmiling, his mouth twisted into a grimace. Though they say *please*, their tone is insistent. "There will now be a short film from our sponsor."

As the lights dim and the room goes dark, I scan the crowd pressing in on all sides until I see my mother. She is making her way to the back of the room, her face clouded with anger, her stride long and effortful. She must be going to get security. She knows the program, and this is obviously not on it.

I look to the doors. When we came in, there was security everywhere. Bulky men in tuxedos with wires in their ears and blank expressions. But I don't see any of them anymore.

Behind the line of four grinning cater-waiters, a huge white screen lowers down from a small slit in the ceiling on the far wall. "I don't think we want to see this," Ford hisses. "Where is security?"

I put a hand on his arm and signal that we should split up, cover more ground. "Let's go look."

Zahra is three people over from me. She looks ready to be amused. I whirl around, moving backward through the crowd, conscious of a thin white beam of light coming from a projector at the back of the room. I thread my way through people clumped in groups, everyone looking worried in the darkness. Ford heads the opposite direction.

Then the film begins to roll behind me.

No.

My heart sinks when I hear the static, though a part of me knew this was what was coming. I whirl around again and am met with the drawing of Invisible's placid, all-seeing eye emerging from gray and white, growing darker at the bottom, lighter at the top.

And then the dark curls framing the white mask, the crude, crayoned-on features. *It's him.* The person who is supposed to be in the maximum security wing of Bedlam Prison. "It was touching how you thought I'd been locked away. You were all so happy." A staticky laugh, the chuckle coming through the plastic of the mask. Did he escape? Was he set free?

"But I'm not as easy to catch as you all thought." His words slice through me like a knife. Suddenly it's obvious. It was all too easy. The person I captured was a decoy.

My heart thrumming louder than an outboard motor, I start to creep toward Ford, past dozens of people who've known me for years. I can't attack the cater-waiters. There are too many witnesses.

"We need to disable the projector," I hiss when I reach Ford.

"I need it to be dark so I can stop them."

I move around a cluster of older women. There are just a few more rows of people to move through before I reach the back of the room where the projector is. I can feel Ford beside me in the darkness.

"I like to think we can all be happy together, don't you?" the masked man drones in that computer-altered voice of his. "Once the city is evened out, everyone can find a little piece of happiness."

I thought I took care of you, I think as I glare at the masked man.

"And I'm afraid most of you haven't begun paying your share," he continues. "I asked for half of your money, but it appears you need a little help handing it over. So today, we've come to collect."

I'm almost to the projector when there's a commotion in the center of the crowd. Three cater-waiters—not the ones at the front of the room, but others I hadn't accounted for—lift a white glass globe full of cash off a pedestal in the middle of the room. This is the globe people have been putting money into all evening, for charity. For the museum. A roar goes up from the crowd as tuxedoed men start shoving the waiters in an attempt to grab the globe, and for a moment there are so many bodies I can't see what's happening.

The roar gets louder a second later, when the globe smashes to the floor, along with several guests, shoved down or clocked by the cater-waiters. It's horrible, but at least it creates a good distraction. Nobody will notice us in the back. Nobody's going to see a girl jumping much too high. Nobody's paying attention.

When we reach the back of the room, I look at Ford and

gesture with my chin toward the ceiling, the beam of light.

He nods, dropping down on one knee and turning his back to me. I take a running start toward him and jump, bouncing off his back and shoulders and up, up, flinging myself into the air, my heart spinning, legs pumping air, my arms straining until I'm high enough to reach out and grab the lens. I grab the black eye of it and yank as hard as I can. It snaps, creaking for a split second before it pops off in my hand.

Blackness fills the room. People are yelling. Screaming. We move toward the edge of the room to avoid the crowd, feeling along the walls. I race to speed up, and in a moment I'm at the front of the room, just a few feet from one of them. Shaking, I leap onto the cater-waiter nearest me. It's dark. He doesn't make a sound, barely struggles. Nobody can see my hands battering him, reaching around his throat . . .

But then, just behind me, there are a series of clicks. A hissing sound. And I feel my grip on his neck start to weaken inexplicably.

"All of it," I hear under the crowd's shouting. "Now."

And then, directly in front of me, a series of clicks, metal clattering on the wood floor. And the whoosh of something sinister opening up.

Just then, someone turns the lights back on, and I see too late what's all around us.

Two of the cater-waiters are fastening gas masks on as they fling several white, shiny cylinders into the air. Thick plumes of pink smoke spew from each one. I am already surrounded with the gas. I stagger backward, away from the one I'd been choking. He grins and slips a mask over his head.

I can fight it is my last coherent thought before I'm engulfed entirely in the cloud of noxious pink spewing up from the canisters on the floor. I cover my mouth and nose with my hands, but it's too late. I've already inhaled enough for the giggle gas to do its job. It tastes of cotton candy and gasoline and pure horror.

My feet feel as if they're glued to the ground, and a moment later I'm convulsing with painful laughter, each spasm of it hitting so hard it hurts my rib cage.

HA HA HA HA HA.

The sound of it echoes all around me. Everyone's faces twisted, bodies shaking.

HEE HEE HEE HEE.

HA HA HA.

Staccato laughter like machine-gun fire fills the air, spilling from hundreds of mouths. So much hysterical laughter, it blends together until it sounds like a collective wail of pain. I laugh so hard my stomach convulses to the point of cramping. The feeling is violent and unstoppable.

Tears begin to stream down my face. My vision blurs with the pink smoke, and the room becomes a fun-house mirror, everyone distorted and elongated, the whole room tilted and bending toward the corners, the room stretched taut like a drum.

The sound of my own forced, painful HA HA HAs scrambles in my ears, messing with my cerebral cortex, my inner ear, my center of gravity, and then I realize I'm falling over from it.

I fall to my knees, my shoulders shaking, unable to fight the gas's hold on me.

Using every ounce of strength I have left, I manage to turn my head slightly. Behind me and to my right, Ford is bent over, his face twisted, both scary and scared, a violent shade of red. He is frozen where he stands. I can't find my parents in the crowd—all I see are dressed-up people convulsing, doubled over, mouths open wide as if on hinges, howling, shrieking, all of whom appear to be dying with laughter.

And to my horror I see they've somehow got the video running again. This time the projection is faint and much smaller, but the audio is loud.

"Until you start leveling the playing field, we're going to borrow your most valuable possessions," the voice on the video drones.

Where are the cater-waiters? I've lost sight of them. Pink gas keeps billowing up from the floors, but I force myself up, make my knees unlock and support my weight again. I take a huge gulp of air through my hands and nearly pass out from the painful giggles it produces, but manage to stay upright.

"We want a hundred million dollars donated to the South Side in the next forty-eight hours. And every day after that, if you don't pay up"—the computer-altered voice pauses just as a guffaw rocks through me, nearly sending me to the floor again—"one of those valuable possessions will be destroyed."

I can hold my breath longer than most people. I can push through this, I tell myself, where others cannot.

My heart punching my ribs, I lift my feet step by agonizing step and slowly move out of the crowded middle of the ballroom, toward the edge of the convulsing, shrieking crowd, tears streaming down my face, agonizing laughter still ricocheting through my body.

As I drag my feet along, I kick dozens of broken champagne flutes, their stems snapped when they were dropped.

And in the back of the room, near the farthest exit, I see the precious possessions. A small group of kids my age and younger, maybe eight or nine of them, are convulsing with laughter, their faces twisted in agony, and simultaneously being dragged across the ballroom by six cater-waiters, each of them wearing hoods fitted with plastic breathing apparatuses, tubes springing out in all directions. *No no no.* I'm too far away still to see who the kids are, but if they're here at this party, they are likely to be children of important families. *Valuable possessions.* Their bodies limp and still convulsing as they're dragged by their armpits across the marble floor.

There is a hundred feet between me and them, and I'm still holding my breath. *Go,* I order myself. *Push.*

It feels like walking with thousand-pound weights on each leg, but I do it.

I drag my legs toward the back of the room, stars appearing in my vision because of lack of oxygen. I do not dare to breathe for fear of inhaling more gas.

I'm seventy feet away, then fifty, then—when nearly all of them are out the door—thirty. Most of the kids still wear their masquerade masks, but a few do not. A couple of them look really young and small. I recognize Celestial Deal, a junior at my school, and my heart twists when I spot a little kid, born of famous parents: Jasper Cawl. He can't be much older than ten. He's so small and delicate, it looks like his arms are going to snap the way they're pulling him. And then I spot Will. He's big and strong at six foot two and 190 pounds, and two aproned waiters drag him across the floor as he kicks in what must be agonizing slow motion, crying out in pain that sounds like laughter.

Just before the masked waiters drag him out the door, his eyes meet mine. Though tears stream from them, they are ablaze with something like horror and something else, too. Something like *help me.* Or *forgive me.*

I stagger forward, my vision darkening from all sides, trying as hard as I can to reach them on the other side of the room. I take a tiny breath of air and push on, my reflexes diminished from the gas. When I get to the door a minute later, all traces of the kids are gone. I breathe more freely in the hallway, a few loose *ha-ha*s still working their way through my cerebral cortex as I listen for them and run silently past eight burly guards passed out in a row on the floor, their hands bound tightly with white plastic zip ties.

I move through gallery after gallery, running in a slow-motion zigzag through marble sculptures from Greek antiquity, beautiful headless women and boys, men with no arms, lovers entwined.

Where are they? Why can't I run properly?

Finally I drag myself to the room that opens up to the scar line of the museum. It almost looks like an art installation, with all the black ash flung against the walls and ceiling and the wall at the end missing, covered instead by a thin gray tarp flapping at the corners, not quite concealing the seam of the bomb site, where wires and metal studs stick out in all directions, all of it coated in a thin layer of drywall dust.

I dash to the tarp and pull it back, my breath held. In the dark night, there is absolutely nobody. Not a trace of the kids or the masked waiters. Not a trace, even, of their screams.

It's almost dawn, and he's been tossing and turning for hours. Finally he gets out of bed, moves to the window. The view of Exurbia in the dust-gray night—the seven stars he can count in the sky where the city lights are dimmer—it feels like a promise.

He turns away, assesses the darkened space. It's only four rooms—living, bed, kitchen, bath—but for now it's all they need. Just outside the city, before the winding lanes and farmland of Exurbia open up, there are two massive C-shaped brick apartment buildings with intermittent heat, brown water pouring from their faucets that needs to be boiled for fifteen minutes before it's drinkable. There are holes in the plaster ceiling that leak every time the upstairs neighbors take a bath, and the floors are so full of splinters, it's best to wear socks.

But for now, it's a roof over their heads.

She's furnished the place with rugs she dragged here from other parts of the city, chairs she found on curbs on trash day. Before her money ran out, she splurged on a love seat. A few pots and pans.

He looks at the clock: 4:06 A.M. Moves his gaze to her, asleep in their bed. Her newly shortened hair springing up in all directions.

They've been living together for eight months. He's found a job down by the river, hauling goods delivered by boat onto the docks. He goes out less and less at night. The riots he's inspired have been gathering momentum all on their own. People demanding safety, fair treatment, jobs. He's still in the news all the time, even though he now rounds up what's left of the criminal element on the streets at night only about twice a month.

Because the spark he lit is spreading through the city, all by itself. They both hope it builds to a blaze. Maybe then the riots will lead to something.

His thoughts return to his usual worries. They need to move farther out. Live off the land. Get away from the city altogether. It's not just him who's got a reward on his head. It's her, too. Though in her case, she's wanted alive.

When she finally told her parents about them, it didn't go well. Her father threatened to send her to boarding school on another continent if she didn't end it. She'd come to him the night it happened, eyes swollen shut from crying. "I'm never going back," she said. "This is it now; it's just going to be us. We can do whatever we want." That was two apartments ago, with the Bridge of Brotherhood twinkling out the window.

"He'll come looking for you," he'd said.

She nodded. "They will. We need to get farther away."

And so they landed here. Where their neighbors mostly speak no English. Where people fight late into the night, where they can hear grown women and babies crying through the heating pipe in the bathroom. Where everyone is too busy trying to get by to suspect Regina Fleet is in their midst. Nobody here seems to notice the girl whose father offered a cool million for her safe return, or the boy the Syndicate will pay several hundred thousand for, dead or alive.

She's dyed her hair now, to disguise herself. It's blue-black and short, cut like a boy's. Almost as short as his. She's become a different person, almost. Going to the dusty marketplace ten blocks away, carrying her meager, careful purchases back and making them into meals that stretch every dime. She's learned from Selina, a woman on the seventh floor, to boil dried beans with a bit of meat, to cook rice with spices so tasty you'd never know it was prepared by a girl who was raised with a full-time cook.

He looks out the window again, feeling the pull of motion, wanting to get outside and move around to calm down. In an hour, it'll be time to leave for the docks. No point in lying back down under the six thin blankets they've scrounged up. It's warm enough in here at night if you arrange them just right, the heaviest on top. A leaden worry sits on his chest. Makes it hard to breathe.

Calm down, he tells himself. *Things are fine. They'll get better. You'll figure something out.* This is what he tells himself whenever he can't sleep, which happens often lately. He repeats it over and over, like counting sheep.

Silently, he slips on his jacket, grabs his wallet off the kitchen counter. He'll run to the outdoor market, he decides, where they're likely just setting up before dawn. He'll pick up milk and fresh rolls. Maybe come home with a treat. Something that will make her smile. When she's in a good mood, he'll broach the subject of their leaving here again. They need to make a plan, to get out before something goes wrong.

With a price on both their heads, this is no way to live.

He opens the door, tiptoes out, closes and locks it from the other side. *Cherries*, he thinks. If he can find some, that's what he'll get.

Regina wakes to the shuffling of feet in the hall. A heavy tread. Someone paused just outside the door. Instantly, she's alert. They've come for him. Today is the day the Syndicate finally catches up to them and tries to take him out. She reaches out in the dark to wake him, but there're just blankets there, a cold pillow. Where is he? She looks at the clock. It's 4:53 A.M. Has he left early for the docks?

She's up like a shot, racing barefoot to the bathroom. Empty. She checks the rest of the tiny apartment. The meager alcove. Absurdly, in desperation, she even checks the coat closet.

He's not here.

What should she do? She stares at the door, frantic. Then she moves toward it as silently as possible, terrified but suddenly filled with resolve. She needs to be the protector now.

If the Syndicate breaks in looking for him and they find what's in here, they'll use it as bait for him. God knows what they'd do. Before she can even process what she's doing, she darts to the pile of dirty clothes at the foot of the bed, throws on whatever she finds over her nightgown. His blue sweatshirt. A pair of his pants. Then she goes to the spot at the side of the mattress where he's carved out a compartment. She digs around inside, her fingers groping in the dark. There is cash here, a small stack of bills that is everything they have. And then her fingers graze what she's been looking for: the cool metal of the gun muzzle. She digs deeper, pulls the gun out, then finds the second gun behind it. Which means that wherever he is, he's unarmed.

She yanks them both from the mattress, pulling out some batting in the process. Her hands are shaking so badly, she's not sure how she'll be able to shoot.

She knows where he keeps ammunition, in the drawer in the kitchen. She darts barefoot toward it, his jeans catching twice on the splintered wood. From the coatrack by the door, she snatches a baseball cap and puts it on. Anything to look intimidating, to feel like someone other than herself.

She moves to the kitchen drawer, where she finds a box of ammo behind the scissors and a bunch of plastic bags. She slams the cartridges down into the guns, first one, then the other. Her hands shake worse than ever. She holds her breath and listens. The door handle rattles, as if the person on the other side is testing it. If they get it open, she will fire. It's that simple. The calculus is clear. Everything that matters to her is on this side of the door. She lives with a man who has a price on his head. She cannot take chances.

As quietly as she can, she tilts the dining table up onto its side to make a barricade. She ducks behind it, rests the gun muzzle on the edge of the table, and aims it at the door. *Stop shaking*, she orders herself. *You have to do this. You only stand a chance if you shoot first.*

There's a creeping silence now, no more jiggling of the knob. Maybe they've given up and gone away.

But then the doorknob starts not just to jiggle but to turn. She hears the bolts sink into place.

And now she is not afraid.

Her hands have stopped their shaking. *I am a defender*, she thinks. Ready for whatever comes. *I was born to this. Born to the wrong family. This is what I was meant for. To make sure he gets away, to protect him so he can save this city. To protect what we have made together. The only thing that matters. This is my path.* A South Side tag on several tall buildings, written in a child's scrawl, floats into her mind: *Defend until the end.*

She will trust in fate to guide her. There is not a trace of fear in her now that she has put her faith in something bigger. In a plan. In *the* plan, the one they've made in case she disappears. He'll come; he'll do whatever it takes to make things all right again.

All these illogical, desperate thoughts soothe her as the door opens. They hypnotize her enough so that she can hold the gun, kneel behind the table in the pitch-dark of the kitchen. No moon tonight. A small blessing. It's so dark in here. If they can't find her, they can't shoot her. She cocks the gun and listens to the bolts move in the lock.

CHAPTER 17

The museum is under police lockdown for hours. We wait our turn to be questioned by a team of two detectives, both of whom have faces that look as if they were formed by having been hit flat with frying pans. I stand with my mother and father in the kitchen, numb and furious, staring at all the uneaten food laid out on the counters. Ford hovers nearby and sometimes stands quietly with us.

All of it wastes so much time. When it's my turn for questioning I tell the police everything I saw, but the trail is surely ice-cold by then.

It's midnight by the time we are told at last that we can go home. But all I want to do is search for Invisible. I need to talk to someone about how to track them down. I need to get Ford alone.

"Mom?" I ask as we trudge through the glass-strewn ball-room. "Could Ford walk me home instead of us taking the car? We'd be careful and only go on busy well-lit streets. It's just, our date was sort of . . ."

"Ruined." My mother nods, her eyes bloodshot. "Your date was ruined by a group of monsters." She looks at me nervously, weighing out her fear, trying to decide. "Fine. I don't want to live in terror. If we are terrified, it means they win."

"Does that mean . . ."

"That means go," she slurs, having downed maybe a little more leftover flat pink champagne than she should have back in the museum kitchen. "Quick, before your father comes and says otherwise."

"Thanks," I whisper, and kiss her soft cheek. Her eyeliner is a mess, forming black wells beneath her eyes. Mine probably is, too. She's shocked me by being okay with this. With me and Ford. Alone. At night. After all that's happened.

I run to get him, stopping to hug good-bye to Zahra, who has been photographing everything with her phone—for the school paper, she claims—and we leave through a back hallway so as not to run into my father.

Outside, I realize my dress wasn't cut out for all it's been through tonight. It's baggy where it should be tight, and the train is all twisted. There's even a rip, where a piece of shantung flaps loose like a bandage at my waist.

"So," I say miserably. "Great night, huh?"

"Yeah." Ford has been quiet for hours.

"I need to get those kids back."

"But how?"

"If I knew how, I'd already be doing it." I turn to glare at Ford, struggling to keep the irritation out of my voice. "I should have been stronger, been able to fight the giggle gas faster—"

"I couldn't believe you could move at all." Ford shakes his head. "I thought that stuff was going to kill me."

"It was awful. I'm sore from the convulsions." I rub my abs, which are used to being worked, but never like this.

"Me too."

We walk in silence for a few minutes. "So . . . the guy in jail? Who was that?"

I sigh bitterly and feel a hot humiliation rising in my cheeks. "Must have been a decoy. I should know better by now, after everything . . ." Rage chokes my voice.

Ford stops, turns to face me. "Don't be so hard on yourself, okay?"

"It's my fault this happened. There wouldn't even have been this party if people didn't feel safe enough to have it because of my stupidity. Invisible wouldn't have had the opportunity—"

"Stop." He puts a hand over my mouth. "You're not doing them any good by focusing on this."

"Fine." I nod. "Let's talk about where they might be. They are clearly well-funded and organized. They would have to go deep underground to hide all the hostages."

"How many are there?" Ford says.

"Dunno," I say glumly. "Maybe eight or nine. They'll release their names soon, I'm sure." I think about them, locked somewhere.

"Maybe something in the videos," Ford suggests.

"Any clues from the video could be traps."

Ford nods and is quiet, brooding now. "What did they ask you in the questioning room?"

"The police?"

"Yeah. They had a lot of questions about what I was doing at the party. Since I'm not from around here, they said."

"Jerks," I mutter. "They're useless. They looked bored when

they were talking to me. Just kept asking if I'd seen their faces, and of course I had, we all had."

"You should have just told them you were the New Hope," Ford says, knocking his shoulder into mine playfully. "They would have listened more carefully then."

"Probably wouldn't have believed me." I smile faintly.

"Ford," I say, still brooding over the glassiness of their eyes, the strange clipped way they moved. "Did they all seem . . . off . . . to you? Drugged, somehow?"

He's quiet, thinking about this. "Maybe, yeah. Think he keeps them that way?"

"Who?"

"Their leader. Maybe he gives them something. To keep them loyal. To make them tougher, or more dependent on him, or unquestioning. I've heard stories about this guy they called the Hammer, a long time ago, big player in the Syndicate, who kept all his goons on the same drugs. If they got out of line, they lost privileges to his primo smokestacks. The stuff he gave them was laced with something, stronger than the stuff on the streets."

I nod, thinking about this. It does seem like the Invisible people are all on the same strong drugs.

We've walked along the river away from the museum until we've ended up in Riverfront, the warehouse district of the North Side. Not exactly the well-lit type of street I've promised my mother we'd stay on. Someone has thrown a rock at all the streetlights here, or disconnected the electricity, because it's seriously dark. The shadows the warehouses make are impenetrable—anything could be lurking up against them and we'd never see it.

But something or someone is near. I can hear it. My ears pick up a scuttling of shoes just ahead of where we are. The sounds of marching. I check Ford to see if he notices, and he doesn't. Must be riot police, cordoning off the area.

Up ahead, three helmeted police emerge from the shadows. One of them lifts his mirrored helmet and looks at us suspiciously. A lock of black hair is slicked down over his forehead with sweat. He pulls something from his belt and I tense, thinking it's a gun or a Taser, but then I see it's neither. It's a small cylinder with a flat glass disc on one end. "What's your business here?" he says.

I look at Ford. His lips are pressed together in an angry line. "We're just walking home."

"Area's been cordoned off. How'd you come to be here?" His eyes small and beady, piggish.

"We came from the museum," Ford says. "That a problem?"

"I'm going to need to take your prints." The cop ignores Ford's question and thrusts the device with the glass disk on it toward me. "Place your index finger on the glass, ma'am."

"Fine." I do as he says. After a moment, there's a beep and the glass turns green.

"Your turn." The cop motions to Ford.

"I don't think so," Ford says. The cop looks around. We're alone. Just the three of us. His hand moves to a button on his helmet near his ear, hovers over it, and for a second I wonder if he's going to call for backup.

But the hand drops. "If you choose not to participate in fingerprinting, I'm going to have to book you on charges of suspicious loitering."

"Suspicious loitering?" Ford's voice raises. I put a hand on his arm and the fabric of his tux jacket feels strangely warm. "Ford." I say it quietly, trying to urge him to remain calm. "Just do it. Takes two seconds."

"Fine," he says under his breath. He's breathing deeply, as if it takes every ounce of his strength to stay calm in front of the cop. He puts his finger on the glass and instead of the beep and the green color, the device emits a series of much louder beeps, then glows red. The cop pulls it away from Ford and shines it onto the ground like a flashlight. A beam comes out of it and suddenly on the street it says

3 PRIOR ARRESTS

PETTY THEFT, GRAND THEFT AUTO, ASSAULT

"It was a long time ago. I was just a kid. Already did my time in juvie," Ford says.

"And now you're just taking a midnight stroll on the North Side, with this girl? Who'd you steal the tux from?"

"That's none of your business," Ford growls. And then before I can stop him, he grabs the cop's wrist, twisting it so that the device goes flying. I hear it smash against the sidewalk a moment later, the sound of the glass screen shattering. There's a sickening stillness in the moment, Ford and the riot cop staring each other down, each contemplating his next move.

"Ford," I say softly, trying to lower the tension of the moment. This is bad. He'll get zapped, or worse. In Bedlam, messing with riot cops means jail time. "Officer, he didn't mean to—" I start saying, desperate for a way to defuse a situation that is quickly getting out of control.

"My business is keeping punks like you off the streets," the cop says to Ford, ignoring me, his jaw tightening as he puts down his riot shield on his helmet and moves to grab something from his belt—feargas, a zapper, or cuffs. But before he can get whatever he's looking for, Ford pushes him hard. So hard, he flies off his feet a little and lands face-first against the side of a parked car.

"Stop it!" When I move to grab Ford's fisted hands, scared of what he's about to attempt, they're hot enough to burn my fingers. I let them go, alarmed.

The cop turns around slowly, holding his bleeding head, moaning a little in spite of his uniform and his job.

"We need to get out of here. *NOW*," I hiss, giving him a horrified look. Ford walks in a small circle in this stilted, jerky way, as if hemmed in by a boxing ring, his eyes glazed red, blinking as if waking up from a fever dream. He moves to the gutter and I hear the splash of objects sliding into the drain, the plop of metal landing in the sewer. The cop's gun, maybe the print scanner, too.

Then he backs away, nodding, looking only at me before he turns the other way and runs. *Fast.* Not as fast as I can run, but fast enough so I understand he hasn't just gotten better. He's become enhanced. Like me, only with less ability to control himself.

I follow him, a burning mix of anger and pity thumping in my chest.

"I'm sorry," Ford says after we've been running for ten blocks or so. He slows down to a walk in an alley not far from my house. "I got carried away."

I stop moving and stare at him, still afraid and incredulous. The heat. The uncontrollable rage. "You could go to jail for this. You will, if they catch you."

"He'll be too embarrassed to bother," Ford says. "Besides, they won't find me. They're too busy worrying about Invisible."

I glare at him, fighting to keep my voice calm when all I want to do is shout. "Even if that's true, it was *stupid*. You were out of control."

Ford nods, his eyes no longer the scary red saucers they were before.

"I think it's time to tell me what's going on." I cross my arms, shivering a little in the cold night.

Ford looks at the ground and speaks so quietly I have to get closer to him even though right now I don't want to be. "When Jax gave me those transfusions, they worked. Really well. But the synthetic blood, it . . . changed me." His voice cracks, and in my heart it feels like a rubber band snaps against it. I know all about the changes Jax can make. I live them every day.

I nod, biting the insides of my cheeks in anger and recognition. That's why he wanted me to leave that night.

I turn away, hating Jax in this moment. I would have done anything to make Ford better, but it never occurred to me that it could also make things worse. That the transfusions would do to Ford what my new heart did to me. We're the same now. *Enhanced.* Like me, Ford is no longer all human. He's something more. And something less.

Finally I talk to fill the silence. "I'm not afraid of you, Ford."

"You should be." His eyes don't meet mine.

"What do you think you're going to do, kill me?"

He makes a sound in the back of his throat like he's in agony. Looks at the wall behind me. I lean against the water-stained wall, waiting nervously.

"What happened tonight isn't the real me. It was just like at Jimmy's, only worse. I just . . . lost control."

"It's okay," I try. "I know what it's like to—"

"No you don't!" Ford interrupts me sharply. "Not like *this*.

When I get around you, when I have a powerful emotion, be it anger like tonight, or . . . uh . . . other feelings . . . like at Jimmy's Corner, when we were . . ." Here he pauses, looking up. "When we were on the mat. Bad things happen. I get so hot, and this feeling comes over me, like I can't control myself. Like I'm moving toward a doorway or something, and I can't trust what's on the other side of it, but I can't stop myself."

"From what?" My voice is tiny.

He peers at me for a second, then swallows. Continuing. "From letting go, going to the other side of that door, where I let this new violent version of myself take over. I can't trust myself around you right now." His voice cracks. "It just gets worse around you. I'm sorry. I need some time."

"Okay," I say flatly. Inside, I feel raw and rejected. I'm already putting a hard shell around myself again. Building up a wall where before, with Ford, I felt only tenderness. "I'm here for you as a fr—"

"You're not understanding me." He shoots me a pained look. "I need to work on this, *alone*. I can't see you for a while."

"But . . . that doesn't make any sense," I say, trying to sound reasonable and not just hurt. He can't cut off contact *entirely*. Can he? "We're friends. Before anything else, we're friends. You don't just end that, just because . . ." I trail off, afraid to finish.

"Yes I do. I can't risk exposing you to that person."

I open my mouth, but nothing I think of to say seems right. The way he looks at me, the defeat in his eyes, the way he's shut himself off from me, tells me whatever wall I'm erecting between us, the one he's built is ten times as thick. He's already written me off.

"You're not making sense," I say, wondering why I'm bothering. He's clearly made up his mind.

"Maybe not. But this is the only way I know how to be right now." His mouth is pinched with that fighting determination I've only seen before in the boxing ring.

"Fine," I say. But I give him one last look, hoping he'll change his mind, realize how this seems, and start to backtrack. Say something to let me know he still cares.

But his face only hardens, and I feel the punch-in-the-gut pain of rejection. This is how he's chosen to end things. Because of the masquerade ball, and meeting my parents, and renting a tux that smelled like another man's cologne. Because of the way the police questioned him, as if he was a suspect. All of it told him we were too different to be together.

I search his eyes for ulterior angles, but all I see are eyes that won't meet mine, flickers of pain moving across his face.

Against my better judgment, I still reach out a hand and touch his shoulder. Hoping I'm wrong, somehow. That he doesn't really want to end this. "Maybe we should talk this thr—"

"I'm not asking you," Ford interrupts me, his voice gruff. Shrugs my hand off his shoulder. "I'm telling you. Go home, Anthem." He shuts his eyes for a minute and turns away from me.

"Fine." I back away slowly, then turn around and walk away, trying to keep my breath level and calm and not give in to the hurt twisting inside me.

I turn back once, and he's still standing there in the gray alley, his hands balled into fists. Staring at me.

"Bye," I mutter under my breath. And then I'm running, in the cold, as alone as I've ever felt.

CHAPTER 18

The next day the kids are all over the news. There are nine of them. Five of them go to Cathedral, and four are rich and famous enough in Bedlam that I know of them from the papers, even though they go to Lakeside Academy. They range in age from ten (Jasper Cawl, scion of the Cawl Paper Products family) to eighteen (Astrid Weathers, the only child of tennis champion Pete Weathers and MegaMart heir Patti Selz). The only one I know well is Will, but three others are a few grades below us: Sheldon Mandell, a sweet-looking freshman at Cathedral whose family inherited the Huntley car fortune; Celestial Deal, a wild junior who's been suspended from Cathedral twice but who will never be kicked out because she's part of the powerful Deal Hotel dynasty; and Mik Elder, son of actress Meeka Post and Reginald Elder (lead singer of the Broken Bottles, a band that was huge when my parents were young), who's only in eighth grade but who is so handsome and sweet that it doesn't really matter that he can barely read.

The rest of the kids are all from high-profile families, too. The news anchors speculate that this is why they were taken. For maximum media exposure.

The next morning, two of the families give a press conference about enormous checks they're writing to the South Side Children's Hospital. "Because it's the right thing to do," Meeka Post says, her beautiful face puffy and quivering with emotion in front of the news cameras. "We are proud today to donate seven million dollars to Children's Hospital. And"—she looks directly at the camera, her green eyes blazing—"we would like our son back now."

Pete Weathers goes on next, talking about personal responsibility and about doing the right thing for the city. "So many of our friends are making sizable contributions," he says. His tanned, surgically perfected face is devoid of emotion, but his voice catches, betraying his worry for his daughter. "Please, everyone. Give what you can. The money is going to good places, and our children need your help."

The morning brings endless thrumming of police helicopters in the skies. Mayor Marks, looking medicated and doused in grief, his eyes ringed in dark circles, does his own press conference, encouraging the city to "go about your business as we hunt down these maniacs and work to retrieve your children."

School is not cancelled. What is there to do but to go? Sit around here with my mother, who's taken to her bed? No thanks, I decide. So I go. And after a long day of sad talk among students and emotional, unfocused teachers, everyone consumed by the missing kids, I head to ballet.

Even though the day is mild, a shiver rocks through me as I wonder how many of those kids are going to come out of this alive. I resolve to try to follow up on Ford's idea about the drugs, see if I can follow the trail. Maybe someone in the South Side will know something.

Normally, I would ask Ford to go with me. I push thoughts of him away, until I can almost ignore them. I'm on my own now.

I'm five minutes early for ballet, so I take my time arranging my boots and socks and changing my clothes in the small dressing room. When I emerge, five of my fellow level sixers, each already bunned and burnished in leggings and leos for practice, are gathered around Constance and her tablet.

It's an Invisible transmission. *Again*. I can tell by the hush in the room. By the hum of electronic static. But this time it's different, because now they have collateral.

I pull a pair of boy shorts on, a high-necked tank top covering the faint line of my scar, and creep out of the dressing area, tentatively stepping toward the crowd.

"She's amazing," Constance says, her ankle in her hand as she stretches her quad, standing like a flamingo in her hot pink cutoff sweats and white sports bra.

Liberty Sewell sighs with admiration. "Graceful and scary at the same time."

I lean in slightly to see a slice of the tablet, and my heart whirs with surprise. It's new footage, of the night I captured their decoy. Even though I took the camera, somewhere there was a second one, filming me.

I see myself lunging at him in the surgical mask, the black mesh band covering my eyes, attacking the decoy on the fourth floor of the hospital in Lowlands. But I'm so covered up, even I can barely tell it's me.

I move closer to the tablet when Invisible's masked face

comes into view again, the curved mask revealing his chin and hair and nothing else. His voice robotic and disguised as always. This time, the wall behind him is blank and white. He could be anywhere.

"Citizens of Bedlam. We would like to encourage you to come forward with any information about this masked girl. We'd like to have a word with her. Post a video if you know anything about who she might be, and we will reward you handsomely."

The mask moves and the hairs on the back of my neck stand on end. He's smiling underneath it. I'm certain of it. The girls hiss and boo around me, but they quiet down as he keeps talking.

"And now on to more important matters. Today was a record-breaking fund-raising day for the South Side Children's Hospital, the South Side Orphans' Association, the South Side Food Pantry, and the South Bedlam schools. We congratulate you on your contributions. Many of you, hundreds of you—" Here he pauses, then laughs, though it sounds like a wheeze. "We are keeping track, dear friends, and we know your names—" Pause for throat-clearing. "—have complied with our requests. But it's not enough. If we do not reach one hundred million dollars in donations for South Side public works projects by midnight tomorrow night, we will be forced to say good-bye to our youngest little friend, Jasper Cawl."

I feel the bile rising up in my throat as a feed of the kids flashes on the screen, this one in color. All nine of them sit slumped against a wall, eyes glazed with boredom and lack of sleep. They look filthy and hungry. Celestial waves her fingers in front of her face, as if batting away a bug or perhaps just to make sure it's still attached to her body. The others stare straight ahead with blank, hollow expressions. Jasper, ten years old, is the only one sleeping. His head is on a girl's shoulder, a sweet shock of his dirty blond hair sweat-stuck to his cheek.

I start shaking involuntarily, my hands and even my teeth vibrating with the cold forces of fury and fear.

I need to find them. And I only have thirty hours to do it.

I imagine making a video of myself, showing the world it's me, that I'm the masked girl. Would they let the kids go, if I offered myself up? He didn't present it as a trade, and I wonder if it would be yet another trap.

"Enough of this." Madame has arrived in a swirl of red scarves and jingling jewelry. "Put it away, dancers. We will have none of this Invisible in this studio, thank you very much." She flashes a disgusted look at Constance's tablet.

I look from one face to another as they scurry to tie up their hair, or begin to stretch alongside the barre, or wrap their ankles. But nobody pays me any mind. They keep chattering with each other.

"She's so graceful. The way she kicked that guy in the neck, like it was nothing? What a badass."

"Wish I could move like that," Liberty Sewell says.

"Yeah, you *do* wish," Constance jokes, raising an eyebrow.

"Who d'you think it is?" Sadie Lockwood asks.

"Some South Side girl raised by pro fighters," Constance says. "Trained to kill."

"I hope nobody outs her," whispers Clarissa Bender, moving from first to second to third position before we start our barre work.

Me too.

"Someone will," says Constance, always a know-it-all.

"Who would do that?" Liberty asks.

"Someone who wants money." She shrugs. And she's probably right.

As I move through our battement, all I see is little Jasper Cawl, asleep on someone's shoulder. A little boy whose luck it was to be born famously rich, whose luck has turned into a curse.

I lift off into the air, leaping into a *grand jeté* and landing hard, watching in amazement as the other dancers follow suit, not one of them paying me more than the usual attention. Not one of them hearing the violent revolutions of my heart.

After practice, Serge drives me home.

"I saw the video," he says as soon as I shut the door. I wait a minute to answer, fiddling with my ballet bag, putting it next to my school bag on the seat next to me. I peek at the rearview and see Serge's dark eyes staring at me. Eyebrow raised.

The air in the car is close and humid and full of things unspoken.

"I have some information I think might be of use."

"What is it?"

"I was reading about a series of security breaches that happened a couple of months ago. A large group of young people escaped from the maximum security ward of Weepee Hills, where the worst psychiatric cases are sent."

"Weepee Hills? Is that like Weepee Valley?"

"Similar, but state-funded instead of private. It's where the mentally disturbed are sent when they can't afford to pay."

He hands me a manila envelope, filled with news stories about the escape. He's circled a few of the people, and I sit up straight with recognition of one boy in particular. I'm sure he's the blond kid from the arena.

LINKS SUSPECTED IN ESCAPES AT WEEPEE

In a string of what police and hospital officials suspect are related incidents, a total of 18 youths under 21 years of age have escaped from the high-security wing of Weepee Hills, a state-run psychiatric facility for the criminally disturbed, in the past four months. Most recently, last night five young men, ranging in age from 16 to 20 and all diagnosed with dangerous impulsivity, violent tendencies, and delusions of grandeur, appear to have escaped through the facility's trash disposal system. They are believed to be unarmed but nonetheless may be highly dangerous.

The rest of the article is harder to read, the print on the copy blurred.

"You'll notice they all have something in common."

All of them were sent to Weepee Hills for addiction issues. Most of them were droopers, with a few of them hooked on drugs I've never heard of, pharms of various kinds or smokestacks or BodMod injections.

"Drugs." I nod. Ford might have been right about Invisible ensuring loyalty with drugs. I shake my head slightly, willing myself not to think of last night. The hurt is still so raw.

"We could try to find their families, see if anyone knows anything," I muse, refocusing myself. "But I think it might be smarter to talk with people who know about the drug trade. I think they're all on the same thing." I flash on the smears of shoe polish, the glazed red eyes they all have.

Serge nods. "There isn't much time."

I stare out the car window as Bankers Alley smears past the windows, all navy blue and gray with pops of white and black, people's faces, umbrellas opening up on sidewalks as a sudden burst of rain falls on the windshield.

We turn onto Foxglove Court, and Fleet Tower rears up in front of us, all lit up with spotlights, two of the doormen standing outside at attention, umbrellas floating above their heads. Three police officers are stationed on the block, guns raised, standing still as statues. Everyone is on high alert again.

"Do you think my parents have figured it out?"

"I am assuming not," Serge says.

"Nobody else seems to have a clue," I say. "It's . . . weird."

"People see what they expect to see," Serge says. "They often don't notice what's right in front of them."

"Do you think Jasper Cawl will die?" I breathe.

He doesn't answer. Serge's silence is worse than any false hope he might be able to give me. Again, I feel the bile in my throat rise up. He leans forward and reaches under the car seat, then hands me something inside a zippered velvet pouch.

I unzip it, knowing it's a weapon. What I find is matte black, small, and light. With a box of bullets. I look at Serge in the rearview and nod, unable to speak. I don't want this. I don't want to use it. Just like he doesn't want to have to give it to me. But the fact that I might need it is something we both understand.

"Thanks." We're getting close to home. My heart revs with urgency. I need to do something. Now. "Would you be able to drive me somewhere later?"

Serge is quiet in the front seat. "A study session, perhaps," he says quietly. "Yes. Of course."

I'm already composing a white lie for my parents. An emergency study session. Certainly plausible. It's midterm time in my classes. Before I exit the car, I make eye contact with Serge in the mirror. "Study session is at Hades. I think I know someone there who might be able to help."

My mother waves me toward her in the sitting room and flashes me a sloppy grin. Her neck, below the line of her makeup, is flushed from wine. Asher and Melinda Turk sit beside her on the L-shaped white couch, flanked on the other side by my father. The four of them are huddled together, all of them staring at my father's wide-screen laptop.

"Five hundred thousand dollars per family, bare minimum. Much more if possible. That's what we should suggest," Melinda says, her deep olive skin and coppery hair burnished and shiny in the evening light even though her eyes are tired.

"Hi, darling." My mother motions me over. "How are you holding up?"

"Fine." I peer at the laptop. There's a spreadsheet on it. "What's going on?"

"We're just putting together a donation protocols sheet," Asher says. "Nobody wants that child to . . ." He trails off, his dark eyes moving to the corner of the room, unfocused. And the silence in the room buzzes with his unfinished sentence: Nobody wants that child to die.

"Have you all already donated?" I hope they aren't waiting until the last minute.

They nod. "To the Children's Hospital. We each gave substantially," Melinda says. "If only it were enough."

"You know, we always give a lot of money to charity, Anthem," my father says, appraising me as if I've said something out of line. "Whether or not an extortionist is forcing us to. It's not something we talk much about or do publicly, normally."

"Of course. I know that." I move from one foot to the other and try not to think about the weight of the gun in my Seven Swans bag. I don't dare set it down here, in front of them.

"We're also working out secondary funds for a private investigation firm, since it appears the police are useless," my father continues.

I nod, curious what they think of the other part of the video. The part where they request a meeting with me. "And this girl they're looking for, do you think anyone's looking for her?"

"Heavens no," Melinda says. "We're all very supportive of that girl. She's done something nobody else can."

"A helluva lot more than the police have," grumbles my father. "How they can walk the streets and hold their heads up high, I can't imagine. This is a travesty, what's happened to those children on their watch. And the mayor is just out to lunch, for obvious reasons—"

"Harris, we know," my mother says plaintively. "We've gone over this. It doesn't help getting all worked up about it again."

"How are you holding up, Anthem?" Asher smiles. He's known me since I was five, and usually likes to keep things light. "You'd never let yourself within five feet of these people, wouldya? I know Zahra wouldn't. I've been telling her where to kick a man who gets close to her . . ."

"Yes, dear. We all know where to kick a man when he gets too close." Melinda smirks.

I can't manage much more than a half-smile.

"Do you think they'll . . . do you think people will donate enough?" I feel the blood rush to my face when I say it, my words trembling in the air.

"It's a long shot. Some people are refusing. But it's very possible that this is a classic bluff," Asher says. "Give me this, I give you this, and then at the last second . . . nothing. Who's to say he'll release the kids and make a fair trade? All we can do is try to convince people, and hope it works."

"People are giving," my mother says, falling back against the pillows of the couch. "I just hope it's enough."

I feel a surge of tenderness toward both my parents. For all their faults, for all my mother's drinking and pills and being checked out over the years, for all my father's obsession with work and buildings and his babying my mother in her endless grief—they're what I have.

Two genetically blessed (and slightly injected) middle-aged people who look much younger than they are. Two people who have lost a daughter. And somehow have gone on, together, to have one more and to raise her.

I only wish I could live up to their expectations. Again, the kidnapped kids flash in my mind. Especially Will.

"How are the Hansens?" I ask.

"Will's father is pulling every string he has. He's talking about bringing in the military, about finding the girl, using her as a lure . . . he's just very upset about poor Will," Asher Turk says. I'm conscious of both my parents looking at me then, to watch my reaction. After all, Will and I have a lot of history. Some of which they know about, a lot of which they don't.

The blackmail, for example. The secret taping of me in my room. The extortion, the stalking.

"It's so awful." I shake my head, saying what they expect to hear. But the truth is, I *do* feel bad for Will. I think of the footage, the way he was sitting against the wall, just staring into space, his eyes empty and his mouth slack. He may have put me through hell, but I don't want him to end up dead. "Poor Will."

I try to imagine what's going through his head in captivity. What will happen if people don't donate enough money before the deadline and Invisible follows through on his threats? How long until the Invisible focus on killing Will?

But then a trickle of ice makes its way down my spine. Will has something Invisible wants—information about the New Hope.

If I don't find them, how long until they find me?

CHAPTER 19

Serge parks in the former mall's vast lot, and we head across the dark parking lot and go inside through one of the side doors. We walk through a dark, liquor-scented hallway until we reach the mall's atrium, lit up brightly with Klieg lights running on generators. The bottom floor is as loud as ever, with barkers selling car parts, weapons, food, drugs. In all, there are about a hundred makeshift booths set up, several aisles crisscrossing through them.

I look up and notice that a line of six huge men pumped up on pharms and wearing Uzis stands on the second floor, glowering, observing the lower level. Nerves twist inside me and I look away, focusing on finding the pack of children I know lives here. I motion to Serge to move faster, toward the back wall where the children of Hades tend to congregate.

When we reach the back wall behind the black market, a group of kids between seven and thirteen years old are playing marbles. I scan their skinny faces until my eyes land on a frizzy head of caramel curls. His hearing aids looped over each ear, glowing blue.

"Hey, Rufus." I crouch down beside him. He's got three wrinkled dollar bills riding on this marbles game; they sit in front of him on the ground. "Remember me?"

He scoops up his three dollars, tucks them away like a skilled gambler, then turns to see me. His big eyes light up with recognition. "You're alive." He grins. "Why'd you take so long to come back?"

I shrug. "Got busy, I guess. But I'm here now. And actually, I need a favor."

He stands up, nods. "I'll be back," he says to the marbles players. "Got a client," he adds, jabbing his thumb in my direction. Then I follow him down the hall in the direction of the Chop Shop. The smell of formaldehyde is noticeable way before we get there. But then Rufus ducks into a storefront with the windows blown out and a pink door falling off its frame. It clearly was once an ice cream parlor, but all that remains of that is a pink counter and a few pink plastic tables and chairs. The ice cream cones that were once painted onto the wall are now mostly graffitied over. The three of us—me, Rufus, and Serge—all sit down at a table.

"Who's the big guy?" Rufus asks me.

"A friend. Trustworthy," I assure him.

Rufus nods. "So what can I do for you?" He wiggles his small eyebrows winningly, and I wish again that I could make sure he never came back here, that he wasn't growing up in this place.

"Well, I'm sure you've heard about Invisible," I say quietly, my eyes darting toward the doorway. Nobody's here but the occasional field mouse darting across the floor.

"Yup. Guys here say they're all from the loony bin," Rufus

says, obviously parroting something he overheard from someone older.

"Interesting," I say. "We had the same suspicions, and we think they're using a new drug. Something different than the usual droops and giggles. Have you heard anything about that?"

Rufus shakes his head. "But I have a friend who might. I can get her. Wait here."

In a few minutes, Rufus is back with a girl of around twelve with four blue braids running down her back and suspicious gray eyes that never seem to blink. There's a scar running from her hand to her elbow that looks like it hurt a lot. "I'm not saying anything without getting paid." She pouts.

Serge calmly takes out his wallet. Lays out a twenty.

"That's a lot of money," Rufus remarks.

Serge lays out a second twenty in front of Rufus. "For your help with the referral."

Rufus beams, then squirrels it away in his pocket.

The girl looks from me to Serge, grabbing her braids and twisting them nervously around her wrist. "Rufus says you're okay. I'm not telling you my name. You didn't hear this from me, okay?"

"Right." I nod. "Of course."

"They were making this weird purple stuff here for a while, on the third floor. But then they needed to expand. So they moved the lab. It's way out in Exurbia now, past Weepee Hills."

That doesn't tell us enough to find it. Serge raises an eyebrow at me. "Can you be more specific?"

The girl sighs. "Why should I help you?"

"Have you seen what Invisible is threatening to do?" I ask. "How they're holding those kids ransom? Jasper Cawl is younger than you. He's only ten. We don't think those kids deserve to die. Do you?"

The silence in the ice cream parlor is thick and expectant. I watch her absorb this, think it over. "No," she says at last. "It's wrong, what they're doing."

I nod, waiting. Hoping she knows more. Serge folds his huge hands on the table. He is good at being patient.

"Okay," she sighs. "I know this lady named Jessa who goes back and forth from here to the factory. She's really tall. Sometimes I help her out with deliveries. She's a runner for the lab. She makes deliveries here twice a day, once around lunchtime and once at night. I can show you where to wait for her."

"Jessa Scorpio?" I ask. Jessa was one of the people involved in Gavin's faked kidnapping. She matches the profile. But I thought she was still in jail.

The girl nods. "But if you ever tell her you heard about this from me, I'll—"

"We won't. Not ever," I promise her. "Jessa owes me a favor." *Or she will, anyway.* I think back to my last encounter with her, when I wrapped a metal pole around her and called the police. I guess she copped a plea and ratted someone out so that she didn't have to go to jail. "Can you show us where to wait?"

We watch a side door of the mall through Serge's car's windshield, hoping to spot Jessa.

And soon, we're rewarded. A lanky woman with long tangled hair pulls up on a motorcycle and slips inside, a leather satchel slung over one shoulder, heavy and packed with product. Serge moves to the car door, to follow her inside.

"No," I say. "Better to wait. We don't need a shootout in

Hades. She'll be heading straight back there, I'll bet."

Serge nods. I shoot a glance his way, studying his face. It's funny that I'm the one in control here, not him. After so many years of him watching out for me, now I'm in a position to watch out for him.

An hour later, we're trailing Jessa's bike down the highways of Bedlam and into Exurbia. As the houses and stores grow fewer and the fields and trees start to proliferate, I have a good feeling that she isn't going home, that we're going to find the place where Invisible manufactures its preferred drug. Jessa seems oblivious to our car trailing her, even though soon we're the only two vehicles on the road. Every ten minutes, another car passes going in the other direction, toward the city. Soon we're so far out that it's dark enough to see actual stars in the sky. "Ever want to move out here?" I ask Serge. "It seems nice."

He nods. "It does. But it's dangerous here. So much poverty that everyone steals from each other. I wish it wasn't that way."

When Jessa turns onto a dirt road that looks like a steep driveway, Serge pulls the car over, and I leap out and sprint to overtake the bike as she chugs up a steep dirt path. At the top of it, visible through a bunch of scrub and trees, is a squat house. The windows are covered with what looks like cardboard but light shines around the edges of it. I spot steam pluming out from a vent to the side of the house. Someone's inside.

I speed up, overtaking Jessa's bike on the driveway before she reaches the house. I stand in the driveway and wave my arms, frowning like I'm part of the drug operation.

Her bike slows when she sees me. It's not until she stops, and

I move close enough to put my hand on the bike, that it clicks for her who I am.

"You!" she gasps. Her beetle-shell helmet is askew on her head. She moves to start the bike again, her hand twisting the handlebar, revving the engine, but I'm faster and stronger than her, and she knows it. My hands are on the handlebars, too, on top of hers, squeezing. "Turn the bike off if you want to live, Jessa." I say it crisply in her ear. "Remember, I'm stronger than you."

I guess our encounter at her old place of business made a big impression on her, because she lets the handlebars go. "What do you want? To send me to jail again? I had to become a snitch because of you!" she hisses.

"So that's how you got out so fast," I say, cutting the engine altogether and twisting the key from the bike. "Guess you didn't snitch to the cops about this little drug racket, right?"

She presses her lips shut. They're painted a dark magenta. Her long hair is dyed blue-black, and she's over six feet tall. I won't pass as her up at the house, but I can tell them I'm her replacement today.

"I needed money," she hisses, her eyes darting nervously toward the house. Whoever's in there obviously scares her. "They shut down my club, thanks to you."

Her club, where she kept binders full of "companions" to be rented out by men. "Forgive me if I'm not sorry for you," I say. "But I'm not here to bust you. I'm just going to need to borrow your bike. And your bag of cash."

Her eyes widen. "No *way*."

"Be smart." I hear a voice behind me. Serge has joined us, having walked from the bottom of the long driveway. He points a gun at her chest. "You have two choices right now. Wait in the backseat of my car at the bottom of the hill until we let you go home, or wait in the trunk."

She looks from Serge to me. "Fine. Go ahead. Enjoy yourself in the drug lab. You always were absolutely out of your mind."

She gets off the bike and makes a sweeping motion with her hands, presenting it to me sarcastically. "It's all yours."

"The bag," I remind her. Serge walks toward her, cocks his raised gun. A small animal skitters in the shrubs at the side of the dirt driveway, and Jessa jumps. I move my gun higher, point it at her long neck.

"Jesus," she mutters. "Fine." She takes off her messenger bag and drops it at my feet with a thud. "They're going to count it. Don't steal any, unless you want them to kill you. These aren't like Syndicate thugs. They're weirder."

I pick up the bag and open the flap to find eight bricks of cash wrapped in paper, in denominations of $1,000. Serge motions with his gun, telling Jessa to start moving toward the car. "What's the drug called?" I call out as she walks away.

"SoftServe."

"SoftServe?"

"Because it comes on slow and easy or something. I don't use, I'm just a runner."

"For the Invisible?"

Jessa nods. "I work with a guy named Nat. I don't ask questions. I tried to, but he said if I got nosy I was out." She shrugs.

"What's with the black streaks on people's faces?" I ask.

"Some people add to the 'Serve by huffing shoe polish."

Gross. I make a face, incredulous. Jessa makes it back at me, a mirror to show me she thinks I'm prissy and naïve.

Serge pats her down to make sure she's not armed. He removes a gun from an inside pocket of her jacket and empties the chamber onto the ground. "Come with me, please."

When they start walking down the driveway, I get onto the bike and start the engine. Then I'm roaring the last little bit up the hill toward the tiny white house, hoping there's a chance I'm right about all this, and that they'll let me in before anyone recognizes me.

CHAPTER 20

"Jessa couldn't make it tonight," I say, shifting from one foot to the other on the cracked cement porch, trying to act like a drug runner in front of two long-haired, scruffy guys in dirty button-down shirts, aprons tied around their waists, both with a week's growth of five o'clock shadow, both of whom definitely use their product, judging by their glassy eyes and the smears of black grease on their mouths and hands and aprons.

They gape at me standing there in the dark, slack-jawed, a ripple of violence lurking underneath their zonked-out eyes. They could almost be twins based on their demeanor and the length of their hair, but one of them has a stubbier nose and a thicker jaw, and the other—the thinner, slightly taller one—has a wall-eye that keeps drifting off to the right. Wall-eye reaches a hand out and pulls me inside by my shoulder. "Let's see the cash. Then we talk," he says. Then he shuts the door and I'm standing in a dim entryway, the walls stained with purple fingerprints, the reek of something chemical filling the air.

I hand Jessa's bag over to Snub-nose and follow them to the living room of the tiny house, all the while scanning every wall for a seam, hoping against hope that the kids are here somewhere. They don't bother to pat me down for weapons. I assume I look too harmless to bother with.

The low-ceilinged room has peeling wallpaper that was once covered in tiny yellow rosettes. On it is a spray-painted unblinking eye that spans the entire width of the wall. The mark of Invisible. I almost trip over a stained mattress on the floor, a television in front of it set up on a stool playing a talk show on mute. Crowded next to that is a torn love seat with springs popping out of it, and a narrow black plastic coffee table covered in baggies and scales.

The rest of the room is all beakers and expensive-looking tubes and scales and large plastic barrels marked with scientific-sounding names I don't recognize. An old yellow stove on one end has two large beakers bubbling on it. The substance inside is deep purple, black foam forming a layer on top.

But I'm not interested in the drugs. I'm only interested in the kids. I look from one of these drug cooks to the other and wonder if they know anything. How high up they are in the organization.

Then a faint clanking sound reaches my ears. It sounds like it's coming from underneath the floor. Two beats of sound, then silence. The drug cooks don't seem to notice—their hearing isn't like mine. The hair on my arms rises, my skin prickling to gooseflesh. I listen, hoping to hear more, but all I detect is a shuffling sound that fades to silence.

"It's all here," Snub-nose says. He stares up at me dully for a beat before turning to Wall-eye. "Should we kill her, though? He said no outsiders." I straighten, ready to grab my gun, which is wedged into the back of my jeans, coated in sweat.

"Yeah. I guess he did," Wall-eye muses, calmly, as if they're talking about what kind of toppings to put on a pizza, or what color shirt they've been asked to wear. His glassy eye lands on me, the other drifting off to the corner of the room. "We're gonna have to put you somewhere until he comes and decides."

Then, as leisurely as if he were picking up a remote control to change the channel on the TV, he leans down and pulls something from under the couch. Before he has time to raise what looks like a very big Uzi, I prepare to remove it from his hands.

I race toward them and the drug cooks' mouths open slowly, their vocal cords working to produce sounds of surprise, then they're rising to their feet, and time has become molasses-slow as Wall-eye attempts to hoist the gun in the air. I can see the threads of saliva in his mouth, the way the gun knocks against a mug full of cold coffee, the way the coffee vibrates inside the mug, the black hairs on Wall-eye's knuckle—

And then I slam a foot directly into his chin so that the huge gun goes flying through the air, front over back, twisting in air until it makes contact with the purple beaker at the front of the stove, shattering it and producing a cloud of black smoke with a fetid smell like burning hair.

He falls backward against the couch and I begin to pummel and hit and hurt him, fist over fist, until Wall-eye is out cold. It only takes a minute, but my hands, when I pull them away, are bloody and aching.

I turn as Snub-nose is coming up behind me, a thin cord looped around both hands, stretched taut between them as if he intends to strangle me. I grab the cord, throwing it to the stained carpet. In a moment I have him in a chokehold so that he's writhing, desperate to get away. I pull my gun from my waistband and press it to his temple. The smell from the spilled beaker is making both of us cough.

I cock the trigger of the gun. "Where are the kids?"

"Don't know what you're talking about," he says. I can feel him shaking in my chokehold. He has seen the way I move. Knows what I can do.

"Do you want to die today?" I hiss. I bear down on his throat, squeezing it with my elbow and forearm, jamming the bullet end of the gun against his forehead until he yelps. "Because I can kill you right now and wait for your friend to wake up. It makes no difference to me."

I feel him shake his head.

"Talk, now." I press the gun harder against his head, grinding it against his skin so that he yelps in pain. "Or I do it."

"Downstairs," he says. "We're not hurting them or nothing."

My body floods with relief. They're here. I'm not too late. "Take me there."

I let his neck go and press the gun to the back of his head until the tip of it is buried in his long greasy hair. "Now!" I yell. The smell of the cloud of spilled SoftServe is making me a little dizzy. It might be disorienting to him, too, because without a word, he does what I say, weaving down a dark hallway carpeted in puke-green shag. He comes to a metal door and digs for something in his pocket.

"Stop it," I hiss, reaching into his pocket in case what he wants there is dangerous to me—a razor, a knife. But it's just a set of keys. I hand them over and his hands are shaking so much the keys rattle. At last, he unlocks the door. Then we're in a linoleum-floored laundry room. "The floor," he whispers. "We peel up the floor."

"Do it."

He drops to hands and knees and lifts up the linoleum. Underneath is a metal trapdoor. He fumbles for the keys and I smell the reek of the drugs, the other vat of them surely burning now on the stove, and bark at him to hurry up. "Okay, okay," he mutters. Manages to find the right key after trying two others, twists the lock. Then he pulls the trapdoor open.

And then I hit him once with the side of the gun. In the temple, like Ford taught me. The knockout spot.

He crumples where he stands.

I take a breath and head down a set of stairs, into a flickering room that smells of urine and stale sweat, terrified at what I'm about to find.

My gun still drawn, I head down the stairs, into a dark basement lit with one flickering candle. Someone in the corner gasps and I move toward the sound. In the candlelight I make out a group of people crowded into the corner of the wood-paneled basement, sitting close to one another, probably for warmth because it's freezing down here, at least ten degrees colder than upstairs.

"I know her," someone whispers. "She's not one of them."

"Ask her," another voice whispers. It's someone really young, maybe twelve.

"You go to Cathedral, right?" She gets to her feet, swaying a little.

"Yeah." I move closer and see it's Celestial Deal. We've met a few times. I'm about to introduce myself, but it seems suddenly like a bad idea. "Let's get you guys out of here, okay?"

They begin to stand up, looking wobbly on their feet. "The

people who took you will be looking for me," I add, pulling a small, thin girl onto her feet. "I don't want them to know who freed you. I was never here, okay?"

I see heads nodding. The thin girl coughs and I hear the rattle deep in her chest. They all look so scared. So exhausted and hungry.

"So," I say, suddenly nervous, afraid for their safety more now than before. There are two candles set up in the center of the room that provide the only light, but it's enough to see that their eyes are swollen and puffy, and their clothes—satin dresses and suits, all still from the party—are filthy and torn. "Can everyone walk?"

Once they've all stood up, I begin to count them. My chest contracts with the horrible realization that there are two kids missing. "Where's Jasper and Will?"

Mik, who is only twelve, moves toward me. He's trembling. "Are we really getting free?"

I nod. "Yes. But we need to hurry. Just tell me where we can find the other two . . ."

His big eyes widen. "Will left this morning. When they took Jasper. He said he needed to talk to their leader privately. We don't know what they did with Jasper. They took him away—"

A fat tear escapes and he paws it away.

Horror rocks through me as I absorb this news. "Never mind," I manage, my voice husky. "Let's just worry about getting you guys out of here for now."

"Thanks," Celestial says. "We won't tell anyone who you are. We'll just say we escaped. I'll make sure the little ones understand."

I nod and thank her, but there's a very good chance Will has already used information about me as his bargaining chip.

The kids ready themselves, smoothing their unwashed hair, buttoning their jackets, and slipping on discarded pairs of high heels, Then we head up the stairs. They step gingerly over the still-unconscious body of Snub-nose and move single file toward the front door, squinting even in the low light of the living room, coughing from the fumes coming off the stove. I'm the last one out, and I dash over to the stove and turn off the burner. Then I grab a roll of duct tape sitting on the kitchen table and quickly tie up the two unconscious cooks as best I can, securing their wrists to heating poles in the living room.

I fill up two glasses in the kitchen with water, and bring it to the kids on the porch.

Next, I call the police and give them all the information they need to find the house. I remind the kids: "Remember, tell them you escaped. Or that you don't know who set you free. Just don't mention me," I say. They nod, each of them fighting their own particular brand of shock, isolation, and confusion.

We walk down the long dirt road about a half-mile. When we reach Serge's car, I stop. "Hide in the ditch," I say, pointing to the side of the road. "If you see any cars that aren't police cars, stay low. The police will be here any minute. When you hear sirens, it's safe to come out."

They nod, murmur *thank you.*

"I'm sorry I couldn't get here sooner," I stammer, not wanting to cry in front of them. Then I run down the driveway, over the sprawling dirt hill to the road, where Serge's car is parked across the street.

With a sick feeling, I get into the front seat. "Let's go," I say to Serge, staring at the empty, glazed faces of the seven remaining kids. "We can't be here when the police come."

Serge nods. "I sent the girl away. She thinks she's coming back later to get her bike."

"If she comes back soon, she can get arrested, too," I grunt.

"How was it in there? I assume you found the children."

I nod. "I did. They were in the basement, below a drug lab," I say. "They'd already taken Jasper. He wasn't in the house."

Serge shuts his eyes. Opens them again, two puffs of air released through his nose. "And William?"

"Gone. He must have told them what he knows. I think the Invisible know who I am now."

CHAPTER 21

Jasper's body is found the next day. He was killed with an injection of poison, his body placed outside the police station, a few carnations clasped in his small hands. They pinned a note to his chest before putting his body in a long, unzipped duffel bag and placing it on the front steps.

> *Poor little Jasper. $56 million. So much money, and yet it wasn't enough to save him. We'll be seeing more of your children soon, we're afraid.*

> *The Invisible*

All of it's on the evening news. I watch the broadcast in the kitchen with Lily, staring at the horror of Jasper's narrow body being lifted onto a stretcher and covered with a sheet, my insides twisting at the sight of it.

The story about Jasper's death is interrupted by breaking

news about the other hostages being free, interviews with the other children, and panicked prognostications about where Will is. Some "experts" worry he's joined Invisible's cause, that he's been brainwashed. Others are certain he'll turn up as the next victim.

The story the kids came up with for their interviews is that the door was unlocked from the outside, and when they climbed the basement stairs, they found the two unconscious drug cooks in the house and nobody else. Reporters hang on their every word. Their parents hover beside them, their expressions pained in the bright lights with a mix of relief and horror at how close they've come to the unthinkable. Behind them, there is a vigil for Jasper going on, thousands of people gathered in a square downtown, holding candles inside paper cups. My parents are among the people at the vigil. They wanted me to come, too, but I convinced them it would be less traumatic for me to stay home.

"This came for you." Lily's soft voice in my ear. She slides an envelope across the table. The return address is the Bedlam Ballet Corps Summer Audition Program.

I open it, not caring what it says. It's clear from the first line that I'm in.

Dear Ms. Fleet:

We are pleased to inform you

It's all I need to see. I'm in. If I do well this summer, I'll get to enter the professional corps in the fall. It feels hollow. Like it's happening to someone else. To the girl I used to be.

Because even though I've hoped for this letter for almost my entire life, it seems vulgar to think about the future right now, when Jasper's body is zipped into a bag. When Will is missing, and god knows what is happening to him. How can I plan my future when I know that they're probably coming for me?

Slowly, methodically, I tear the letter into long strips. Then I tear the strips into shreds.

"Anthem," Lily says, watching me tear up the letter and shooting me a concerned look. "I'm proud of you. And so are your parents."

I nod. "Thanks," I say, and keep tearing, the pieces getting smaller and smaller. I wonder vaguely what Ford is doing now. If he's heard about Jasper. If he even cares. Since he sure as hell doesn't care anymore what's become of me.

The next morning, I walk out the lobby doors and head to school, unable to enjoy the palpable sense of relief on the streets now that most of the children are home and safe. When I turn onto Cathedral Way, two blocks from school, a dark-haired boy in a baseball cap is sitting on a stoop across the street from me. He wears black dress pants, shiny with wear, and a grubby white dress shirt under a dressy suit jacket, one sleeve of the jacket ripped from elbow to shoulder, lengthwise, as if it's been cut. He's got a KillBall hat pulled down low, and he's looking down so I can't see his face. There could be something familiar about him, I think, squinting in the bright afternoon.

I move closer to him, drawn by that initial spark of recognition. When he looks up, I'm so startled I jump. "Will!"

"Shhh, let's walk," he hisses as he jumps up and takes off down the sidewalk. I catch up to him and jam my hands in my pockets. They're tingling with worry now. Everything about this spells trouble.

"Everyone's looking for you," I whisper as we move quickly

down the sidewalk.

"I haven't been able to face going home yet," he says, his words rapid-fire, his breathing quick and labored, manic. "I slept in the park. I needed to talk to you. I think they're watching me, Anthem. We have to be fast."

"Okay." I look around us as we move down the sidewalk and don't see or hear anyone, just a few birds squawking in the trees. There's a nasty yellow bruise on Will's cheek, and the remnants of hair dye at his hairline, a blue-black color that must have been done in a hurry. His pale blue eyes are bloodshot, his expression hollowed and lost. "You changed your hair," I say stupidly.

"They made me. They're crazy." Will stops abruptly so that I walk into him. I take a step back. Will looks terrified and helpless and lost. "I'm so sorry," he says, his voice thick. "After it was clear they were going to kill Jasper, I had no choice. I could have been *next*. I'm sorry."

"Sorry about what?" I whisper, a sickening dread spreading through my limbs. "Will, just tell me."

"I—I—they wanted—there's only one thing I had to trade! Only one thing he wanted bad enough. I didn't want to tell them, but—"

Just then my phone buzzes loud in the pocket of my plaid skirt. I spin around, peering at each quiet town house in the spring morning, suddenly worried he's right—we're being watched. In the distance, apartment towers around us warp as if I'm seeing them in fun-house mirrors, their glass façades glittering against the too-bright sky as my panic spreads.

"Who is it on the phone?" I shout. I spin around, frantically searching for Invisible's followers. But nobody's there. I dig around my bag as the phone bleats.

But of course I already know who it is. Because Will told Invisible how to find the girl he's been looking for.

"I'm so sorry!" he says again, then he takes off at a sprint, his arms flailing wildly, that strange black hair under the KillBall cap making him seem like a totally different person than the postrehab Will I studied a few weeks ago at school.

I pull my phone from my pocket with shaking hands. But it's just Zahra.

I take a rattling breath and pick it up. "Hello?"

But all I hear is a weirdly labored breathing. As if through a paper bag.

"Zahra? I can't handle weird jokes right now, Z. I just saw Will! They released him after . . ."

"I released him."

My blood turns to ice. It's him. The voice no longer computer altered. A voice that is calm. Smug.

"Where is Zahra?" I spin in a slow circle, suddenly certain there's a sniper's gun trained on my head. But there's nobody.

"I think it's time we met," he says, avoiding the question. "Don't you?"

"Where is Zahra?" I ask again, frantically looking up at the top of every building. I see nothing, nobody.

"I have your friend," he says evenly. "Come alone to the Shmuts and Company scrap metal yard if you want to see her again. You have one hour. Oh, and don't bother with the mask. I know who you are now."

And then the line goes dead.

A howl of rage erupts from deep inside me, bouncing off the town houses, reverberating in my ears. I half-expect the houses around me to crumble into piles of brick. I imagine smashing all their windows as I gulp sour-tasting air and look at the sky.

No help there. Stupid helicopters still patrolling the city, and they've done nothing but make noise. One of them dips below the tree line over by the lake, a skittish mechanical dragonfly.

And then I bounce off my heels and lift off, my legs kicking out behind me, taking me back home. Because I need to get the gun. I'm not showing up there empty-handed.

As my feet fly over the sidewalk and I turn onto a busier street, I speed up, conscious of all the police, the helmeted riot cops still on alert, still looking for Invisible. They're standing around, shifty with tension as their radios squawk. "The last hostage has been located. Attention, the last hostage has been located."

I zoom past them, one thought like a drumbeat, over and over, as if I can telepathically communicate with Invisible: *You take my friend, I take your life.*

CHAPTER 22

I run all the way there, the barrel of the gun chafing against my ankle, shoved between my sock and boot. Extra ammo in the pocket of my denim jacket. As instructed, I left my mask at home.

As I run, I wonder what he wants from me. To help him kill people? Does he actually envision me cooperating on anything he proposes?

Or maybe he just wants to kill me himself. Keep it personal.

I run until my lungs burn and my eyes tear. My body craves speed; the faster I go, the more energy I seem to find to push through the knife-blade sizzle in my shins. My feet seldom make contact with the pavement.

Way out in South Bedlam, I move from the sidewalks to the center of the street. There are very few cars out here at the ragged edges of the city. I run past the factories at the city's outer ring, past the bald sprawl of landfills and fallow fields. At last, up on top of a foothill, is the Shmuts and Company scrap metal yard.

It is flanked on three sides by giant, skeletal cranes. A tall chain-link fence with a padlock the size of a Christmas ham bars my entrance. I'm so filled with fury that I wonder if I could just pull the padlock, snap it in two. But then I notice a section of the fence is loose where it attaches to the dirt, and I'm able to bend the fence upward. I have to strain to bend the chain link, but it yields to me. I slip beneath it, my heart hammering out a violent Morse code.

I move into the scrap yard between two hulking piles of smashed cars, curtains of shattered windshield glass hanging down the sides. There are shipping containers stacked high all around the yard, and flattened metal scraps from walls, from cars, from boats.

But no people. I stand stock-still in the center of it all. Nothing moves but the morning sun glittering off all the chrome and glass.

Nobody.

"I'm here," I scream out. No echoes. The space is too open. The sound just ebbs away. "You wanted this, so come on out! Or did you bring me here to kill me from afar, you coward?"

All I can hear is the mad pulsing of blood in my brain. I keep turning in a circle, more frantic with each revolution I make, each second that ticks by with nobody here.

Then something catches my eye between two piles of burnt-out cars.

Something I really wasn't expecting.

It's a boy in a *wheelchair*. Pigeon toes. Stick-thin legs. Upper body wide and strong. Arms defined and sinewy in a black mesh muscle tee. With a head of brown curls, full red lips, an aquiline nose, and olive skin. And a pair of intelligent green eyes lined with black eyeliner. He's young and vibrant, and almost preening. In a way that makes me think the word *glamorous.*

"Surprised?" he says. I think of the computer-altered voice on the videos. This could be a match. I look at his hands. Those are the hands I've been studying on video. The same bitten-to-the-quick fingernails.

It's him. My thoughts spin, trying to catch up with what I'm seeing in front of me.

"But how do you . . ." I trail off, not sure what I'm even asking.

He smiles. Perfectly white, squared-off teeth. Orthodontically perfect, gleaming pearls. The teeth of a North Sider. "I have people help me do things. You'd be amazed at how easy it is to find muscle in this town. Or . . ." He pauses, looking at me sideways, kohl-lined eyes gleaming with the satisfaction of having lured me to him. "Maybe you wouldn't.

"I was shot when I was around your age. A bullet hits your spinal cord and if you live, this is what happens." He motions flamboyantly to his sparrow-thin legs, then shrugs as if to say *big deal, happens all the time.* "But enough about me. It's you I want to talk about. Your impressive"—he looks like he's gagging on the word—"*rescue.* Of my hostages."

"How about we talk about Zahra?" I press my lips together and wait, the area around my ankle suddenly throbbing, the gun rubbing too tightly inside my boot, communicating through my skin. It takes everything I have, every ounce of energy to control the urge to beat Zahra's whereabouts out of him with the handle of the gun.

"I know things about your family," he continues, pushing the wheelchair closer to me, his hands (in red pleather half-gloves with Velcro fasteners at the wrists) gripping the wheels and shoving them forward, his body folding over his knees as he pushes. My heart stutters in my chest. *What kinds of things?* I want to ask, but I don't dare give him the pleasure.

"When the Hansen kid told us it was *you* of all people, I couldn't believe it. Anthem Fleet. Daughter of Harris and Helene, the golden couple of Bedlam real estate."

I take a step back and he stops the chair. Something in his face, the way his eyes are trained on me, searching for what I am, feels invasive.

"What have you done with Zahra?" I ask again, trying to refocus him.

"I'm getting to that, supergirl. First, let's talk about you. And what you can do for our cause."

"Your cause is killing children," I say coldly. "I'm afraid I can't help you with that."

I look past him at the scrap yard, teetering towers of crushed cars as far as I can see. No movement. Not from people or machines or even rats.

"I know you weren't born this way, Anthem." He sighs, irritated with me. "Someone made you the way you are."

"What way?" I shrug theatrically, opening my empty hands upward. "I have no idea what you're talking about."

"We've all seen the footage. Do we have to go over this?"

I look away. Up at the graying sky. At the enormous sheets of metal leaning like huge thin dominoes against a teetering pile of drywall studs. The piles of flattened cars appear to shake slightly in the scrap yard and I tense up, alert for signs of anyone else here. But then the moment passes and all is still.

"I want to know who put those stitches in your chest, Anthem. The stitches Will told me about. That's it. Easy peasy. You give me that, I give you your foul-mouthed friend Zahra back."

So this is what Invisible has wanted all along. To be fixed. To become "like me," though he has no idea what that really means. And Zahra is his bargaining chip.

I think of Jax alone in her lab, a pit of dread expanding deep in my stomach. If she runs to the police, she could be jailed for life for crimes she committed long ago. And if she doesn't run, if she helps him—who's to say he'll ever let her go?

"And if I don't tell you?" My voice shakes. Part of me already knows. But I want to hear him say it. I lift my leg slightly off the ground, prepare to grab the gun from my boot.

"I think you know the answer to that. Let me show you a little live feed I've got going on." He pulls a phone from his pocket, looks at it, then flips it over so I can see it.

It's a surveillance camera image, green and black, of Zahra sitting on a concrete floor in a narrow room the size of a garden shed, unfurnished. No windows. Her chin rests on her knees.

When the camera pans upward, I gasp.

Hanging from the ceiling above her, like party decorations, are hundreds of sticks of dynamite.

CHAPTER 23

I look around me for a quarter-second. The scrap yard is empty. I am able-bodied and armed. He is in a wheelchair, holding a phone, with a smug smile decorating his glossed lips.

"Take me to her," I whisper, walking toward him. He looks amused. There's something in his eyes I don't like. Something assessing and impervious and proud. "Or I'll finish what that bullet started."

"Do it," he calls out, sounding bored.

I feel something bite into my upper thigh.

When I look down I find a purple plastic dart sticking to my jeans. It looks almost like a child's toy. I fight a queasy slow-motion sickness rising inside me, grit my teeth, and pull it out. The tip of the dart is over an inch long, metal and wet.

I start to stay upright, turn to face whoever did this, but the poison is already working, radiating outward from my right leg, which is now refusing to move.

My vision starts to fade, purple creeping in from all sides, reminding me of the pink gas at the masquerade ball.

I'm too weak now to do anything but try and grab my gun and hope I can hold on to it long enough to get off a shot or two. I'm not thinking straight, can't quite put together how shooting anyone is going to save Zahra, but somehow I sense there's a connection.

The purple, hazy world of the scrap yard is slanted now, all the people—*so many goddamned people!*—moving toward us, out from behind the mountains of cars and metal.

It takes everything I've got to pull the gun from my boot, but I wrench it out at last. Only my fingers will not cooperate, and my hand refuses to close around the gun.

"Don't hurt Zahra," I say, but it's garbled, my jaw floppy and uncooperative now.

I fall to the ground. The gun falls from my grasp. He looks down at me with a clinical sort of interest as I fumble for it on the ground. I'm touching the edge of it. The signals my brain is sending are getting scrambled, my body attempting to respond, but everything's in sickening slow motion.

I try to ask if I'm dying now, but all I hear are loose syllables, just a string of nonsensical vowels where words should be.

"Look how long she's fighting it. Amazing. She should be out cold." The others nod. How many are there? Five? Ten? A hundred? I can hardly see now, the figures are ghostly shadows.

My head lolls backward until my skull smacks against the ground. I barely feel it. White pinpricks of light dot my vision. I can't lift my head up anymore.

They've surrounded me, the Invisible army, over my shoulder, and they are coming out every which way, people dressed in black and white, the stupid eye on their shirts. They are young people, many younger than me. The purple goes gray, sweeping in from the periphery to cover everything so that I cannot see at all.

And then everything goes black.

"Hello? Hello hello, fast girl?"

I open my eyes. A man in a white lab coat snaps his fingers above my head. "Blink if you can hear me," he says in a thick foreign accent. So help me, I blink.

"You are still a bit blue, but I think out of the woods. The IV did the trick. Sensitive system you've got. Whatever's in your chest is a tricky one."

"Where am I?" I try to ask, but it comes out garbled, like *whaama?*

"Few more minutes, and I think the muscle relaxers will be out of your system. They gave you animal tranquilizers. Double dose of Tremorga. It should have been enough to take down a charging elephant instantaneously. All very amazing how you kept moving," he said. "I look forward to meeting him."

Who? I breathe. It sounds right. Intelligible. *"Who?"*

"Oh good. Mouth starting to work. Very very good. Your doctor, of course. You will lead us to him. And you have my word he will not be hurt. Unless he doesn't cooperate. But we seldom find people unwilling to cooperate."

No, I breathe. *No no no.*

"But fast girl, I am sorry to inform you that you do not have options." The doctor genuinely looks sorry. He wrings his hands. The bags under his eyes are massive. He looks like a sea turtle. "You see, they will blow up your friend in three hours. Timers are set. It is the way of the leader of Invisible. He is wild about timers."

The man sighs, as if it's a tragedy that cannot be helped. As if he, a lover of peace and nonviolence, would never condone such acts.

"*Don't let him*," I whisper.

"It is not in my power, speedy girl," the doctor says. "Do you want to see your friend? I have a screen. I am authorized to show you. You can look at her. You can see the clock."

I lift my head from the gurney and look around me at the all-white, spotlessly clean room.

"You'll be good to the doctor," I whisper. "She's a genius, you know. You'd be losing so much knowledge if you hurt her. You'd be hurting humanity."

"Her? Very interesting indeed, I had not pictured a woman. We will not hurt her," the foreign-born sea turtle–like doctor assures me. I wonder where he came from. Why anyone would leave their country to come here, to this place where nothing is fair and everything is tainted with violence. He seems kind. Crazy, but kind. "We only want to use her science to help our leader."

"Why is he your leader?" I ask.

"We believe things have gone too far in a certain direction," he says. "We believe it's time for a . . . correction." He blinks, hard, then he smiles down at me in a kind way. He pulls my hand up off the table and examines my fingers, which I see are still horribly blue at the tips. "We believe he will change things for the good."

"By killing people?"

"Oh no, not at all. He's absolutely nonviolent by nature. Violence inflicted on the very few is only a means to an end. For less everyday violence toward the very many."

I nod, but in my head I think *lies*.

I reach down and feel for my gun. Of course they've taken it away.

"Okay," I say. "Let's go."

My head feels like someone sawed it in half and put it back together, but I think my legs work, and at least I'm forming sentences again. I slip down off the gurney and stand on my two feet, walking slowly around the large white room and swinging my arms over my head, rolling my neck, stretching and moving and testing to make sure all my muscles work again. The walls are coated in a shiny white plastic, like we're on the inside of a balloon. As I stretch, I study an open cabinet full of medication. Most of it in plastic-wrapped clear syringes.

When I see a box of syringes marked TREMORGA™, I wait until the doctor begins to gather his tools with his back turned slightly away, then grab a handful and stuff them under my shirt, careful not to break them or snap their delicate metal tips.

As the doctor gathers up his tools into two black leather bags, I look at an open laptop set up on a table. I see Zahra, still sitting in the dark room. Terror is etched across her face.

And in one corner of the screen, red digital numbers of a timer, the seconds ticking down in three decimal places, the numbers slipping and slipping closer and closer to zero.

2h56m2945s to go. I take a deep breath as the doctor swings the door open.

"After you, speedy girl."

I nod and step outside.

CHAPTER 24

The door to Jax's lab has a complicated code inspired by the formula for the composition of sodium. I try it a couple of times, but my hands are shaking too much to get it right.

In the end, I knock. My chest whirs with foreboding, but beside me, the doctor appears relaxed. He straightens his tie under his lab coat, as if he wants to make a good impression.

After a long wait, Jax's shadow appears in the peephole, then the door swings open. "Anthem," she says, pulling me inside. "You look terrible."

"Hello hello," the doctor sings, stepping inside behind me. Then he carefully closes the door behind him.

"Who is this?" Jax looks at the man in the white coat. "A doctor?"

Already she's nervous. On her guard. Ford and I know not to bring anyone here. Jax is very private. As a wanted fugitive, she has to be. Her door is always locked to outsiders.

"I'm sorry." My voice cracks. I stumble over my words,

tongue-tied. How can I possibly explain this? "He is hoping you can help him with a project."

She nods, her silver curls springing out in all directions. Her big blue eyes wary. "A project?"

"This is . . . Doctor . . . uh, what's your name?" I ask feebly. My eyes bore into Jax's, trying to communicate many things—how sorry I am to have brought him. How she needs to be on her guard.

"You can call me Dr. I," the man says, his eyes big as saucers, taking in the lab with its twenty-odd animals in cages against one wall.

"Fine, this is Dr. I. He'd like to work with you."

"Work with me? I don't really . . ." She trails off, sensing danger.

I move closer to her, conscious of the syringes under my shirt.

"We would like to consult with you about a difficult case," Dr. I says. "And we can pay you very handsomely for your trouble." He opens one of the bags and reveals dozens of paper-wrapped stacks of bills.

Jax turns to me, eyebrows raised. I nod, pressing my lips together. I let one of the syringes peek out from the bottom of my jacket.

She averts her eyes quickly, but she's seen it. "That's a lot of money," she says to Dr. I.

"Half now, half when finished." Dr. I smiles broadly. His teeth are very white. He has a deep dimple in his stubbly gray chin.

"When what's finished?"

"Our project."

"And what is that, exactly?" I ask.

"Medical rehabilitation." Dr. I speaks as if he has nothing to hide. As if this is just a routine visit, doctor to doctor, and not the "rehabilitation" of a wheelchair-bound maniac with a taste for killing children. Obviously he'd like to walk again. And with Jax's help, he probably thinks he can do that, and maybe more.

"Right. Dr. I, can I please say good-bye to Jax privately before I go?" I say, forcing my mouth to curve into a civilized smile.

"Of course, your time is running out," he says, bowing a little as if it's us who are in charge, and not him. "I will acquaint myself with your animal subjects," he says to Jax. And he crosses the room to look in Mildred's monkey cage, to study the dozens of white rats running on their wheels.

"What is this?" Jax asks, panic creeping into her voice. "Why are your lips so blue?"

"I'm so sorry," I say. "They captured me with a tranquilizer gun. They're going to kill my friend."

"Who?"

"Invisible."

Jax gives me a blank look. I remember that she doesn't get out much, doesn't keep up with the world too well from inside her underground lab. "Have you heard about the group that calls themselves Invisible?"

"Ford mentioned something. It didn't seem important. I may have not paid much attention."

"Their leader is a pretty scary guy. Turns out he's in a wheel-chair. He thinks you can help him walk again. They've promised not to hurt you. I'm sorry, I had no choice."

"I'm not a miracle worker," Jax snorts. Figures she'd be stuck on the *help him walk again* part and not the *scary killers* part of what I've said. "I can't fuse the spinal column back together,

I can't splice severed nerves . . ." As she talks, her hands flap around like two out-of-control birds.

"But you can bring a girl back to life with a hummingbird heart," I remind her. "He knows about my . . . enhancements."

"I mean, who knows. Maybe I can help, maybe not." She blushes slightly. "I certainly haven't helped Ford as much as I would like."

Ford. My insides rattle at the mention of his name. A momentary terror passes through me, that he'll walk into the lab and see this. But I can't do anything about that right now. There isn't time. I just have to hope he'll stay away until this is over.

I unzip my jacket and push the jumble of syringes into her hands. There are six. "Keep one of these on you. Stash the rest. Tremorga. Some kind of high-powered tranquilizers. They'd take out an elephant, supposedly. You probably won't need them, but just in case."

"Okay." Jax nods, her lips pursed. She is calm and steely now. "Go. Get your friend. I'll be fine." She smiles to reassure me. "I do my best work under pressure."

"He doesn't deserve to walk. He's a killer," I whisper, leaning in to give her a tight hug.

She shakes her head, mouth open to respond, but I put a hand on her arm to stop her because Dr. I is approaching us.

"Time is short, speedy girl. You should go to your friend."

"Your turn to give me what I need," I say. "The address."

He hands me a lined index card with an address chicken-scratched onto it—*351 Azalea Ln.*

"Go with God."

"God has nothing to do with this," I spit back.

"Very good, very good." He smiles, infuriatingly polite. "Now is not the time for theological debating, I suppose."

One last look at Jax and I've got my hand on the door.

"See you soon, okay?" I say, too loudly, as I turn the handle, my heart spasming, a ticking clock inside my chest. I close the lab door behind me and despite what I just said about God, bow my head for a moment and put the flat of my palm on the peeling door. "Please let her be okay," I whisper.

Then I bolt eastward along the back alleys of the South Side, toward Azalea Lane.

CHAPTER 25

When I get to 348 Azalea, I cross the street and locate the number on the sidewalk, 351. But instead of a house, all I find is a slab of concrete foundation with wires sticking up at various spots, a few metal pipes sprouting from its corners. And sitting on the metal slab, three boys my age, two holding paper bags, a third dealing playing cards in the pink light of sunset.

One of them has streaks of black shoe polish around his mouth, his eyes entirely red under a curtain of scraggly brown hair hanging limply to his shoulders. The other two have that peppy, manic look I've come to associate with Invisible's posse. Slightly unhinged on their cocktail, their eyes glassy but their movements precise, their smiles—always smiles, it seems—creepily smug.

One of them notices me, elbows the one with polish streaks. "She's here." He's got an Invisible patch on his ragged red hunting jacket. The eye stares at me, unblinking, rage-inducing.

"He said she would come, and she did," Streaks replies, look-ing up at me with that glazed SoftServe stare. The others nod sagely as if this is religious wisdom.

"Take me to her." I cross my arms and wait, anger surging through me at how stupid and drugged they are. "Now."

"Calm down," the biggest one says, his frizzy red hair match-ing mine. He's stooped over, gathering up his playing cards. "It's this way."

We walk down the street that way, past 351, 353, 355. At 357, a house that was once nice but now has trash in its scabby lawn and a car on blocks in its driveway, they turn and walk along the gravel side path to a wooden fence marked with a few tags in metallic pen. One reads *INVIS*; another is just an elabo-rate *I*. The ink looks fresh.

Streaks lifts the lock on the other side of the fence and the gate creaks open. In back there's a wooden skate ramp flanked by two lemon trees, an above-ground pool that smells like something died in it. And a little cinder-block shed. My throat constricts as we move toward it. Zahra must be inside.

The one with the Invisible patch on his shoulder produces an enormous set of keys, the kind of keys a janitor would have, and starts leafing through them. I check my phone again. Twenty-one minutes until the timer winds down. At which point I assume the dynamite will blow the shed to bits.

"Hurry," I bark.

I look around the bald lawn for anything I can use as self-defense if I need it. A dozen beer bottles are scattered to one side of the skate ramp. There's nothing else here.

At last Patch seems to have found the key he wants, and he moves toward the padlock, the door and roof made of corru-gated metal, the rest of the shed made of poured concrete.

I hear the barrel click inside the lock and I sprint toward the shed.

"Zahra!" I'm yelling, not thinking about the drugged-out boys outside, yanking open the door and falling forward, missing the two additional steps downward into the shed. I land on my palms and they sing with pain.

"Anthem?" She sounds shocked and scared. "They've got you, too!"

There's a single red lightbulb hanging above her, and in the almost-pitch-darkness I make out her shape as she moves toward me and helps me up. I search her face. She looks terrified, but unharmed. Thank goodness.

"No, no," I say, hugging her hard. "We're leaving here. Let's go. You're not hurt, are you? I'll explain everything—"

But her eyes widen. She shakes her head slightly and pulls me behind her.

I whirl around just as the door slams shut. The click of the bolt when they lock it is like a nail in a coffin. "We're dead," Zahra says flatly. "They're about to kill us both."

I shake my head. "Don't worry."

I look around at the concrete walls, then focus on the ceiling. Above the hanging sticks of dynamite, it's just corrugated tin.

I go into that space where all I hear is static. Then I jump up and tell myself *feet first*. I flip in the air, my feet over my head, and kick as hard as I possibly can. The edge of the shed's roof pops off, the opening letting in a narrow sliver of light. Zahra shrieks. "Anthem! What was *that*?"

Then I do it again, and the roof opens up enough so that a third jump might let me through it.

But the red-haired boy's face is there, as is his gun. The air vibrates between me and my target. And this time when I jump,

I kick him in the head and manage to grab his gun before he falls off the roof.

When I land inside the shed, I aim at the metal door. It takes two bullets to shoot the lock off.

It swings open, and I pull Zahra out of the shed.

She stands there squinting even in the mellow light of sunset. How many hours has she been inside this bunker?

The red-haired boy is on the grass, clutching his head and gasping, but Patch is coming at us, gun raised.

Zahra's scream is shrill and deafening in the dead air of the backyard.

I lunge at him, spinning around until my foot makes contact with his chin with an audible snap that breaks through the static rushing of blood in my ears. He flies onto the grass twenty feet away and his gun clatters against the concrete wall of the shed.

I leap to grab it, aiming both guns at Streaks. He looks unsure of what he wants to do, but decides to come at me. I shoot, aiming for and hitting his arm.

Streaks clutches his arm and moans, but continues running toward me. I look away from the blood pouring through his fingers and move to shoot him in the foot this time, but there are no more bullets in the chamber of the first gun. I squeeze the trigger on the second one and hear the click of the hammer coming down on an empty chamber. It's not loaded. "Of *course* you don't have enough ammo," I spit, tossing the guns into the grass.

I grab two bottles by their necks, break the wide parts against the wooden corner of the ramp, and hold them in front of me. "Want your faces all cut up?" I shout at all three of them. "Is Invisible worth hundreds of stitches to you?"

"Oh. My. God," I hear Zahra say under her breath. I turn to make sure she's okay, and she's staring at me, eyes wide. A hand over her mouth. "You're *her*."

Streaks looks from me to Zahra for a minute, deciding. Then he backs away and moves to sit against the wall of the house. Judging by how white his face is, he's about to pass out.

I hear moaning in the grass. The redhead is moving to stand up.

I race down there and pull him away from the shed, because even though I will kill him if necessary, I don't want him blowing up from his own dynamite. I drag him up, hoisting him from under his armpits, then using all my strength to throw him against the skate ramp.

"Get out of here!" I yell. But he somersaults the ramp and recovers enough to launch himself at me. All two hundred pounds of him. I jump in midair and direct both legs at him, kicking him so hard in the chest that he goes flying twenty feet or so up in the air, landing smack on top of an anemic-looking lemon tree. I hear branches crack as he falls against them. A few lemons roll out from behind him after he falls.

"Bedlam's balls!" I hear Zahra yell behind me. "How could you not tell me this?"

I turn and grin at her, shrugging my shoulders. She smiles back, and a bit of the Zahra I've always known comes alive in her eyes.

"I'll explain everything. Soon as we get out of here." I spot a garden hose in the grass and move toward him again, this time punching him in the side of his head, hard, in the knockout spot Ford taught me about, just above the ear. Pain explodes into my hand, but the punch hurts him even more.

I take a close look to make sure the redhead is passed out. His eyes rolled back in his head, he's unconscious, but his chest still rises and falls.

As quickly as I can, I start to wrap him in the hose, but then I hear a crash.

I whip around and see Patch.

He's climbed on top of the shed, so big on the tiny structure that he's almost caving in the tin roof. He holds a long knife he must have taken from the kitchen of this dilapidated house. And beneath him, not running away fast enough, is Zahra.

"Run!" I scream. And just as he jumps down, she does. He grabs at her ankle, tripping her. She lunges at him, her eyes wild. She looks like she's going to rip his head off, but he's still got the knife in his hand.

I'm there in a quarter-second, stamping hard on his wrist until he lets the knife go. I toss it into the grass ten feet away and struggle to get both of his arms behind his back. I use all my strength to pick him up and toss him toward his unconscious friend by the lemon tree. He goes flying at least ten feet into the air and lands with a thud and a yelp. He puts his hands up and cowers on the ground as I move toward him.

"Watch him," I say to Zahra, handing her the knife. Then I go to where Streaks is, his arm soaked in blood. He's still conscious. "On your feet," I tell him.

When he doesn't move, I twist the hand of his shot arm just slightly, and he yelps. Instantly, he gets up. "Come with me," I say, leading him toward the tree where his friends are. When he reaches the tree, he almost collapses against it.

I grab the garden hose and wrap it around the three of them again and again, tying them to the tree.

"Let me help," Zahra says, moving behind me. Of the three of them, only Patch is fully conscious at this point. He watches us mutely. We loop the hose around and around, knotting it tight.

She grins when we make the last knot. "So *this* is why I've always felt like you're keeping something from me."

I nod, distracted by what still needs to be done. "We need to get rid of that shed," I say. "I don't want them hiding anyone else in there. It's supposed to blow in . . ."—I check my watch— "in a little over two minutes. He could be watching the cameras right now, though. He probably is."

"Okay," Z says, though her voice doesn't sound so sure.

"Got a light?"

Zahra shakes her head. I search Patch's pockets. "Leave me alone," he growls.

"It's this or I make you unconscious like your friend," I say.

He falls silent after that and just stares straight ahead of him into space.

I find a book of matches in a low pocket on his crusty jeans. It's smeared with shoe polish, but it will do. I grab a couple of smashed cardboard beer cartons from behind the skate ramp and rip them up a bit. Then I open the door to the shed and light a match, then the whole matchbook, on fire. The cardboard from the beer carton smokes for a few seconds before it catches. In a minute this should be a good-size fire. I pull one of the sticks of dynamite from the ceiling and arrange its wick end a few inches from the fire, near a strip of cardboard that's about to catch.

I close the door behind me. Z's waiting a few feet away.

"Let's bolt," I say. She nods, speechless for once in her life.

And then we tear through the yard and out the gate, running down the street as the last orange rays of sunset die away, two ordinary girls again, like old times. Like it always used to be for us, sharing something nobody else would ever understand.

When we get to the end of the block, the shed explodes

with a metallic pop. We turn around to watch a gray cloud of debris expand in the sky, a whorl of orange smoke eight feet high spreading over the house.

"Do you think those boys will be okay?" I ask her. "They were kind of close to the shed."

"Those people are like roaches. Indestructible. They'll outlive our entire civilization," Z assures me. "But if not . . ." She shrugs. "I wouldn't shed a tear."

"I'm so glad you're all right. And I'm so sorry this happened to you."

We walk quietly for a few minutes, arm in arm, one or the other of us turning to check out the smoke now and again.

"I was sure I was going to die in there. My life flashed before my eyes," Zahra says, visibly shaken at the memory. "And then there you were."

"You can't tell anyone, you know."

Z nods. "Clearly."

I get out my phone and call the tip line, reporting Invisible activity and giving the Azalea Lane address.

"Ant. It's time to tell me everything," Z says when I hang up.

I nod. She's right. It's time. I open my mouth, searching for the right words. And then I begin at the beginning.

CHAPTER 26

After I get Zahra home and make an appearance at my apartment, I wait for my parents to go to sleep, then head back to Jax's lab to make sure Dr. I kept his promise. It's after midnight when I arrive.

Yet again, I can't seem to type the code correctly on the lock's keypad. I've pounded on the door for ten minutes and nobody's come. My hands are clammy when I finally think to try the knob. The door surprises me by giving easily.

I swallow a scream when I walk inside—the lab is wrecked. Jax's wall of file cabinets is gutted, drawers spilling out at odd angles or thrown onto the floor. Papers covered with Jax's scrawled scientific formulas are scattered all over the floor. There isn't much equipment here anymore; the banks of machines that used to be crowded into the corner are gone, with just a few wires left snaking across the floor as evidence that they were ever here.

I move toward the tables that used to hold the animal

cages. Mildred's cage door swings open, creaking on its hinges. Mildred herself, little black monkey with the white tuft of fur on her chest and crazy eyes, is nowhere to be found. Her red plastic water dish is overturned on the floor on top of a wet stack of books.

I spot one of Jax's albino rats—maybe one of the ones she first showed me when I came out of surgery; judging by how fast it moves it also has a hummingbird heart. It races along the floorboards, so fast it's a blur. It is the only sign of life in the ransacked room. I force my feet to take me to the back, where Jax's small bedroom, her office, and the operating room are.

I peek into her office first. The desk is knocked over, her computer is gone, and another filing cabinet is on the floor, the piles of papers and files on the ground too tall to walk through. They must have taken her with them. Right now, she's probably in the same operating room I was in before, the all-white one, so much cleaner than her own, going over Invisible's chart with Dr. I.

But then why did they destroy her lab?

I walk into her small bedroom down the hall. It's neat as a pin, the bed made with hospital corners. One corner of the room has a little table with a mirror above it. I move toward the mirror, where a few photos are stuck into the frame. Jax, laughing, her small daughter in her lap. Noa looks two or three. She's a frizzy-haired moppet with Jax's big blue eyes. They're outside, in a park somewhere. Jax's now-estranged husband probably took the picture, back when they were a family. Before Noa's heart condition was discovered. Before the marriage dissolved. Before Noa began to die. Before Jax tried something risky to save her. Before it all went so horribly wrong.

I'm not sure why, but I pluck the picture from the frame. When I do, a folded piece of lined paper falls out onto the table.

I slip the photo into the back pocket of my jeans, thinking to save it for Jax in case the lab gets raided again, and I smooth open the paper.

Dear Jax,

I don't know if this letter will ever reach you. I gave it to a woman you used to work with, who said she might be able to send it to the right place. She looked a little terrified when I told her who I was. ☺

I just wanted you to know I'm out here, in case you didn't know already. I've been in a children's home since I was four, and though it's not the easiest life, I'm all right. I've never been able to remember exactly what happened when I was a little girl—it's all scrambled, somehow. All they can tell me at the children's home is that I was sick, that I had heart surgery that went wrong, and when I got better, the hospital turned me over to them because I had become a ward of the state.

Anyway, I've always been able to do things physically that aren't exactly normal. I won't say more, in case someone's reading this, but it's kind of crazy, the stuff I'm able to do. So I started digging through old newspapers, trying to find out what might have happened to me. And I found some things about a sick girl named Noa, and her mother, who was a medical researcher at the university and who tried and failed to save her.

I think I must be Noa. I can sort of remember my name, and being sick. That hospital smell, I guess it's alcohol, always makes me picture a mom with curly hair. I just wanted you to know—I didn't die like it says in the papers. The surgery worked. You saved me.

If you ever get this, here's where you can find me:

Bedlam Children's Society Home for Girls
80 Willoughby Lane

Your daughter,

Cleo (they named me Cleo at the children's home, but you can
call me Noa if you want)

So this was what had Jax so rattled the day I came over to talk about Ford. I say her name out loud. *Cleo*. Could this really be her daughter? The one she thought she killed on the operating table? How is it possible she survived? And not only survived, but by the sound of it, flourished? And who is this woman who used to work with Jax, the one who Cleo says agreed to take her the letter? Very few people know about the lab.

I'm so focused on the questions the letter brings up that when I leave Jax's bedroom, I almost skip the operating room across the hall. But then I stop in front of it. Something nags at me. I put my hand on the knob.

I want to skip it. I don't like that the door is shut. Which is exactly why I have to force myself to make sure nobody's inside.

Just do it, I order myself, stuffing the letter in my pocket.

I gulp air and push it open. And then I see how desperately deluded I have been. Because here she is. Her face blue-white, eyes wide open with surprise, gray lips open in a shocked O. My whole body shakes as I move toward her. The wail that has been sitting in my throat opens up into a howl.

She is in her blue operating scrubs, her silver hair tucked into the blue shower cap she wears during surgery. Her body sits slumped against the wall, her head tilted, no visible wounds, but of course there wouldn't be, not with Dr. I around. He would do it with injections. On the floor, scattered near Jax, the needles

I slipped her as protection. Each one emptied and used, on her.

My hands shake too badly to pick them up.

Is that why they killed her? Because she tried to fight back?

When I get a foot away I notice writing on the wall just to the left of her head. The narrow lowercase letters were carefully formed with a pencil, traced over and over so the words show up. The note says *nice try*.

I fall to the floor and sit there facing her. I reach out and lower her eyelids. It's not easy. Rigor mortis has begun. Her body is cooling. She has been dead for a couple of hours, perhaps more.

"I'm sorry," I whisper as the tears fall. "You didn't deserve this."

After a long time of sitting with her and giving myself over to a wracking grief so awful it feels like it's ripping me apart, I decide the least I can do is give her body a little dignity. I hoist her up—in death, she feels heavier than even Serge—and lay her as carefully as I can on the operating table. I arrange her hands, which fall off the table, alongside her body, finding the marks where they got her with the needles on her upper arms. Six neat holes, three on each arm. Enough to kill anyone. Like vaccinations gone horribly wrong.

Not only did I bring killers to Jax's door, I even handed them the murder weapon.

I find a sheet underneath the table and unfold it with shaking hands to cover her.

The sheet billows across her still body, falls softly over her frozen white face. I pull off the shower cap and smooth her curls, then pull the sheet up over them. A stray tear falls on it, a smattering of weather in this room so stale with death.

I tuck the sheet around her, done crying for now, when I

notice the rats in the corner are still in their cages, still running on their wheels. I move to open the doors. No creature deserves to starve in here with Jax's body hardening next to them.

They're out in an instant, their white albino bodies no more than blurs as they speed across the table, onto the floor. Following the floorboards along the walls, they make their way to the door and are gone.

CHAPTER 27

Half an hour later I'm pounding on Ford's apartment door. He hasn't answered my calls, and I need to tell him. He deserves to find out about Jax from me and not from the nightly news, and certainly not by discovering her body himself. I wouldn't wish that on anyone. No matter that he wants nothing to do with me anymore, I owe him this.

"Abe. Ford. It's Anthem," I'm calling in the hallway, half-hoarse from the tears I've shed tonight.

Behind the door there is the shuffling of feet, a heavy, slow gait. I brace myself in anticipation of seeing Ford, how awful it will be to look him in the eyes and tell him Jax is dead—but it's Abe who greets me.

"Anthem. Hi."

"Hi. Sorry to come here so late." I try for a smile. No way do I want to burden Abe with the death of someone he doesn't even know. "I need to see Ford. Just for a few minutes. I'm sorry to wake you."

Abe looks pained. "Don't worry about it. Had the late shift last night, so I'm sleeping weird hours. It's no problem. Only thing is, uh, Ford's not here."

"Not here?" I crane my neck, peek into the dark living room around Abe. My heart revs with alarm. Is he so repelled by me that he's having his uncle lie for him? So adamant about things being over that he's hiding from me?

"He's been gone for a while." Abe clears his throat. "Want to come in anyway, sit down? I can make you some tea . . ."

I shake my head. "Where is he?" I ask, my voice nothing but a dull croak now.

"Well, see . . ." Abe gets a weird look on his face, a half-wince, half-frown. "He made me swear not to tell you. Said he needed to be alone a while."

He stares at the floor, his feet inside a pair of blue slippers. An awkward silence sits between us now.

"Okay," I say, not wanting to make this any more uncomfortable. "If you speak to him, can you tell him to call me? I have news for him. It's important."

"Sure thing." Abe smiles weakly at me. "I shouldn't tell you this, but he's left the city. To recuperate more, and to lay low so the police lose track of him. Gonna be back in a couple of weeks, he said."

I turn away before he can see I'm upset.

Heading back out into the drizzly night, I wonder if I've ever felt quite this alone before. Even when Gavin was taken from me, it was just one person. Now it feels like I've lost an entire family. Jax is gone. Ford has vanished. Jasper is dead. Martha is dead. And I'm no closer to knowing what's happened to the man in the wheelchair. For now, he's all I have to focus on.

But I don't know where he is, or what ungodly thing he may have become.

I fly along Hemlock—my legs bicycling through the air, arms pumping, pushing as hard as I can, the pain of exertion needle-sharp in a way that feels soothing in my current state of mind—when I see it.

It's so jarring, I fall forward, nearly careening onto the ground, my momentum cut off so fast. Then I right myself and stare. Am I imagining it?

In front of me are two prominent apartment towers on the corner of Hemlock and Holly. One across the street from the other. Both with gold awnings. Affinia Tower East and Affinia Tower West.

I could swear I just saw both buildings start to *sink into the ground*.

Just then, the pavement starts to rumble and shake under my feet, and a hideous mix of pipes snapping, valves hissing, earth and rock crumbling fills the air. Fire alarms in both buildings begin to bleat, along with several car alarms. And people begin pouring out of Affinia East's lobby like sand from a bucket. They run onto the sidewalk, half-asleep, wrapped in bathrobes, a few people with coats slung over their pajamas, many with little kids and babies still asleep in their parents' arms.

All the while, the inexorable movement of the buildings is downward. They're being sucked into the sidewalk. It's happening fast enough that I can see the tops of each building lowering a foot or so every few seconds.

After half of both lobbies are swallowed into the ground, the sinking stops. But the damage is done.

Affinia East is now slightly tilted, listing to the left. A cloud of white dust pours out of Affinia West's lobby doors.

People stream out from both buildings now and stand on the sidewalk, staring at their homes with dismayed eyes. Many seem unsure of what to do or where to go. The one on-duty uniformed doorman in each scurries in and out of the building, desperately hurrying residents outside.

I'm moving closer when the glass doors and front windows on Affinia East explode, followed by Affinia West twenty seconds later. The pressure against the rising ground is too strong. The columns holding up the buildings have bent and warped.

I skirt the block and brush by a woman in a blue terry bathrobe, now covered in tiny chunks of shattered glass. Her eyes are hollow, ringed on the bottom with old makeup. She carries a big black purse and carefully brushes glass from it before clutching it tightly to her and walking away from the building. People stare open-mouthed as the buildings smoke. Taxis start to appear on the street, to take them away from here as the first hints of predawn light appear in the sky.

Water is trickling from Affinia East's lobby now. Hundreds of people have no homes to go back to.

Invisible did this. He must have. This is all part of his bizarre system of punishments for the North Side, now that I've ruined his plans for their children. I remember a line from one of his videos: *Leveling the playing field.* This is how he's going to do it—by leveling the city.

I move away from the two towers and run toward my own, all the while checking the skyline to make sure Fleet Tower is still standing.

CHAPTER 28

Ten, fifteen, eighteen feet. It's not even half a story, but it's enough to destroy an entire building. Once the foundations go, so does the whole structure. Cracks crawl up walls. Pipes burst. Wires tangle; electrical innards combust. Buildings begin to smoke. Dust pours from the higher floors. The lower floors flood or buckle.

On the streets below us, people wrapped in blankets and robes race along the sidewalks, the adults all talking frantically on cell phones, making arrangements, getting into cars, driving away to summer homes, weekend homes. Hotels. Helicopters land on some of the structurally sound buildings, taking the wealthier families as far away from here as they are able.

People pack into their cars and drive off. I've been home less than an hour and already the traffic is at a near-standstill, cars honking endlessly, on all the streets in the neighborhood. As far as I can see in every direction from the penthouse windows, lines of cars crawl down the choked streets on their way out of town. Most of the residents of Fleet Tower have evacuated. We've watched them stream out of the building. Announcements have been blaring through the speakers: *For your own safety, evacuate immediately.* My father made the call. Directed the building manager to sound the alerts. It's his flagship apartment building.

My mother and I quickly packed three bags for us. They sit by the door, waiting.

And yet, we haven't budged.

Fleet Tower remains untouched, unsunk for now. And my father refuses to leave.

The only reason I'm still here and not already out there is that I need to know they're leaving. Otherwise, I have no reason to believe they won't die up here.

So far eleven buildings in the North Side, two of them just around the corner from Foxglove Court, have sunk.

And yet my father refuses to budge. And my mother is starting to lose what little sanity she may have had. No amount of Vivirax can cure the sense that we're doomed.

We are on the terrace now, at 6:22 A.M. All around us, buildings keep sinking. Not a lot, just enough to be ruined. There's at least one on each block, sometimes two. Not ours, though. Not yet.

My mother plays the latest Invisible transmission again on the laptop, set on the white metal table next to the potted rosebushes. "Watch it, Harris. Really pay attention. This is not going to end just because you refuse to believe it's happening!" She puts her hands on my father's shoulders and physically turns him toward the video. I think what she'd really like to do is shake him.

"I don't want to watch, Leenie. We've seen it already. They're all the same, these *transmissions*." He says the last word like it's filthy.

"Too bad." My mother crosses her arms. She's come alive; deep in crisis mode might be the place she's most comfortable. "You can't strong-arm your way around this, Harris."

My father looks at me as if I'll give him permission to escape. I shrug, because what else is there to do but watch, either this or the chaos on the streets far below us. He sits down petulantly in a wrought-iron chair and stares as the static warms the screen. He's wearing jeans and a gray sweatshirt. I've rarely seen my father look so rumpled and lost. His age is showing. Normally they both look so young. But their regimen of injections has been stalled lately with all the trouble in the city. His cheeks droop. The stubble on his chin is graying. A web of wrinkles around his eyes, on his forehead, deepens more every day. I have the horrible thought that we are about to die here and now, but I push it away. Worst-case scenario, I would grab them both and jump to the next building. I've done it before and lived, and I'm sure I could do it again. I'd take my mother across, then my father.

We will stay alive because of what I can do. But what about everyone else?

There have been reports on the news of people jumping from burning buildings. Six people have died already. Surely that number will only grow, unless I figure out what's happening and put a stop to it.

Static lights up my mother's laptop screen, and the dispatch begins. It's all over the Internet, all over the news. Playing as if on an endless loop.

This time, seeing that white mask with the child's marks for eyes and mouth fills me with more than just disgust and anger. My hands tingle at the sight of him. I imagine curling my fingers around his neck. The monotone sound of his computer-altered voice is so maddening, I have to walk to the edge of the balcony. I can't look, I can only listen.

"Your buildings are sparkly and tall, but their foundations are rotten," he says. "Soon we'll all be on equal footing. All us fishes together, swimming in the same sea." He threads his fingers together on the flag-draped desk. The mask moves. Underneath, he is probably smiling.

"He's destroying the ground underneath. We need to leave now, Harris. Enough denial," my mother hisses.

There's a *crack-snap-thunk* across the street, and my father and I leap up and move to the rail of the balcony. My mother is beside me, her hands over her mouth. Eyes wide with horror.

Across the street is a shorter building, another Fleet project. Five years old. The Smithson. Thirty stories. And it's being sucked into the earth. We watch, horrified, as it sinks several stories, faster than the other ones. A woman's shrill scream rings out into the street. A minute later, my father stretches out his hand to the right. "It's on fire."

"That's it," my mother says. "Everyone inside, now."

The sound of sirens is deafening. I need to get out of here. I need to help. But I have to convince my father to leave here first.

In the sitting room, my mother shuts the sliding glass doors to the terrace and locks them, a final-looking set to her mouth. "No more waiting. We are leaving. Right now."

"Leenie, I won't do it. I've worked too hard building Bedlam. I can't abandon my buildings now." My father crosses his arms, defiant.

"You care more about your buildings than you do about this

family. Always have." My mother's voice is raised now, shaky with anger. "How will you feel if one of us dies up here?"

"Stop fighting!" I can't listen to this anymore. "Dad, you need to listen to Mom."

And then I walk toward the door while they're still arguing.

By the marble statue of the griffin, there's a small table with a notepad on it. I scrawl a quick note and impale the paper on the griffin's claw.

Had to take care of something. Let's meet at the office at 4 p.m. It's on higher ground.

Love,
A

They're still fighting on the terrace when I slip out the door.

CHAPTER 29

Even with all the people out on the sidewalks, the sirens, dogs barking out their distress, the cars honking, something about the way the ground feels nags at me. I stop dead in my tracks, ignoring the smell of fire and burnt plastic and charred flesh in the air and trying to focus on the rumbling under my feet. Am I imagining it, or is the sidewalk under my shoes actually sinking, too?

I decide to head toward the river. It's the only way I can think of to measure the movement of the land.

Some corners are so crowded I have to walk in the gutters to get past. Families are huddled under awnings of every building, in the shade, looking anxiously at the cars. Helicopters hired to get people out of here keep landing on rooftops of the intact buildings. And all the while, people lean on their car horns. The North Side is a wall of sound.

I cover my ears, the better to focus on my feet. I think of Madame shouting at us to feel the bounce of the studio floor helping lift us as we worked on our *échappé sautés*. I wonder where she is now, if she got out or if she's still holed up in her townhouse in the hills, wrapped in a shawl and watching all this out her window.

This morning, Zahra left for her aunt's house in Eastern Exurbia. I'm sure Will's family is long gone, probably via private helicopter like most Cathedral families. The people left here are less wealthy. The older people, those with small children, people caught unaware. And the ones who are stubborn, like my father.

My phone buzzes with a text from my mother: *Where are you???*

I'm fine, I write back. *Will meet you at the office in 2 hours.*

Will this possibly work to calm her nerves?

Anthem. What is going on? Where are you?

She knows. She doesn't want to know that she knows, but somewhere inside that Viviraxed, wine-soaked head, she knows who I am.

I needed to help out. Just trust me, I'm safe.

Even though I may not be, soon. Anything could happen out here. But I've got to take the risk. I owe it to Jax, to my father, to everyone out here, all these frantic faces, panicked and afraid for their lives.

A chill runs through me as I walk past the courthouse. There are at least a hundred people gathered on the steps, many of them the bandanna-clad protesters who are always camped out at Bankers Alley. They're banging on the locked doors of the giant old building. They must see it as a safe place to gather for whatever's coming.

Two blocks away, a line of riot police marches toward the

courthouse. The sun glints off their helmets. I shiver at the knowledge of what's probably about to occur, and I can almost taste the feargas they'll use to disperse everyone. I do not want to be here when they arrive.

All the while, the ground keeps vibrating underfoot, like it's alive. I move away from the courthouse and toward the docks, drawn there by nothing more than a bad feeling and the words bumping against my brain—*soon we'll all swim in the same sea*. He could mean anything, or nothing. I head for the river anyway.

Everywhere, I scan the crowds for his face. As if he's going to be walking among us. Which is ridiculous. Invisible may be blunt and an attention seeker, but he's not incautious. I learned that at the scrap metal yard.

Just then the sludge-green mass of the river peeks out in my vision between two buildings. I dart into an alley, jump a low fence, and edge around an old warehouse toward the docks near the Bridge of Sighs, the fetid scent of the Midland hitting me in the face.

However crowded it was a few streets over, down here where there are fewer residential buildings, it's quiet enough to hear the musical racket of birds in the trees. It's startlingly loud. I peer up into a nearby elm and find hundreds of circus birds huddled in the inner branches, their neon yellow and blue feathers ruffling as they jump and squawk. It's like they know something strange is happening.

I move toward the river, and then everything clicks into place. The water is high. Much higher than I've ever seen it. It laps up to the very top of the northern retaining wall—another few inches and it will flood, just like North Bedlam used to do thirty years ago, before my father repositioned the land, built it higher with all that landfill underneath. . . .

I stop short. Somehow, Invisible is readjusting things so that the North is returning to its original height. The landfill mass beneath the asphalt and concrete is sinking. The plan is to flood the North again. It must be.

I flash on a memory of a banquet I attended years ago with my parents. They were talking with an investor, a little old man, about the landfill. This was when I was seven or eight.

"All of it, garbage, under our feet." The old man nodded. "Sturdy, for now."

"Sturdy for *always*!" My father protested at the time, and the man said he hoped that was the case. At the time, I trusted my father. He built it, and it would stay that way forever. But I was wrong. The old man was right.

Invisible is somehow dissolving the landfill.

I stare down at the water sloshing against the side of the retaining wall, the stench of kerosene in the polluted river sharp as a slap.

I squint into it, suddenly certain I'm sinking slowly along with the earth itself. Then I turn back toward the crowds of the residential streets, and it dawns on me.

Why lower the level of the earth unless you also plan to raise the level of the river?

And how do you raise the level of the river? You break the dam at the reservoir. The dammed-up kidney-shaped lake at the eastern end of the Crime Line is the county water supply, holding all the water Invisible would need to flood the whole North Side and turn it into a wasteland like Lowlands—a place nobody wants to live.

If I'm right about what's happening, it won't be long before the dam opens up. And once the floods come—I walk faster now in the direction of the reservoir, into the thickets of people hurrying down the sidewalks, into the wall of noise made by the traffic—once the floods come, the casualties won't be in the tens or even the hundreds. They'll be in the thousands.

I hurry through downtown and into the banking district, threading my way through crowds of people hauling cardboard boxes from the office towers, their faces wild and scared. The line of cars snaking through the streets moves so slowly that the honking of horns forms a curtain of sound. A woman in a blue blazer and pajama pants holds an accordion file bursting with paperwork.

"Watch it," she growls, pulling her folder close against her body.

"Sorry," I say, and keep walking, jostling shoulders in the crowded sidewalk as I press forward, people all around me pushing and angling to get somewhere. Everyone's face set with hard, tense determination. The atmosphere is starting to feel dangerous, like people might turn on one another at any moment. I wonder if this is what it felt like back when the riots happened, when I was a baby and just before.

The words bubble up in my head from politics class: *mob mentality*. Images from Dr. Tammany's lecture, of piles of people all holding bats and sticks, their faces twisted in anger, the police nowhere to be seen, swirl in my head.

I contemplate climbing a fire escape and jumping along the rooftops instead, and then I notice an entrance to the tube. I cock my ears. Even with everything that's happening, it seems to be running. I haven't been on it in years, not since way before the tube gassing four years ago when two hundred people were gassed unconscious and robbed of everything but their underwear. But it would be fast. It might be the fastest way to get there.

I take a breath and decide to try it.

I'm about to walk down the steps and into the Bankers Row tube station when someone barrels into me, lifting me and running around a parked car toward the street.

"Get off me!" I yelp, struggling. But the arms that hold me don't budge. A second later, I'm deposited gently down onto the street.

"Easy, Green." Those brown eyes. That teasing expression. "It's only me."

Just then, the building I was standing next to a moment ago sinks into the ground a few feet, shattering the glass in the lobby window and sending metal columns springing out of it. If I was still standing there, I could have been hurt, or worse.

"Thanks."

When he moves to hug me, I let him. Even though he's hurt me, I can't help it. It's good to see him, amid all this. To know he's back. But then the memory of him saying good-bye—*I'm not asking*—falls over me, and I pull back a little.

"I heard what was going on." His voice is husky in my hair. "I thought it was time to come home."

CHAPTER 30

"I'm sorry I . . . left like that. Abe told me you stopped by." Ford's eyes are filled with concern. Regret. And something else, too. A new sense of calm, maybe.

"I missed you," I say. It's barely a whisper. My ears burn with the memory of how coldly he brushed me off last time we saw each other.

"Me too. More than you'll ever know." He looks at the ground for a minute, then back at me. "I'm sorry about everything, Anthem. I was . . . scared."

"Scared?" He was the one acting scary. I was the one who should have been scared, but I wasn't.

"The last thing I wanted to do was to hurt you. You're . . . everything to me. You must know that, by now."

I open my mouth, shut it again. Shake my head. But some part of me does know it. And can understand being scared of inhabiting a body you don't understand. "How do I know this is the real you, not just another manifestation of the hot-blooded—"

"This is real. I swear to you. This is the real me talking. The person who's under control. The person who wants to be with you." And then he kisses me, a peck that is soft and tender enough to say everything. "I'm better now. I promise. Give me one more chance."

I stare at him, loving being near him. Soaking this moment in, not wanting to spoil it with words.

"You really do seem better," I say finally.

He nods. "I'm a lot better. All the synthetic blood has been absorbed into my system now, I think. I don't feel so out of control. I guess Jax was right about that. It just took some time."

Jax. I need to tell him. I search his eyes, but he doesn't seem to be thinking about Jax particularly hard. He must not have gone to the lab yet since his return.

"Listen." I clear my throat. "I think I know what he's planning. And I think I know where he is. That's where I'm headed." As soon as I say this, I wonder if I shouldn't have. He'll want to come. But a part of me already knew that. A part of me wants him to.

"Let's go."

"We need to get to the reservoir," I say, scanning the packed streets. "Could be slow going. I was thinking the tube, but I'm afraid it'll flood."

"The reservoir connects to the river, right?" His eyes glitter with his old mischief.

I nod.

"Let's borrow a boat."

I think of how Ford likes to "borrow" cars by stealing them for a few hours at a time.

"You really are back to your old self," I observe as we head to the marina.

* * *

At the marina, there aren't many options. Just a rusted-out row-boat and a sailboat half-filled with water. But then under a lip of metal and a collapsed tree, Ford spots something. He moves toward the tree and pushes the leafy branches aside.

"Here's our candidate," he says, pulling something covered in gray canvas out from underneath the dock. I come over to look and the white gleam of fiberglass and chrome of a speed-boat hood twinkles in the waning sun.

Ford moves efficiently around the dock, untying ropes in two places, while I pull the canvas cover off the boat's hull. He jumps into the boat, bending to detach a panel between the two front seats, using a tiny pocketknife attached to his key chain. He hunches over it while I nervously pace the dock, watching as a few people scurry on the sidewalk edging the river, all of them looking distracted, nobody even glancing at us. The dock itself vibrates periodically, the same way the ground does.

"How long will it take?" I ask his back, covered in the same gray sweatshirt he's always worn. It's a comforting sight, but if the ground lowers much more, we'll be too late.

"Nearly done," he says over his shoulder. His cheek is stubbly. I wonder how it would feel to touch it.

He jerks back, I see a couple of sparks fly out onto the leather seat of the boat, and then the motor hums to life. Ford pulls the cord on the outboard motor, and the engine roars.

He moves aside and motions for me to get into the driver's seat. When I hop in, my leg brushes his shoulder. Even with everything going on, the attraction I feel toward him is still magnetic. My feelings for him haven't changed a bit. The way he looks at me tells me his haven't, either.

We can't really talk over the roar of the motor. I settle into the driver's seat and press the gas on the floorboard, and the boat hurls through the water away from the dock. I turn the wheel hard and a spray of water goes up beside us, the boat cutting into the green murk of the river so hard the nose of the boat seems like it might tip in. I ease up on the gas, and soon we're shooting down the Midland, wind in our hair, heading toward the reservoir.

Twenty minutes later, we've stowed the boat as best we can, partially hiding it under a discarded piece of sheet metal lying near the riverbank. We've hiked through the overgrowth of gnarled bushes and skirted the edge of the reservoir—calm and serene as cut glass but for these weird ripples, as if someone's throwing invisible rocks at it. It must be connected to the rumbling of the ground, the way things are sinking here.

My phone vibrates with another text from my mother: *Tell me you are okay.*

I'm fine. See you soon, I write back.

"Ford," I whisper, stopping moving as he catches up behind me. "Where are the girls? Are they safe?"

"They're home," he says. "With my uncle." He gives me a look like *why do you ask?*

"But what will they do if there's an emergency?"

"People in the South don't seem too concerned." Ford shrugs. "Nothing's changed over there."

Of course. Invisible only wants to hurt the North. I nod and keep moving.

We skirt the trees, stopping when we hear shouts. I motion to Ford that we should cut in through the trees, go deeper in so we're under thicker cover. Now that we know there are people nearby, I'm conscious of the snap of every branch we step on. The last thing I want to do is walk into a trap.

Through the branches, I count six people, all my age or a bit older, all moving with purpose at the edge of the dam that hems in the reservoir above and stops it from spilling out into the river. I lose my breath when I realize that one of them is Wall-eye, his face a mass of bruises and swelling. He must have regained consciousness and gotten away before the cops raided the drug lab. My fingers make fists as I stare at him—I won't let him get away again.

I recognize another one of them, the blond boy from the control room at the arena.

"Roll it out," Wall-eye yells at a guy with blond dreadlocks held back by a red bandanna, whose muscles bulge and strain under a gray jacket and who looks keyed up on extra doses of SoftServe, his movements robotic and his eyes dulled. He and an equally robotic-looking shorter boy start to pull a large bulky object—huge and flat, the size and shape of a twin bed, covered with a blanket—toward the dam.

"What is that thing?" I whisper.

"I don't know. Let's get closer."

We begin to run along the path toward the dam. My heart kicks against my ribs as I try to develop a plan. Ford is faster than he used to be, and his step is lighter. He can almost keep up with me.

"What was in that blood, anyway?" I hiss when he catches up. I've stopped as close to the Invisible thugs as I dare, and now we're crouched behind a scrim of trees where we have good coverage.

"Tiger DNA?" Ford grins. "Dunno, really. Jax started to tell me but I stopped her. Didn't want to know."

We stop about sixty feet away from the crew dragging the huge bundled object toward the dam edge. The edge of the dam is a three-tiered series of steps, each of them with four spouts where white streams of water are released, four thin waterfalls spraying the two hundred feet down to the churning bottom, where the river starts. Each opening is held shut with a complicated-looking electronic lock.

The thugs hit a tree root in the path and the blanket comes loose on the top corner and falls off to reveal a matte surface, black as onyx. Immediately, the one with dreadlocks raises his arm, the back of his hand drawn to the black surface, where it smacks and sticks. His watch is stuck to it. *A magnet.* Ford whispers it the same moment I think it.

The dreadlocked guy unbuckles his watch and leaves it attached. Must be very powerful, judging by the way he doesn't even bother to try to get his watch back.

I remember learning about the dam in the engineering unit I had in school. The locks are computerized. Tamperproof. So why the magnet?

Then I realize. "Magnets scramble digital code, right?" Ford nods. "They must need it to unlock the dam," I say.

"The dam opens, the river floods," he finishes.

"We need to take them out," I whisper. We're moving closer as we walk, cautious but still moving forward. "Are you up to this?"

Ford nods. "Jax built us for this stuff," he says under his breath, so quietly I almost miss it. He's accepted his fate, I guess. Easier than I ever could. And the way he says *us* instead of *me* sends a tingle across my skin, gone as quickly as it appears.

"It's all she knew to do to help us," I say, the past-tense *knew* curdling on my tongue.

Ford nods. "I'm getting used to the idea that this is not going away."

Meanwhile, they keep moving the magnet closer to the center crack of the dam. There are enough tons of water behind the dam to fill a Bedlam-sized basin.

"We need to go in," I whisper. "Now. Two of them know who I am."

"Let me go in first and confuse them. The guns won't come out right away, I'm thinking."

I nod, trusting that he has an idea. I move behind him.

When we reach the path they've used, Ford simply ambles out into plain sight. No element of surprise. I duck behind a fallen log and hang back, afraid to watch.

"Hey, y'all. Sorry I'm late," Ford yells over the rush of the water. Without my sonic ears, there's no way I'd be able to hear him.

"Who the hell is this?" Wall-eye shouts to the others, moving closer to Ford, his hand reaching for what I'm sure is a gun in his jacket.

"He didn't tell you about me?" Ford grins, four, then three paces away from Wall-eye, who's pulled the magnet onto the middle step of the three-tiered edge of the dam, each tier topped with a metal grate to walk on and a single metal railing to hold on to, more for balance than to prevent a careless person from falling off. It's a long way down with nothing to grab if you fell, just the cement dam with the four waterfalls trickling down it, and then the white churn of water at the bottom surrounded by the quiet green murk of the river.

"Narrows, who the hell is this guy?" one of the others says, moving closer to Ford.

"I'm the inspector. He told me to come give a final look-see."

"Inspector?" Wall-eye—he must be Narrows—swivels his bruised head around, as if checking to see if his boss is anywhere nearby. I follow his gaze but don't see anyone else. "What for?"

"Technical specs, doofus," Ford says, moving toward the magnet. There are buttons all around the bottom of it, along with red flashing lights.

"Like, come here and look at this. Why didn't anyone check the rotator switch?"

"The what?" Narrows moves toward Ford. "I don't—"

So fast I almost miss it, Ford's hand is on Narrows' neck, then he slams him against the magnet, hard enough so I can hear the echo of his skull bouncing against metal. Before I can breathe, he's on the ground, rolling off the middle tier and landing with a thud onto the lower tier of the walkway, his arm hanging off it into midair, perilously close to slipping off below the railing and tumbling the hundreds of feet into the dam. His eyes roll back in his head, and he's unconscious for the second time this week.

I'm up like a flash, running toward the group of them. There are four more of Invisible's thugs there, and each of them will have guns pointed at Ford in an instant.

I leap from the edge of the path onto the nearest of them, surprising them enough to turn and look at me as I wrestle the gun from his hand and knock him to the ground. As I'm doing this, Ford has another of them, who's been distracted. He's on top of the younger guy with the blond dreadlocks, yanks his gun away, and almost gently—as gently as can be done with a gun—slams him on the temple so he's out. There are two left, each with their guns out, and now Ford and I each have a gun.

"You know she can jump around bullets, boys." Ford aims his gun at the two remaining minions. "It's a thing of beauty."

Just as they turn to appraise me, I leap. I sail into the air, roundhousing one of them—a steroidal boy with bloodshot eyes. He grunts and falls backward, landing on the metal walkway and nearly flying over the edge of the dam. His gun falls out of his hands and over the edge, sailing into the river far below.

He looks at me, speechless. Suddenly scared. Then he starts to crab-walk away from us, back toward the woods.

The last one looks from Ford to me and thinks better of it. He puts his gun down. "Easy, easy" is what I think he says, but it's hard to hear over the steady stream of water crashing out of the reservoir and into the river below.

"Good move." Ford nods, jumping to the lower step to scoop up the gun, and removing the other one's gun from his unconscious hand. He throws them both into the river below the dam, just out in front of the waterfall, over the edge. We don't hear either one land.

I turn my gun on the magnet, and even from five feet away I can feel the gun wanting to pull toward it. It takes a lot more strength than I would have thought to keep the magnetism from pulling it all the way in.

The magnet seems to be activating something at the dam already, because when we got here the waterfalls were just a trickle and now they're closer to a foot wide, water gushing from their stretching seams. It must be opening something internally, unlocking sections of the dam.

"Should we just cover it up and wheel it out of here?" I yell, the sound of the widening waterfalls deafening now. None of my schooling has prepared me for the best way to dispose of a mattress-sized magnet at the edge of a dam.

"How about we send it over?" Ford yells from the lower

walkway, over the din of the water. "Dam's way up here. The current would carry it far enough away, maybe."

I'm considering this when I hear a clank above me. I whirl around and look up to where the glassy-smooth water of the reservoir meets the cement of the dam. There's a metal walkway from the other side, one I didn't notice before. And Invisible is on it, coming toward me. *Walking.* His legs move fluidly inside strange mechanical braces, made of a shiny black metal—titanium maybe—that's so snug and flexible, it seems almost to be fused to his black jeans. His eyes are again lined in kohl. And they blaze with rage.

"I'd rather you didn't touch my things."

CHAPTER 31

His face is red and sweaty. His brown curls longer than before, spiraling out in all directions like an overgrown shrub. His jaw clenches rhythmically.

And he's with friends. Just behind him, there are six people in black T-shirts with that placid eye illustration done in white.

Each of his friends is armed, and all of their weapons are aimed squarely at me and Ford.

I consider launching myself through the air, aiming a boot at his face, taking my chances with the group of goons around him, when five more men and a woman appear in the trees behind them, each holding a rifle on their shoulder, taking aim.

I do a quick scan and count twelve people altogether.

Invisible is the only one not holding a weapon. "Your boyfriend is cute, Anthem."

"Wait till you see how cute," Ford says at my side. I sense he's about to attack, and I put a hand on his arm so that he sees the shooters in the woods.

"Why are you doing this?" I ask, stalling for time. "I see you've got your legs. What more do you want?"

He smiles. Below us, the water churns and roars, promising the sureness of death. There is nowhere we can turn, and the advantage is all theirs.

Four of the goons—all close to my age, the oldest maybe twenty—move closer.

"I used to live right off Museum Mile, you know." Invisible squints out over the river, staring out at the helicopters swarming like gnats over the towers in the North. A wave of shock runs through me at this revelation, but then I realize how much sense it makes. He's targeting what he once called home. The place he was banished from. "Not far from that monstrosity your father named after himself. Fleet Tower used to be a moldy squat. Before he fixed all that."

"It must make you so happy to see your old neighborhood sinking and burning," I say dryly. My parents could be in one of the choppers by now, waiting for me, not sure how to find me. My mother might be hysterical and overmedicating. My father, if she's forced him to tear himself away from his buildings, might be raging at her about me, asking her what I mean by scaring them this way. "You want it to be a moldy squat again, is that it?"

Invisible laughs. "It was very posh, my childhood. Just like yours, Anthem." He moves closer. I marvel at how graceful he is on his new legs. How smooth his movements, considering he's just gotten the use of his legs back.

"You don't know anything about my childhood," I say.

"Oh, but I do." His eyes twinkle with hate and mischief. "I know more about you than you know about yourself." His face glimmers with a sheen of sweat. "I went to Cathedral, just like you. Before my father got caught doing bad things with other people's money." He laughs, a single bitter snort that is swallowed by the roar of the water.

"And then it all ended for my family. My father was disgraced. All of our money was ill-gotten through pyramid schemes, bad investments. We lost everything. Moved south. He went to jail. Killed himself after just three days in Bedlam Prison. Didn't have the stones for it. My mother was penniless, and clueless about how to get by without money. So I started applying to menial jobs. One day I was putting in an application to be a dishwasher, and I got in the way of a bullet meant for someone else."

"Poor you," Ford says under his breath.

Invisible continues, not noticing or not caring. "And that was when I realized how cruel the world really is. Everything I thought I knew before was just exposed to me to be built upon these . . . glittery, pretty lies. Regina knew all about that, Anthem."

His lined eyes meet mine and something passes between us that sends shivers down my spine. What does he know about Regina? I glare at him and I'm about to ask him what that's supposed to mean, but he continues as if he never mentioned her.

"So I spent the rest of my childhood on the computer, teaching myself about why things were so unfair. Teaching myself to build bombs, to use technology. So that someday, I could teach my old neighborhood what it's like. To be scared, to be helpless. To live in a world that is out of your control."

As he talks, I survey the goons behind him. I count nine guns pointed at us.

"And what you did to Jax? Was that to teach everyone a lesson? I think all you care about is yourself." Ford looks at me sharply. I wince, horrified that this is how he's finding out about the death of one of his closest friends.

"I'm not particularly interested in killing people, believe it or not. That was just the way the cookie crumbled. She was very helpful, until she sabotaged it by attacking us. She's the reason Dr. I's invention worked. What do you think—don't I look amazing in these jeans?"

I steal another glance at Ford. He's absorbing the news of Jax's death. And his face is growing redder. His hands clench. "Ford, don't."

"The foundations are rotten," one of his goons—a boy built like a fireplug, with blue hair and glazed eyes—says. "We're evening the scales."

"Volo, stop talking. You are here for your body, not your brain." Invisible rolls his eyes as if he and I are in cahoots. And that's when I realize his philosophy is all faked. A hodgepodge of buzzwords that even he doesn't quite believe. He doesn't really want to "even the scales." He just wants the kind of people he grew up with to feel the same kind of pain he's felt all these years, sitting in his wheelchair remembering his past, and looking ahead at the future and seeing nothing but a black hole.

"Anthem," Ford whispers.

I nod slightly, just enough to show him I can hear.

"I'm going to knock down those guns in the woods now."

Before I can respond, he fires four shots. Four bodies fall in the woods, like dominoes.

Then the thugs on the walkway begin to fire. Ford and I both jump into the air at the same time, and I'm amazed to see Ford flip his whole 180-pound body in the air, his feet coming down on the neck of another one of the minions, the gun the guy carried flying out of his hand and into the river.

Static echoes in my ears as I attack, kicking guns out of hands, dodging bullets. Ford is doing the same, a few feet away.

Something slams into my head just then. I turn around in time to see a huge fist coming at me. It's the blond dreadlocked guy. I stagger backward and fall, and then I'm tumbling past the flimsy railing, the white crash of the water into the river two hundred feet below all I can see. I flail, and manage to grab on to the bar of the railing at the last second, flipping over it, feet first. I leap into the air and attack him, pausing just before I throw him into the water. Instead, I take my gun and hit him with it, hard enough so his legs collapse and his eyes roll backward into his head.

I have a second to watch Ford, who is smashing his fists into the final two goons, both already bleeding. He's fast and strong and seems to want to kill them. Invisible has a gun in his hand and is aiming it at Ford, looking unsure. I have a feeling he's not accustomed to guns. He prefers remote-detonated bombs and poisoning children. He moves closer. His leg braces are smooth and fluid.

"Ford!" I shout. He whips around just as Invisible is about to fire, and lunges at him, so fast it's little more than a blur.

Whatever Jax did to enhance Invisible, it worked. They seem equally matched. Both of them fast and strong as they roll on the railing. I still have a gun.

I wait until I can find an angle where I won't harm Ford. Invisible pins him to the ground, and I have my shot. I shoot him in the arm, enough to disable him temporarily but not kill him, and not destroy his legs.

He'll need those legs where he's going. The land Bedlam Prison was built on is called Dead Man's Hill for a reason.

When the bullet hits his tricep, though, Invisible barely

seems to notice. So I move toward them and yank him off Ford, using everything I have to toss him into the air. He lands thirty feet away, smashing upside-down against the giant magnet.

Amazingly, his legs stick to the black surface. He struggles and squirms, blood pooling around his nose, dripping into his eyes, but he can't detach the lower half of his body from the magnet.

Ford knocks out the last two minions, and we step over their bodies toward the magnet.

"You know, I wasn't sure I liked those jeans when you first mentioned them," Ford says, reaching out to flick the kneecap of the metal-denim hybrid, which makes Invisible yowl. "But I've come around. They really do look amazing on you, you sick bastard."

"Just do it," Invisible croaks, clearly in pain. His head is down by my feet. "Shoot me in the head."

"Tempting," I say. "I'd love to do that, since you have no problem killing innocent children and since you killed our friend. But I think the city wants something more from you. I think they'd like to *even the scales* themselves."

I dig into my wallet for the ripped business card of Officer Rodriguez. She's the only cop I know who my gut tells me isn't corrupt.

Miraculously, she picks up on the second ring.

"Rodriguez here." The sound of chopper blades thumps in the background.

"Hi, Officer Rodriguez. This is Anthem Fleet. Do you remember me?"

A long pause. "Yes," she says at last. "Of course. What can I do for you?"

"I have someone here, and I want you to make the arrest. I

need to be kept out of the papers entirely."

"I'm going to need a little more information, Anthem. We're kind of busy here, what with the evacuations . . ."

"Right. He's, uh, it's who we've all been looking for."

"You have *Invisible*?"

I look out over the river toward the city. It's gray and ugly and hard, but it's mine. And now maybe it won't sink into the ground. "Yes. I'm at the dam, at the edge of the reservoir. Can you bring a team with you? There are a lot of arrests, I'm guessing. We'll keep an eye on them until you come."

"I'll be there in five," she says. "And Anthem?"

"Yeah?"

"Nice work. It'll be our secret, if that's really what you want."

Then the line is dead. I put my phone away and look for Ford. I spot him dragging Invisible's goons off the dam railing, toward the woods. A few of them look like they're regaining consciousness again. I jog toward him, marveling at how strange—a good kind of strange—it is that I don't have to do this by myself.

CHAPTER 32

"I hear jackhammering in my sleep," Z says, stretching out languidly on my bed. It's two weeks later, and Zahra and I are in my room, the sounds of construction all over the North Side floating up to us, even here on the eighty-seventh floor.

Invisible had poured an industrial dissolving acid into the ground to get the landfill mass to shrink. Teams of environmental engineers, structural engineers, and city planners worked together for weeks to reinforce the ground and swell the landfill mass back up to its former levels. Now construction workers have the go-ahead to repair all the buildings. Only a few of them needed a complete demolition. My parents' development company is busier than it's ever been, working on new buildings for the demolition sites.

Construction aside, things in the city are back to some semblance of normal. Everyone has returned from their summer places. Zahra and I both graduate in a month. I'll be heading to the Bedlam Ballet Corps dorms, and Z is taking a year to "just live life," as she puts it, before she decides what she wants to study. And now that Invisible is gone, she can. We all can.

There are no more curfews. People aren't afraid of being kidnapped anymore. And Invisible is behind bars, awaiting his trial.

Last night at dinner, my father went on at length about his new construction philosophy.

"We need to rebuild higher," he said, his eyes wild. "To show them they've been beaten." He looked so obsessed that I had to look away out of embarrassment.

And Zahra met someone on her journey out of town. A boy named Fred. She keeps texting him, lying here on my bed. "Did I tell you Fred knows how to chop down trees with an axe and that we built this huge fire in the cornfields behind his house? I never thought I'd be into a woodsy guy, but Fred . . ." She sighs, her face screwed into an expression of semi-ironic enchantment, her rosebud mouth (lipsticked hot pink) twisting an unsuppressible grin. "He's got the goods. He hooked me."

"I've been briefed." I roll my eyes. This is the third time I've heard about Fred's skills with an axe. "You're going to be one of those exurban girls who wears long dresses and bonnets, aren't you? One of those back-to-the-land girls?"

"Maybe a long dress. Never a bonnet." Zahra grows serious then, grimacing over the word *bonnet*. "I'll admit it has occurred to me I *might* get bored in the woods. Who knows, maybe it won't last."

"You never know," I say, thinking of Ford. Love sneaks up on you sometimes. Makes you a different person than you thought you were. I never thought I'd spend time in a boxing gym and actually like it. But I do. I like everything about it.

The TV is on in the other room, the news reporting on Invisible, who's been held and questioned for two weeks now. Officer Rodriguez hasn't breathed a word about how she found him, at least so far. Her explanation is that she received an anonymous tip.

Invisible has a name: Aaron Lift. He's thirty-one. The news anchor breathlessly repeats the story we've been hearing for two days already, and it drifts into my bedroom: "Aaron Lift had a normal childhood, until the fateful day his father, Ignatious Lift, was arrested for fraud. Then everything changed for young Aaron." Cue the ominous music. Cut to a commercial for Motoko Cars, on sale this weekend at Bedlam Wheel City. When the commercial break is over, the story will continue: Leaving the North Side with his mother, moving to the Sigh Houses, a housing complex near the bridge. And getting in the way of a bullet not meant for him. He lied about a lot of things, but he was telling the truth about that.

"Ant." Z gives me a serious look, takes a deep breath like she has something important to say. "Aren't you curious?"

"What do you mean?"

"He went to Cathedral. He mentioned your sister. He must have known her. Aren't they around the same age, or would be if she was alive?"

I do the math. I'm seventeen, so if she'd lived, Regina would be around thirty-two now. "I guess so, yeah." But I'm apprehensive. Do I really want to dive into Aaron Lift's life? What's the point?

"Remember when we used to go in there and look through her stuff? I seem to remember old Cathedral yearbooks on the bottom shelf."

My stomach jumps. I stopped looking at them when I was

younger. I decided it was morbid. But maybe it does make sense to look for him there. Just to know. Just to see.

"Yeah. We could look at them, I guess."

"Don't get so excited," Z murmurs sarcastically, pulling me up off the bed.

I let her pull me toward the room, surprised I haven't thought of it myself. I used to spend hours in Regina's room, until I decided it was unhealthy, like trying to conjure a ghost. But I still remember the details of her bookshelf, with every yearbook lined up from kindergarten through tenth grade—the year she died. And I remember Zahra going with me on these snooping expeditions. But is it still snooping if the person is dead? We used to debate this question. Now the idea just seems silly. Of course it's not snooping. It's *research*.

"I haven't been in here in forever," Z says when we move down the hall toward Regina's closed door, separated from my room by just fifteen paces, with a linen closet and a bathroom door between them. Years ago, my mother walled off her entrance to the bathroom our two rooms once shared. She thought it would be traumatic for me to "share" a bathroom with the shrine to her first daughter, I guess. Of course, nothing as simple as drywall could fix the feeling of being haunted by her presence.

"Ready?" Z breathes, her hand on the knob. I nod, butterflies flapping in my gut. What will it mean to see a young Aaron Lift in the same book as the sister I never knew?

Maybe nothing. Maybe something.

We both go quiet when we step inside, our bare toes sinking into the plush lavender carpet Regina chose for her room when she was eleven. The room is dark and odorless, sterile-smelling thanks to regular cleanings in here by the twice-weekly team of housekeepers we've had for years.

When I reach for the light switch, the bulb lights up, emits a loud pop, then dies.

I move to the window and pull back the gray-and-lavender striped curtains, sending a cloud of dust motes dancing in the still air. When there's enough light to see, I join Zahra and kneel at the bottom of my sister's bookshelf, feeling more and more nervous about what we might find.

"Where are you, Aaron Lift?" Zahra murmurs, running her finger along the spines of all the yearbooks, from elementary on up through tenth. She pauses, looks at me as if checking to see if it's okay. I nod, and she pulls down ninth, hands it to me, and starts to page through tenth.

The yearbook is done in ocean colors and says in gold embossment CATHEDRAL SPIRES—THE TIDE IS HIGH. As we flip the pages, I'm transported back to being ten years old again, back when I used to come in here all the time and read all of my dead sister's yearbooks. All the inscriptions, the drawn-in hearts, the scratchy signatures of the boys, the bubbly letters of the girls captivated me. I must have looked at each page at least fifty times, but of course I was never searching for anyone specific, just trying to get a sense of who she was. I look over some of the inscriptions and realize I remember seeing most of them before.

Stay sweet, Reg! Let's party this summer! Love, Luella

To the smartest girl in Dr. T's class. You'll change the world one day, Reg. Or at least throw it a damn fine party. Don't forget about me this summer, okay? I have a buzz hookup. Philip

Pleasure getting to know you, Miss Fleet. Remember what I said about taking your time, okay? No need to rush into life too fast. You've got a brilliant mind and the kind of passion we need more of in politics. With admiration, Dr. T.

I look up and stare into the bookshelf in front of me, the titles swimming, devoid of meaning. Dr. T is Dr. Tammany, my politics teacher. This is clearly a warning to Regina about something. But what? I make a mental note to ask Dr. T about my sister before school lets out.

And then I come to page nineteen, where a beautiful girl with white-blond hair crimped in perfect waves falls like a waterfall down her narrow shoulders. She sits cross-legged atop one of Cathedral's metal tables, her plaid skirt dipping into her lap. I've seen this picture so many times. I remember being amazed that she wore the same plaid skirts I wear, because it meant I really was living the life she left behind.

But now it has a whole other meaning. Because now I know that the boy standing at her side, to whom she is giving her full attention in what looks like a serious conversation, is Aaron Lift.

"Look," I whisper, and Zahra leans over to see.

"Oh my god. It's him." His head of wild brown curls has not changed much, maybe grown a little coarser. Her hand is on his arm. His mouth is partly open, like he's not aware of the camera. They look intensely close, like the kind of friends who tell each other everything.

The caption below the photo says it all: *Regina Fleet shares a secret with Aaron Lift.*

Regina Fleet shares a secret. The words give me chills. Exactly how well did Aaron know her?

"Wonder what the secret was?" Zahra says, reading my thoughts.

"We'll never know," I say.

"They look like they're sharing some serious dirt."

There's a star next to the picture, drawn hastily. I flip through the book until I find another star just like it.

Yo Fleetfoot,

This year has been real. Or maybe surreal is a better word for it. Wonder if we both might not make it back to Catheter next year. Whatever happens, know I'm always on your side. No matter what our stupid parents put us through, we'll always have us. And our good looks, ha ha.

Love,
Liftoff

"Catheter?" Zahra says, her expression blank.

"Cathedral. Not the most creative name." I bite my cuticles and think. Aaron must have already known something was going on with his father. The arrest may have already happened. But why would he think Regina might not come back? He couldn't predict that she would drown in the lake. Did he have another reason to think she wouldn't return? And what was it he said to me? That he knew more about me than I know about myself? "But why did he think my sister wasn't coming back?"

"You should go ask him," Z says. "Call that cop who helped you. She'd set it up. She owes you."

I flip back to the picture of the two of them again. Their heads are tilted toward each other. Both utterly serious. No clowning around, not them. So close, so intent. Like brother and sister.

"Good idea," I mutter. I need to find out what Aaron

knew—what he *knows*—and I need to do it soon. God knows where he'll end up after his trial. I look toward the window and watch the dust motes dance in the sunlight, a mini-scene of chaos. And in my head I start to compose a script full of good reasons to give to Officer Rodriguez to let me have a few minutes alone with Aaron Lift.

The tip came from an anonymous caller. A baby wailing in the background. A woman with a foreign accent he can't place. "Leave one hundred thousand dollars at the corner of Vine and Poppy and wait for my call. I know where your daughter is."

It had been over six months and his leads have all run dry, have been dry for months. What can he do but try it?

He takes the money from the safe in his office. It's nothing to him, nothing at all. Anything to make the apartment alive with Reggie's presence again. Anything to get Helene to stop wailing each night. To bring back his little girl.

Harry is a bad man. He knows this. But he doesn't deserve to have his family ripped away from him. Not when he's done it all for them in the first place. All the bribes, all the payoffs. All the Syndicate activities that have disposed of certain people, that have made the South unpalatable as a place to buy a home and have made the North easier to rejuvenate, to sell. All the "urban planning" he's done over the decades. It's provided well for them. His girls. His loves.

Waiting for the next call in his office, Harry thought of his own childhood, cut short at twelve when he was told by his mother to leave because his father didn't like his smart mouth and she was afraid he'd take a hand to him, her boy. *Harry*, she'd said. *You need to get away from him before things get uglier.* Things were already plenty ugly. His father was the kind of man who would drink, then raise a chair over his head and break it over the nearest child. And there were so many children. More kids than they could properly feed.

So little Harry Flatts left. And after he left, he changed his name. Harris Fleet sounded rich. It jingled like coins in his ears.

Harry began a slow rise in the ranks of the Syndicate. And after the years piled up and he was close to the top, he got out. He moved into real estate development. Not that you ever really got out from under the Syndicate in this city, not really.

He played the part of the sophisticated, cultivated father and husband well. He never beat Reggie when she misbehaved, never lifted a chair above his head and smashed it down upon her small body. Never even raised his voice. He acted the easygoing charmer. Inside he sometimes raged and seethed, but on the surface? He'd become everything his own father wasn't. Not a trace of the person he could have become if he'd stayed Harry Flatts. He shed his accent, his poverty, his South Side manners. And he'd broken the cycle of violence. At least in his home. At work, he did what he had to do to be intimidating, to rise in the ranks. But once he reached a certain position, he had the luxury of leaving the violence to the others.

In this way, Harry Flatts was scrubbed clean. So clean that not even his right hand, Serge, knew about Harry's days as a Syndicate foot soldier. He prided himself on keeping Serge as ignorant of all that as he possibly could.

So why did Reggie leave? Had his explosion when she told them about her boyfriend been that frightening? How could she cut off contact for nearly eight months when she knew that she was all they had? Their bright star, their beautiful girl. Gone.

So of course he put the money in the trash can.

Of course he waited and watched, with Serge, as a woman with neatly braided blue-black hair came and got it, looking both ways before she stuck a ringed hand in the can and grabbed the duffel.

Serge followed her, but he needn't have. Twenty minutes later, Harry's phone rang. He wrote down the address, his hands shaking with excitement. With *love*.

It's easy to find. Close enough to the city dump that the whole street reeks of garbage. A sagging brick monolith, blotting out a big swath of sunrise. When they pull up, it's 5:47 A.M. according to Harry's watch. He leaves Serge in the car. This, he's got to do alone.

When he reaches the entrance, Harry looks down at the scrap of paper written in his own hand. 4B. He considers ringing, but once he speaks and she knows it's him, she won't let him in. The boyfriend will defend the place by force. The only way is to take them by surprise. Then make her see reason.

Back in the Syndicate days, he was a specialist at breaking and entering. But that was years ago. And lock technology has improved somewhat. He moves toward the door, trying not to breathe too deeply for fear of the garbage smell getting in and then never leaving his nostrils. My god, he's gone soft. His shoes, which he keeps obsessively shined, click on the sidewalk.

Turns out he's worried for nothing. Someone in a janitor's uniform is moving quickly toward the building, a young man wearing headphones, oblivious, almost staggering with exhaustion after the night shift. He walks past and Harris can smell the bleach on his hands. The janitor puts the key in the door and Harris waits until he's most of the way inside and the door has swung most of the way shut to push it open again. He walks inside with his head held high. Confident the janitor won't question him, Harris moves toward the stairs like he owns the place.

Maybe he *should* own the place, come to think of it, if this is the kind of home Reggie is going to insist upon. But he's here to talk sense to her. To make her see reason. To finally, god help him, meet the boyfriend. *The Hope*. Such a ridiculous name. He's ready to accept him, even though he refused to even meet him before. Because he's realized during her months-long absence that all he wants is for Reggie to be with someone better than he is. Someone with good beginnings, not foul ones in the bosom of the Syndicate.

He goes up the stairs two at a time, his heart racing at the prospect of finding her at last. He peeks out a tiny barred window when he gets to the fourth-floor landing and sees Serge smoking outside the Seraph, the cream-colored hood reflecting the candy-pink sunrise. Maybe Reggie will be so happy to see him she'll come home with them today, he thinks crazily. He's suddenly so full of optimism as he turns to walk down the hall toward 4B that he does a little hop-step—a dance move he hasn't done since he was a teenager.

After ten minutes of jimmying the lock, sweat pouring down his sides in a way it hasn't in years as he coaxes the bolts into position, he finally succeeds. He pushes the door open slowly, his heart in his throat. Pictures standing over her bed, shaking her awake, her eyes crusted with sleep, offering his apologies while she's groggy, before her anger takes over, before she can get her back up. Meeting the boy. Accepting the boy. Harry will do whatever it takes to get his family back. He was stupid. He'll tell her that. Just needs to catch her unaware, before her fury blinds her to reason.

God, to think she's been living in this building, fire hazards everywhere he looks, not an extinguisher in sight, the hallway smelling of urine and soup and mold.

His daughter, his angel. Harry has done all he has done to make sure he never had to smell this again—it's the smell of impoverishment, of hopelessness. And this is where she ends up, right back in the thick of squalor.

The door creaks on its hinges and reveals a dark apartment, but before Harry can even focus his eyes, can even find his way, there is a *ping*—a bullet released, passing through a silencer; Harry knows the sound as well as he knows his own heartbeat—and he ducks, though not quickly enough.

His shoulder explodes with pain.

What Harry knows is this: Someone is shooting at him. He cries out, can't help it. The shattering of bone is hard to take stoically. Another *ping*. A second bullet barely misses him. His reaction is swift. Instinct takes over. It has had years of practice, this instinct. Decades upon decades as a violent man have ingrained his response, honed his timing. This is what he knows: Kill or be killed. A figure behind a table rises up for a half-second, and the little punk is all he needs to see before he grabs his gun from inside his jacket. Short dark hair, a baseball cap. Grubby punk who wants his girlfriend's father dead.

He will kill the little turd. End it right here. Shoot now, explain later.

All of this flashes through his mind in a tenth of a second and he moves toward the table, kicks it at the kid. The kid goes flying back, eyes shining in the hushed blackness of the room like a forest creature, and Harry shoots.

It is swift, the bullet. Harry is an excellent shot. He's been doing this a long time. Longer than he'd like to admit. No thought of aiming to wound. No, Harry Flatts—Harris Fleet to everyone but himself— aims to kill. That's who he is. Always will be.

But when he bends over the punk kid, something is not right. The cheeks. Even in the pitch dark he can see they are smooth. That pointy chin. The body is funny. Too narrow. The hands are the strangest part of all. So small, so soft.

Oh god. Oh god. Harry's hands fly into the air when he sees what he's done. His gun clatters to the floor. This cannot be. Cannot. Impossible.

CHAPTER 33

Officer Rodriguez leads me into a high-security meeting room with cameras in all four corners underneath the central police station. The walls are brushed metal. The table is brushed metal. The chairs are black metal. Everything is bolted to the ground. And it's sweltering.

"Sorry, the air-conditioning system is out this week," Officer Rodriguez says before she leaves. "I'll be right outside the entire time. This mirror is a window. I can see you."

"Thanks." I wipe sweat from my brow and stick a finger under my black wig to scratch at my hairline. "I really appreciate this."

"Least I can do." She smiles, and her teeth are bright white against her tanned skin. "Gotta get a few privileges for capturing Public Enemy Number One. You just let me know what else you need, okay? Anything, really."

When I had called her and asked to speak with Aaron, there was a long pause on her end of the line. "You want to . . . talk to him?"

"Yes," I said. "I think he has some information about my family." Why not be honest, at this point?

"I'll call you back with a time and place" was all she said next. When she called me back, she told me to come wearing a wig, and to enter through the back of the building. In front is a media frenzy full of reporters, but the back, where all the beat cops hang out, was clear of photographers.

And now that I'm here waiting, adjusting my black bobbed wig to try to make it less itchy, it's obvious she's taken some risks to make this happen. Maybe bribed the guards here to keep it quiet. Because this is the kind of story the media would jump on, if given even a scrap of information to run with.

There's still so much talk about the New Hope. My mother has been giving me funny looks ever since the day the buildings sank—it's not lost on her that Invisible was captured the same day I insisted on leaving my parents for exactly three hours. But she hasn't come out and asked me anything, so I don't mess with the lie.

I smile at Rodriguez from the black metal chair, my heels bouncing off the floor with nerves, and she salutes me, then peeks her head out just as the sound of footsteps—one pair of feet walking normally and another walking with a drag— reaches my ears.

Goose bumps break out across my forearms, and I jump up to stand because sitting feels too passive. Too dangerous, some- how. Anything could happen down here. Aaron will be moved to a bigger facility after his trial, but for now he's housed here, in a maximum-security ward in the bowels of the central police station.

He fills up the frame of the doorway, a bulky guard in uni- form at his side. He's in an orange jumpsuit. His ankles are shackled, a long chain between them. His legs—which still sort of work—appear stiff and bent at slightly wrong angles, the knees bowing out when they should bend forward. He is handcuffed.

I force myself to look at his face. Without the eyeliner, he's just a little less striking. His eyes still have that light in them. That blazing, penetrating blue. His mouth forms a smile that is sarcastic and knowing and cruel and vulnerable all at once. The guard pushes him forward and he nearly falls, but rights himself as best he can, his left foot dragging across the linoleum behind his right, both legs shriveled and strange.

"Sit," the guard says. Once Aaron is seated, the guard produces a huge set of keys and twists one into the hole in the center of the table. A round metal joint in the center opens up like a mouth and the guard shoves Aaron's handcuffs toward it. A moment later, the chain on his cuffs is fastened to the table. He slumps over the table now, closer to me than I'd like. But he has no choice. The chain is so short.

"You have ten minutes," the guard says.

We watch him leave. I wait until I hear the click of the door closing behind him. Then I dare to look Aaron in the face. He's three feet away from me. He has a beard growing in, a dark shadow across his cheeks and chin.

"You're my first visitor," he says. His eyes are blank, focused on my shoulder instead of my face, but I detect sadness in the set of his mouth.

"What about your Invisible army?" I ask. "Nobody come to slip you a shiv?"

"Just a lawyer who says I'll be lucky not to get the death penalty." He just shrugs and stares at the mirrored wall. I wonder what he sees in there. How lonely he must feel. And then without meaning to be, I'm filled with pity for him, thinking about his childhood and what was taken away from him. He was abandoned, left by everyone who'd meant anything to him. And now his goons have abandoned him, too. For good reason, this time. He's a charlatan, a huckster with a half-baked plan. Without his army and his videos, he's just empty words, an empty person. That must all seem so clear now to the ones who haven't been arrested. "All the rest of them care about right now is finding more drugs like the stuff I gave them. They won't, though. Doesn't exist without me."

I think of what Ford said: *Drugs kept them loyal.*

The only one who didn't abandon him might have been my sister.

"Nice wig. You look good as a brunette."

"Thanks. Are your legs . . ." I trail off, not sure what I want to ask, curious to know if Jax put an expiration mechanism on them, if a time will come when they will fail him completely. If such a thing is even possible.

"They took away the braces. Your . . ."—he pauses here, clears his throat—"friend could only do so much. She gave me the spinal cord fusion I needed to be able to walk with the braces. We'd been working on them for years. Without them, I'm still a gimp. Upright, but a gimp."

"Oh." What else can I say? *Sorry?* A shudder of anger rocks through me and for a split second, I'm back in the room where I found her slumped against the wall. And all the pity I might have felt for Aaron Lift melts into white-hot anger again. "I would tell her about it, but as you know, she's dead."

"Sorry." He clears his throat again, a cough. "Really. I'd do it all differently if I could."

"Right," I snort. "You wouldn't be in jail, is what you mean."

"Is that why you came? To talk about your doctor? Look, I'm sorry she's dead. My guys got carried away. They're lunatics, you know. I liberated a big group of them from the psych ward at Weepee Hills. They needed good drugs to function as well as they did, and sometimes they took too much. I tried to regulate it, but I couldn't always keep close tabs."

I nod and sit back.

But I'm not here to talk about that. I'm here because I want to know about Regina. We're both quiet for a long minute, staring the other down.

His neck pulses. I watch the vein go up and down, noting his flared nostrils. I wonder if his hands weren't fastened to the center of the table, if he would lunge. And what I would do in response.

"I came here to talk about my sister," I finally say. It's so hot in here I feel sweat pooling in the small of my back and against the backs of my thighs. Sweat beads up at Aaron's temples, too, and on his upper lip. He nods and shifts in his chair, his eyes flashing with something like pity, the tables turning in who feels sorry for whom.

Don't look at me like that, I almost say. But he speaks first.

"You mean your mother." A prim smile on his face, half-pained, half-relishing the effect of this on me.

A painful heat fills my stomach, the fire spreading outward. My *mother*?

In my head I'm screaming at him *shut up shut up stop lying*, but I say nothing. I'm too stunned. Of course Regina wasn't my *mother*. The thought of it is absurd. Impossible.

So why am I shaking?

I think of all the times over the course of my life when I've wished I looked like my parents. I think of how old my parents are. The injections and facials and doctors keep them looking young, but they're not. They're old. My mother had me when she was forty-two.

I look nothing like either of them, really. And there is nobody in my family with red hair, only stories about an aunt I've never met who was a strawberry blond. But still . . .

"She's not my mother. Helene Fleet is my mother. And hers."

"She ran away because she was pregnant. I was the only one who knew. Then after she died, Helene Fleet had this . . . baby. It can't be a coincidence."

Aaron keeps talking, maybe just to fill the silence. "I tried to tell them about your grandfather."

"Who?" I say, and it comes out like a squeak.

"Harris Fleet," Aaron says, like it's obvious. He flattens his long fingers on the table. "Of course by then my father had been disgraced and nobody wanted anything to do with me. Nobody listened, not even the cops. At the time, I couldn't believe how he got away with it. Now after all these years, I get it. He's been bankrolling the Bedlam Police Department forever. But it was so clear he did it."

Now I'm not following at all. "Did what?"

Aaron looks at me like I'm an imbecile, then softens. "This is all new to you, isn't it?"

I nod, my eyes filling. I blot my eyes with the corner of my sweatshirt, tell myself to toughen up. "Did what? Just tell me."

The door swings open just then. Our ten minutes are up. "Say it," I whisper. "Time's up."

"Killed her. He killed his own daughter. I can't prove it, but I know he did it."

Not possible. No way. "You're lying."

"I loved Regina," Aaron says, and then the guard is unlocking the table hold on his cuffs, pulling him up by his collar. "She was my friend. Why would I make it up? Nothing's in it for me."

"Let's move," the guard barks. And Aaron shuffles away, a diminished figure in orange. I may never see him again.

"You know I'm telling the truth, supergirl," he yells behind him. "No way did she drown in that lake. Harris Fleet faked the whole thing. Everyone's corrupt in the North, you know. Everyone has secrets."

That's the last thing he says before the guard pulls him out the door.

A long time passes before I can force myself to get up from the metal table. Before I leave the sweltering room and have to face the task ahead of me. But eventually, I hobble out of there, down the humid basement hallway where the walls seem to sweat and where secrets go to die.

He pulls off the KillBall cap and strokes the short dark hair he's revealed, his hands shaking with the horror of what he's done. She cut her hair and dyed it black. She became another person. How could he have known? A cry rises in his throat. A deep and howling moan. Quickly, with the side of his brain that is still, even now, operating like a professional mob boss, he closes the apartment door, which has been swinging open on its hinges since he broke in. That side of his brain is panicking. Who else is here? Where is the punk kid who calls himself the Hope, the boyfriend he was supposed to be meeting?

Why was his daughter alone here; why was she shooting at him?

The other side of his brain is still moaning, is hysterical with grief. And some part of him that is neither of these men, neither the professional crime boss nor the father who has murdered the person most precious to him on earth, some other distant part of him slowly begins to notice the strangest sound rising to greet him in the dark apartment.

For a moment he thinks it is himself, but he cannot produce a sound like that.

Crying like that can only come from a baby.

That third part of him moves his shaking body wonderingly toward the sound. A tiny alcove. A crib. Jesus, no. It cannot be. But it is. And all the pieces fit together now. Reggie's disappearance. The months and months. Oh god. And here is the baby. His daughter's clone, in miniature. Except instead of Reggie's blond head, the infant has a shock of red hair. It's *his*, of course. The papers say the vigilante has red hair.

Dangling above the crying baby is a homemade mobile, felt letters tied to fishing wire. Bobbing in the air. He picks up the baby—who is so light it's almost obscene, how can anyone be so helpless and unknowing and new?—and he bounces it like he used to bounce Reggie. As the baby cries in his ear, he cries, too. Choking, unmanly hiccups while he examines the letters. Happy primary colors.

His half-dead heart spasms as he reads the word they spell: A N T H E M.

The boy walks home in the center of the street. A newspaper cone twisted at the bottom holds a pound of cherries from the all-night outdoor market. They were expensive and an indulgence, but he can't wait to see the look on her face, hear her squeal of delight. *So early in the season*, she'll say. *You shouldn't have.* Then she'll pop one in her mouth and grin, that pointed chin of hers wiggling.

I couldn't sleep, he'll say. *So I went out and found these. I wish I could get you these every day.*

He kicks a Buzz Beer can down the broken asphalt and it flies a few feet, then lands in a patch of weeds threaded through with straw wrappers and old newspaper. He can smell the landfill from here, a block away from their building. When the sun rises higher in the sky it will reek to high heaven. They like to tell each other they don't notice the smell anymore, but it's a kind lie.

The smell is putrid and decomposing, and it sends him down the same thought spiral as always, that he needs to get them out of here, Reggie and the baby. Move them somewhere green, not gray and brown and drained of color.

Next month, the month after. The riots have caught fire. He's not needed here anymore. Bedlam citizens are rising up. He can feel it. It's almost time for him to disappear, to stop going out at night. Stop rounding up the remaining criminals and trust that people will demand change.

Next month, two at the most. They will get a car and go, just keep on driving until they get someplace where wildflowers grow. He'll pick up work in a small town, rent a little house with a tree in the yard. Somewhere cheap and simple.

He weaves in the center of the street, daydreaming about the fields of alfalfa and aster he once tromped through as a boy when he was shipped off to relatives, after his dad was killed. Those yellow and white blooms that went on for miles. What baby wouldn't like a field like that to play in?

The daydream is so rich and real, he doesn't see the cream-colored car until it screeches right in front of him and it's too late to run. Even with his fast legs, too late.

He makes eye contact with the man driving, a man with wide licorice-black eyes, dusky skin, the whites of his eyes yellowed, cropped black hair. His mouth open as he tries to swerve out of the way. But the car is coming so fast. The moment stretches out; the Hope sees everything, their future stretched out in front of them, the little tree, a stream, a picnic. Endless waves of pale purple blooms blowing in high grass. The baby growing, a willowy freckled thing like him.

The cone of cherries goes flying as he tries to run, their red-black skins like flecks of blood on the blank white predawn sky.

Another man next to the driver, he sees wonderingly in the expanding, pulsating moment before impact, looks like someone he knows. Handsome, strong jaw. Eyes red-rimmed and wild. Dark hair slicked back. So familiar. *Maybe someone famous*, he thinks point-lessly, even as he senses he will not clear the car, will not avoid the skidding screech of the long cream-colored hood, upon which the precious expensive cherries already bounce, marking it with their dark red juice.

An actor, maybe? Someone imp—

CHAPTER 34

I feel sick when I leave the police station, too destroyed inside to run home. Eventually I catch the bus and stare numbly out the window as gray Bedlam crawls by. I've never seen so much construction in the North Side. So many hard-hatted workers. So many Fleet Industries redevelopment project signs.

Even when the city almost implodes, we make money, I think wonderingly. *No matter what happens, how bad it all gets, my father still turns a profit.*

I decide to go to the office. It's early still. I can catch him at work. And this conversation cannot wait.

The thick gray carpet mutes my footfalls as I move down the halls of Fleet Industries. I've spent many a school vacation filing for my mother and father here, so I know my way around.

Irene, the receptionist, waves me through the secure inner doors with her key card. The urge to smash the glass pulses through my hands, but I hold back as the doors swish open.

"Hi, sweetie. You're getting so big, growing up so fast," she says as if I'm still ten years old.

You don't know the half of it, I think, but I just smile and say thank you. I wonder if Irene knows about my origins. She may or may not, but certain people close to my parents must have some idea. I think of Serge and shudder involuntarily.

"Your dad's just finishing a meeting, great timing," she says, answering a ringing phone. I'm free to walk the halls on my own. The walls are lined tightly with hundreds of pictures of Fleet Industries buildings, both finished and at the blueprint stage. Half of North Bedlam must be on these walls.

By the time I reach the office door with the placard that says HARRIS FLEET, CEO, my heart is a ticking bomb, my blood boiling white-hot with rage.

"Tell me about my sister." I lean against his office door, breathing funny, shallow breaths and fighting to stay calm, to keep from screaming. The city stretches out in front of him the way it does at home, seemingly endless from this high floor. Only here, his office has a curved window that encompasses three sides of the building, so the view goes out in all directions but due north.

Maybe there's still a reasonable explanation for all of this. Maybe Aaron was just messing with me. Or maybe I'm just grasping at straws.

"Kitten, what a surprise." My father smiles flatly from his desk chair. His canines seem longer than I remember; his face appears suddenly wolfish and grotesque. I shudder inwardly, take a tentative step inside.

"What are you doing here?"

"Someone told me." I move closer to him, not wanting to call attention to myself and have someone interrupt us. I lower my voice to just above a whisper. "You killed Regina. And a lot of other things besides."

My father goes pale. Clears his throat. "Who said that?" he growls. "Who would say that to you?"

"Doesn't matter. I can see from your face it's true," I say calmly, though inside I'm breaking into a million pieces. I need to act like I already know everything or he'll charm his way out of it like he did last time.

"Of course it's not." He won't look at me. He stares at a pile of papers on his huge desk, gathering them up roughly in his hands. There's a tremor in them I've never seen before. More confirmation that Aaron was telling the truth.

"Tell me now or I walk out that door forever. I disappear and never come back. I spend the rest of my life investigating you. I already know most of the story," I lie. "I just want to hear you say it."

My father looks like he might pass out. He sucks a noisy breath in through his nose. "It was *him*. He killed her. He took her away, he ruined all our lives. I wanted her as far away from him as she could possibly be, and I was overruled." This all comes out fast and so quiet I almost miss it. "If not for that animal she took up with, she would be alive."

Do I tell him I don't know who he means? Better to let him keep talking. To think he's confirming what I already know.

"Did Serge tell you about him? Serge is fired, by the way. As of this moment. Had to be him who told you. Nobody else knows."

I shake my head, opening and closing my mouth like a fish as I accept the awful fact of Serge lying to me my whole life. "No. It wasn't Serge."

"You want to know why we have all this?" My father's eyes

are wild as he stands up behind his mammoth desk. "All our money, all the nice things, all your ballet lessons, your education, this office, the billions we're about to make from the stadium project? Everything we own? It's because of me. I made it all out of *thin air*," he hisses. "The success of this company all depended on people moving north. Fleeing crime. I made sure crime stayed where it needed to. I made sure the North would become off-limits to the thugs who terrorized this city. For Regina. I did it for her. And then I did it for you. And for your mother," he adds, as if she's an afterthought.

"Don't call her my mother," I say, feeling that same shattering in my chest again, that gaping, whooshing hole.

I'll never know my mother.

My mother is my grandmother.

"When that egomaniac started changing things, it wasn't going to be good for me and my family." My father pauses here, stands up and moves toward the window, his voice shaking. "Real estate prices began to drop in the South. Young families started moving there. He just . . . Anthem, he wanted to destroy the whole social fabric of what I'd created. All of it, just . . . *poof.*" My father snaps his fingers.

"You'd created? But how?"

"Doesn't matter," my father murmurs. His eyes travel over the buildings, the factories, the steaming gray beneath and around where he stands. "I had ways of reining in the Syndicate, but it doesn't matter now. I'm out of that, for the most part."

"So you lied to me before, when you said you had no knowledge of what Gavin was doing."

"That's not what we're talking about!" my father explodes, moving toward me in his socked feet. I note his wingtips lined up neatly under his desk. He's close enough to me now so I can see each of the hairs growing in his five o'clock shadow. "I don't know why you are so *insistent*, Anthem, or how you came to know all this, but I intend to find out."

"You were talking about her boyfriend," I say softly to veer him back on course. The words echo in my head. I'm afraid of them. Even though I'm terrified, I force myself to say it: "My father."

"I'm your father! *Me*. I *raised* you." His hand darts out, fingers wrap around my chin to force me to look into his eyes. I glare up at him, my lips curling with disdain. I can see the fine lines around his eyes, the wrinkles on his forehead that he and my mother usually work so hard to erase.

I don't know who I'm looking at, I realize. But I know it's a bully. A man who's done terrible things to this city, to strangers. And who's done the worst thing of all, maybe. Killed his own child. We stay like that for a second, glaring at each other, then I twist out of his grasp.

"Don't touch me," I whisper.

"You've got to see it from my point of view," he goes on, his words buoyed by a sort of mania I can hear in his voice. He is afraid, I realize. That I will expose him, or maybe that I'll leave him. "Because one guy gets really good at sneaking up on criminals in the act, because one guy decides to take a stand, the city started to treat him like some kind of hero. He started *riots*, Anthem. The city was disintegrating. Law and order, what little of it works here, was crumbling before my very eyes! Everything I'd built. And then I find out my own daughter is involved with him? Of course I didn't take it well. You wouldn't, either, Anthem, believe me. Because I know you. I *get* you. You are a pragmatist. A workhorse. You would react the same way. Especially after what happened with that boy. The pain you went through."

"You don't know anything about that," I snap. "Don't talk like you know me. You know nothing."

My thoughts stutter as I try to catch up with what my father is saying. A man who started riots? A man who went after criminals? There's only one man like that. My sister's—my mother's—boyfriend was the freaking *Hope*? I try to remember what we learned in politics class about the Hope. Is he dead, alive? Disappeared, I remember Dr. Tammany saying. Just . . . gone.

"Anyway, *he* did it," my father growls, his hands fisted, staring away from me, at some distant point in the sky. Staring, maybe, at his past. At memories he's long tried to bury. "*He's* why it happened."

"I don't understand," I whisper. "How did he do it?"

"By taking her away. Turning her paranoid. Cutting her hair. It was like she was in a cult, Anthem. I didn't recognize her until . . . How was I supposed to know my daughter, who, let me tell you, who was a *princess*, the way we raised her, a goddamned princess who never worked a day in her life? How could I know my daughter had learned—"

"Learned what?" I cry, impatient, disgusted with this stranger. How can I believe anything he says? But I've never seen him this agitated, this hollowed-out and panicked and trapped. It feels all too real.

"How to shoot a gun." It all comes out in a rush, the words tripping over themselves falling out of his mouth. His eyes are unfocused, like he's back there. In the place where she died.

"I was given a tip about where she was. I'd been looking for so long. I wanted to sneak in, catch her before she ran away from me again. Just to talk. Just to convince her to return. She heard me coming, I guess. She'd become violent. Paranoid. She was armed. It all happened so fast." He pauses, looks around him, but his eyes are turned inward. His face a mask of horror. Then he continues. "I thought . . . I thought she was someone else. I responded the way anyone would. And then I realized it was her—" His voice breaks, and I wave my hand in front of me to get him to stop, not wanting to hear any more.

It's too horrible, what he's saying. Too brutal to imagine. That little tow-headed girl sitting in the field of wildflowers in the picture in my parents' bedroom—how can he have woken up and seen that every day of his life? It's unthinkable.

"So she shot at you and you shot back," I whisper numbly. A comment, not a question. My father's—the stranger's—shoulders sag, and the stunned rawness on his face translates to *yes*.

"Where? It wasn't in the lake," I whisper, trying to reconstruct it. The lake must have been a place to dump the body, to buy time. "You moved her later."

Harris nods, looking at the floor, all that thick gray carpeting. His socked feet. I stare at his shoes peeking out from under his desk, neatly side by side. Shiny black. And for a half-second I am full of self-pity. Those shoes belong to a man I call my father, the familiarity and security of seeing his shoes under his desk all wiped away now. He turns away from the window and faces me, his eyes red-rimmed. Underneath them, black hollows. He looks a hundred years old. "I never told a soul. How could Serge do this to our family? To your *mother*."

My mother. That shattering sensation in my chest again.

"All this time, the two of you have been keeping this from me." The room starts to blur and tilt, my knees locked for too long. A circle of black opens up in the center of my vision and starts to expand. I clutch the back of Harris's leather desk chair for support. All the pills. The drinking. Her numbed state. Her near-suicides. She had so much more inside her than grief over a dead daughter. Harboring a murderer. Sleeping in his bed, night after night. Lying to me about everything that mattered. She built a fortress of lies, and lived inside it alone.

"Your mother—Helene—" He pauses, checks my face to see if there is revulsion there. Finds that there is. "Doesn't know all of it. Not about the shooting. Helene knew you were Reggie's baby. That's all. I said I found you, that she'd dropped you off at a police station before killing herself in the lake."

"But the papers don't say suicide," I say. "They say it was an accident. And what about the gunshot?"

"The police left it alone because they thought suicide. And I had friends at the papers," he says gruffly. "They printed what I wanted. Especially back then. There was one story for the papers, another for your mother. Another for me, and only for me."

"Until now, you sick son of a bitch."

We look up. My mother's standing in her stocking feet, leaning against the wall near the door. She padded in so quietly I didn't hear. "You bastard."

"Leenie." My father moves toward her. "You've got to understand. It was his f—"

"Did you kill him, too?" Helene's eyes are so wide with anger I can see the whites all around her irises. "The Hope? Is that why he disappeared?"

"I don't—I don't know what happened to him. We may have—"

"Enough!" I say. "I can't be near you anymore. Either of you. My grandparents."

My mother is weeping uncontrollably. I need to stop. I

should stop. But I don't.

"It's over." I fight to sound calm as I walk toward the door, though every part of me is shaking. "We're not playing this game anymore where I'm your daughter."

And then I run out, turning around once when I hear my mother screaming at my father, watching her batter his chest with her fisted, manicured hands. He reaches for the door, not to go after me but to shut it so that others don't hear. That gesture says it all. Always the calculator, Harris Fleet. Always conscious of his secrets.

And then I'm walking out on that deathly silent ocean of gray, shaking all over, while at the same time aware that something has lifted from me. No more secrets. No more burdens. I can be anyone I want now, because I'm not their daughter anymore.

I'm the daughter of a dead girl who was brave enough to shoot a gun, and a vigilante who I'll never know.

My whole life's been a lie, an empty story built on top of death. There's nobody to disappoint anymore. No way to throw away my potential as the Fleet girl. My murdering grandfather has taken care of all that for me. There is nothing more to screw up.

The only place I can possibly go from here is up.

Up, and away.

CHAPTER 35

"When you were eight or nine, I finally tracked him down," Serge says, folding his hands on the table between us at the Scrambled Yolk. Both our coffees sit untouched in their mugs. It's a Sunday in early September, my one day off from the eight-hour practice sessions that have become my life since accepting a spot on the Bedlam Ballet Corps last month.

I nod, absorbing this. We've met here at my request, to talk about my father. My *real* father. Not Harris. I'm still not talking to Harris. But I'm getting stronger all the time, both as a dancer in the dorms, and emotionally, too. Strong enough after a few weeks to forgive my mother for lying to me all my life. And strong enough now, after a few months have gone by, to understand that it wasn't up to Serge to tell me the truth before I was ready to hear it. My father was his employer. No matter how sick he felt about what happened, he couldn't expose the truth before I demanded it. And I wasn't fully ready to have this conversation until now.

"So he lived. After the accident." I stare down at my hands in my lap. Shaking, just slightly, when I picture Serge slamming the car into the Hope, the way my father ordered him to, keep driving, don't stop. And imagining how he held me, a tiny infant in his lap in that car, all he had left of Regina.

What could it mean that my real father is alive, out there somewhere? Will I ever meet him?

"I always suspected he did," Serge says, "because there was never anything in the papers. So I kept looking. Put out whatever feelers I could. Finally, an old friend of mine found him living outside a tiny mountain town, entirely off the grid. He'd gone there to recover from his injuries. I went to see him."

"You did?" My heart revs wildly in my chest. I look into Serge's eyes, trying to understand. "Did he know I was alive? Did he care what had happened to me after he left?"

Serge nods. "I know it must seem like he abandoned you. But he was a very broken man, Anthem. Not just his body, but his spirit, too. I urged him to visit you, and I know he wished he could. I gave him some money he tried to refuse, and then I left."

I sit back, stunned, absorbing this news. Serge looks like he's aged. He works for a friend of my mother's now. Harris fired him the day I came into his office and blew up our family. "I'm sorry about what happened," I say quietly. "I wish it hadn't affected you."

"Nothing to be sorry about. Your mother has been very good to me," he says. I've been seeing my mother once a week lately. She's quit drinking, thrown all her pills away. Moving out of Fleet Tower and into her own apartment has made her into a braver person. Serge is still in her life, as a friend now and not an employee. She is still considering telling the police about what my father did, though so far we've kept it between us. In part because we suspect he has enough friends inside to exonerate him. Neither of us speaks to my father now. I'm not sure we ever will again.

"The only apologies are mine to give, to you," Serge continues. "I wish I could have told you the truth. When you began fighting, I was tempted to. You were so much like him, suddenly." A wan smile twitches across his mouth and vanishes.

"It's okay," I whisper. It took me a few months to stop being angry at Serge, but all that's over now. I'm glad to have him back in my life. I open my mouth, barely daring to ask my one remaining question. Something I would never dare ask my mother, who is still unsteady when we talk about the past. "What is the Hope's real name?"

"Jacob Lokhem." It feels like a key to something, hearing his name. Like the syllables could unlock something scary and yet vitally important.

"Do you think . . ." I can't finish the sentence. It feels too loaded. I don't know if I want to meet this person. After all, he abandoned me. He knew right where I was, all these years. And yet he never showed up.

"That you could meet him someday? Yes. If you feel ready, I think he would like that."

We sit in silence for a while, the clattering of the diner a welcome cacophony. I look out the window and imagine what it might be like if he walked in right now. I know from looking up old news stories that he has red hair. He's where I got my red hair. And a lot more things, besides.

Serge takes a long envelope out of his pocket and slides it across the table. "I've been holding on to this for six years," he says. "He wanted me to give it to you when you were ready."

I pick it up. It's light, but the moment is heavy enough to choke me. My hands are shaking again, but I don't want to wait and read it alone. Better Serge is here. Safer, somehow.

Dear Anthem,

We named you Anthem because you lifted us up and gave us hope. It was an exciting and scary time, and you felt like the embodiment of everything we'd ever wanted. For the city, and for the world. That's how magical you were, to Reggie and to me. You were a perfect baby. A miracle. We couldn't get enough of looking into your big eyes.

I hope you've found some happiness in your life, and that it's not too great a burden to bear to know you came from Regina and me. I assume that by now, you know the truth about your parents, or Serge wouldn't have given you this.

I loved your mother very much. Maybe too much.

When she was taken from me—and more importantly, taken from you—I couldn't recover. It's funny, they called me "The Hope," but nobody has less hope and more sorrow in their heart than I do. Reggie was what allowed me to do what I did. Her optimism is what kept me going. Without her, everything turned gray and dull and dead for me. It became impossible for me to go on, almost. I wanted to die, to just disappear, but I wasn't brave enough to join Reggie in the next world. Nor was I brave enough to take you away. I thought about it a hundred times a day at first, for a few years.

I came once to the city, when you were five or six. I waited outside Fleet Tower, thinking you'd recognize me somehow, that you'd see it was your dad and I would belong to someone again. When you came downstairs with your grandparents I stood on the opposite side of the street, frozen, watching you. You were happy, laughing as you pulled a new-looking wooden zebra on a string. You were dressed so beautifully, and you had on new shoes you were excited about wearing. I saw you were taken care of in a way I could never care for you myself. Your grandparents had all the money in the world to give to you, and I didn't have anything.

Please know that nothing has made me happier than hearing about you over these years. I think it's why I've stayed alive, to hear about your dancing and to see your picture sometimes in the society pages. Reggie would have been so proud of you. You are the best thing we ever gave to the world, Anthem.

Your parents—Reggie's parents—can't be all bad. They have raised an amazing girl. I work every day on forgiving your father for what happened.

I would understand if you could never forgive me for what a coward I became. But if you would ever like to meet, nothing would make me happier.

Yours always,
Jacob Lokhem

Tears slip down my cheeks and onto the table as I read, and when I'm done, I look up at Serge and see his eyes are glassy, too. "Don't go crying on me, Serge."

He nods, solemn and kind as ever. "He's a good man. If my opinion matters to you, I can tell you that much," he says quietly.

"It matters a lot," I say. I glance up at the clock on the wall of the diner. Almost eleven. I fold the letter up carefully and slip it back inside the envelope. Then I get up from the booth, folding the envelope in half and slipping it into the pocket of my jeans. "One of these days, I'll meet him," I tell Serge. "But for now, there's somewhere else I need to be."

CHAPTER 36

In the South Bedlam Cemetery, the sky is a startlingly vibrant shade of blue and dotted with cotton-ball clouds. I'm walking the gravel pathways through the graves, Ford's calloused hand in mine. In the easy silence between us, I listen to the wind blow through the trees and hear the faint rhythm of a metal shovel against wet earth, a gravedigger working somewhere on the other side of the hill.

With my ballet schedule, I only get to see him a couple of times a week lately. It's been a big shift after seeing him every day—I moved in with him and Abe for a month after the confrontation with my father, before I was able to move into the dorms at the Bedlam Ballet Corps Summer Audition Program. With my ballet and Ford boxing in real matches again—so far the Syndicate isn't going after him for it—we're glad to take things slow. And the occasional nighttime sweep of the South when we hear about something bad going on is much more fun, now that we can do it together.

What my real father did meant something to this city. And I've finally accepted that what I'm doing means something, too.

We are here today to visit Jax's grave, no longer fresh. And we're also here to meet someone.

"It's this way." Ford points off the path to one side of a willow tree sagging under the weight of its downturned branches. He comes here more often than I do—it's not far from his house—and my schedule at the ballet corps is so demanding that I seldom get out during the hours the cemetery is open.

We turn off the rock-lined path onto the grass, careful not to walk across the graves. I spot a flat, smooth stone and add it to the three I've already got in my pocket.

The solid mass of the stones is comforting somehow. Permanent. They'll still be here long after all of us are dead and gone.

Up ahead, I spot someone with frizzy honey-colored hair, thick plastic horned-rim glasses, and narrow shoulders sitting on a tree stump. She turns and looks at us with incandescent blue eyes, then scoots off the stump and waves a tentative hand. The way she moves, the tidiness of her gestures, leaves no doubt in my mind about who she is. It's uncanny how like her mother her features are. For a moment, I almost think I see Jax standing there.

But then I blink and Jax is gone, the girl in the graveyard herself again, threading her way through the gravestones. She looks about fourteen.

"Here it is." Ford stops. We've reached the grave.

Ford and I arranged for the headstone together, after we did the research and uncovered Jax's birthday. Ford came up with the wording:

JAXON MAGRATH.

SCIENTIST, DREAMER, MOTHER.

GONE TOO SOON.

I added something she once said to me at the end:

"IT'S THE PEOPLE YOU HELP THAT GET YOU THROUGH."

I stack two stones on the side of the granite grave marker and let out a shuddering sigh. "I'm so sorry, Jax." It's what I always say. Today is the four-month anniversary of her death.

The girl's feet crunch on the gravel, and then she joins us at the grave. She's carrying a bunch of white wildflowers, and she squats to place them in front of the headstone.

"Hi," Ford and I say at the same time. We're nervous. We want her to feel comfortable.

"Hi," she says. "I'm Cleo."

"You look just like her," Ford says. "It's uncanny."

"You think?" She shrugs, but I see from the way her cheeks turn pink that this pleases her. That she wishes she'd known her mother. I can relate.

"Thank you for coming." I smile at her. "We really loved her. Your mom. And I know she would have given anything to meet you." As I say the words, I'm more sure that I'm going to visit Jacob Lokhem. Soon, maybe. Before winter comes.

"I'm glad you found me," she says, biting her lip and staring at the gravestone. "Was she really a scientist? Like with a lab and everything? Even after she left the university?"

Like me, there are so many puzzle pieces swimming around in Cleo's mind. It's hard to piece everything together. "She had a lab, yes. It's still there, actually. I was there last week."

"I'd love to see it. I'm into science, too," she says, moving from one foot to the other. "Ever since I figured out my heart wasn't like everyone else's, it's been a hobby of mine to try to understand why."

"We'll take you there. We can go today, if you like," Ford offers.

"Sure," Cleo says, her eyes huge behind her thick glasses. She smiles broadly and rocks back on her heels. "I'd like that."

"You know, Jax worked on my heart, too," I confess, raising an eyebrow. "I can do some pretty unusual things. Ford can, too."

Cleo fixes her big eyes on me, then Ford. Sizing us up. "In that case, want to race?" she says casually, almost yawning. But she's bouncing on her heels, her black canvas high-tops flexing.

I look at Ford. He's grinning. "Sure thing," he says. "Here to the cemetery gates?"

And then, as if a starting shot has been fired that only we can hear, all three of us take off. We barrel down the grassy hill in the direction of the gray city, laughing and whooping, nobody here but a thousand silent graves to see the way our feet barely touch the ground, to notice the strange blur of our bodies against the sky.

ACKNOWLEDGMENTS

To Joelle Hobeika and Sarah Landis for their tremendous insight, wisdom, and patience in every step of the writing process. To Josh Bank, Les Morgenstein, Sara Shandler, Liz Dresner, Kristin Marang, Phyllis DeBlanche, and KB Mello for their big brains and eagle eyes. To everyone at HarperTeen, especially Jennifer Klonsky, Gina Rizzo, Alana Whitman, Margot Wood, Aubrey Parks-Fried, and Lauren Flower for their endless enthusiasm and promotional genius.

To readers and friends near and far, especially Rufus Misrok, Alison Gould, Tom Grattan, Thaïs Jones, and Shasta Lockwood for embracing Anthem's story so wholeheartedly. (See what I did there?)

To my amazing sisters, Jeannie Kahaney and Cory Kahaney, for their fierce loyalty and audacious spirit. And to the rest of my family in New York and San Diego, most especially Gabi— their love and support is everything. Thank you, thank you, thank you.

SEE HOW ANTHEM'S STORY BEGAN.

Don't miss the prequel to *The Invisible*.